Top Hats

and

Treachery

Bonnie Cavaliere

eBook ISBN: 979-8-9857928-4-3

Print ISBN: 979-8-9857928-5-0

Mind's Eye Media, Incorporated

United States of America

Contents

Chapter 1: California Dreamin'

My plane touched down ten minutes late (head winds) and I anxiously checked the time on my phone. As soon as we hit the gate, people were trying to stand. I absolutely HATE when people all start crowding into the aisles before the cabin door is even opened, but it's as if all airline passengers are spring-loaded. The minute they can unfasten their seatbelts, they are up and grabbing their gear out of the overhead compartments, narrowly missing the heads of fellow passengers in a rush to get off the plane. And then they stand for three or more minutes while everything is secured.

Today I was one of those people. I have learned to sit as close to the front of the plane as I can. I was in Row 7, aisle and my laptop was already in my carry-on and my carry-on was in my hot little hands. There was a gust of hot, dry air as the cabin door opened and the first-class passengers started their slow file out. I had about seventeen minutes to get to the baggage claim area, grab my checked bag, and find the shuttle to the resort. And I had to pee. Hey, it's a long flight from Florida.

Fortunately, John Wayne Airport in Orange County, California is small, only 22 gates spread out over three terminals. I wove past the slower moving people, following the signs for baggage claim, moving at a clip just below a run—the advantage of having long legs. I made it to baggage claim before my luggage which gave me time to hit the ladies' room. #WINNING!

I took an extra minute to brush my hair, reapply my lipstick, pull a long red hair *out* of my fresh lipstick (why does my hair always end up stuck in my lipstick?), and pop a cinnamon Altoid. I went back to wait at the carousel just as the bags were starting to slide from the conveyor belt. I looked around for signs for the hotel shuttles while waiting for my one checked bag. I watched other people grab their bags and go and a little knot of anxiety started forming in my stomach. Then my bag popped up the chute, I felt my stomach unknot, and waited until it circled around to me.

I tried to pack light, but I had no idea what kind of clothes I needed which means I packed everything from jeans and boots to a black cocktail dress with emerald green accents. My friend Ali told me to "dress for success" and helped me pack. She's a genius at putting outfits together—something I have no flair for. She mixed and matched pieces and I ended up taking pictures of the outfits because I was pretty sure I'd get mixed up and default to jeans and a starched white shirt. Nothing wrong with that, really, except Ali could add the right shoes, top it with a jacket of some sort, a chunky necklace, earrings, and a cuff bracelet, and make me look pulled together. If I'm ever rich and famous, Ali is going to be my stylist. In the meantime, I keep hoping they'll start making Garanimals for adults.

I'm Kasey McCormick, by the way. I'm a stand-up comic and no, you've never heard of me. I've been getting work as an opening act, which is great, but I really needed to start making some real money. When I heard about this seminar on the Business of Comedy, run by Juliet Hartwell ("America's Comedy Sweetheart"), I figured the timing was perfect, even if affording it was a bit of a stretch. I managed to get a cheap ticket from Tampa to Southern California and the hotel had special rates for seminar participants. And it included breakfast. The schedule had us in seminars and trainings during the days. There was a welcome cocktail mixer scheduled for tonight and opportunities to showcase our acts to a real Los Angeles agent. And at least one other event marked "TBA"—to be announced. It didn't sound super-organized but the trainings were what I was after. And to be honest, the showcase. I mean, a real agent? I was in. I signed up and put the hotel on my credit card. In for a penny, in for a pound as they say.

As I hurried towards the signs for the hotel shuttles, I saw a movie-star pretty brunette. Should I know her? I wasn't sure. She was hovering over a porter who was stacking several Louis Vuitton suitcases onto a luggage cart. They seemed to be waiting for a fourth and I could hear her fretting to him about being late. I felt her pain, but at a lower socio-economic level. I made my way to the shuttle area, hoping I hadn't missed the resort shuttle. It ran once an hour and I really just wanted to get to the resort, settle in, and have some time to get my butt organized before things started rolling.

I stepped out through the sliding double doors and was hit in the face with a wall of dry heat. It felt like I had opened an oven door. I couldn't decide if this was better or worse than Florida's sticky, humid heat, but I knew one thing: I was going to have to use more moisturizer. I looked around, trying to get my bearings. I saw a second sign for hotel shuttles and walked over to wait. I was pretty sure I hadn't missed it. I checked my phone. The resort shuttles ran at a quarter after each hour. I had five minutes to spare.

There was a small knot of people waiting. I found a spot next to a handsome, mixed-race man who was deeply involved with his phone. He knew how to pack light; he had one carry-on bag with him, with a suit jacket draped over it. I checked his shoes. They looked expensive. He was wearing dress pants and a starched white dress shirt with the sleeves carefully cuffed up, not rolled, exposing a Tag Heuer dive watch. I don't know much about watches, but there are enough divers on the Florida Gulf Coast that you get to know a good dive watch when you see one.

Another guy looked like he might be heading to the same conference I was. Jeans, a black T-shirt, Maui Jim sunglasses, too much product in his dark hair, and an attitude of being too hip for the room. (Spoiler Alert: He wasn't.) All the signs of a comic. A Hilton Hotel shuttle pulled up and a couple of people got on. I felt like I was baking in the heat, but I wasn't sweating for some reason. Did sweat dry instantaneously here?

The first guy's phone rang. From the one-sided conversation, I could tell that the airline had lost his luggage.

"Oh, good. Thank you." Pause. "San Diego? Well, that shouldn't be too hard to get. Tomorrow? Really? San Diego is less than 100 miles from here." Pause. "Yeah. Okay." He sounded resigned. He was taking it much more calmly than I would have. But then, men can wear the same clothes for a week and no one notices. If a woman walks into work just once wearing the same thing as the day before, she'll never hear the end of it. Or so I've heard...

"I'm staying at Santa Ana Winds Resort. Yeah. Yeah. Under Nicholas Hill. Definitely tomorrow then?"

Well, the weekend just got better. He was staying at the same resort I was. And he definitely didn't look like a comic. That could be a positive. Then I noticed the wedding band on his left hand. I sighed inwardly. Just as well.

I watched a Springhill Suites shuttle come and go while Nicholas finished up his conversation. He slid his phone back into his pocket with a sigh.

"Lost your luggage?" Duh, Kasey. Nothing like stating the obvious.

He shrugged. "One of the joys of traveling."

"Sucks to be you, man," the other guy piped up.

"Indeed." There was silence.

"I'm heading to the Santa Ana Winds, too. Hope the shuttle gets here at some point." I said it to Nicholas, but the other guy jumped in.

"Me, too. I'm Chad Warder." The hair gel guy said his name like I should recognize it.

"Kasey McCormick."

"Nick Hill. Though you probably already got that."

We watched another hotel shuttle come and go.

"Are you here for the comedy seminar?" Chad asked.

"Yes," I said. I had called that right.

Nick said yes, too. That was a surprise. He did not dress like your typical comic. There was another silence and I saw the resort shuttle approaching.

"Here's our ride." I slung my computer bag over my shoulder as the van pulled up and I grabbed my bigger suitcase. Chad had a backpack. The driver opened up the back and started loading in the few bags.

"Wait! Wait! Don't go!"

The pretty brunette from luggage was running for us—in spike heels no less—and her porter was trying to hustle the luggage cart behind her. It was stacked with four matching Louis Vuitton bags. I had a suspicion they weren't knock-offs.

The driver smiled at her. "No worries."

The porter brought the bags around the back. Nick, Chad, and I got into the van. The air conditioning was running full blast. I could hear the brunette thanking the porter and saw her hand over a tip. The porter looked at it and grinned. "Thank you!"

She climbed into the seat behind me, next to Nick. The shuttle driver closed the back and side doors and we were on our way.

"Hi, I'm Gabby. Short for Gabriela, of course, but my father says it's because I talk too much." She paused. Then, apologetically, "I talk too much."

I had to smile. But in the back of my head I was already thinking her father must be a piece of work. We all introduced ourselves again. Gabby lived up to her name.

"You're all comics, right?" She looked around. "Me, too. I'm just starting out, really."

She had an innocent charm. I twisted around in my seat to face her.

"I'm not too far ahead of you," I volunteered. "Trying to move into feature work."

"I'm headlining these days," Chad announced from the back. "Looking for TV opportunities. People have been sniffing around, of course, but I want to make sure I get the best deal I can."

"Wouldn't your agent do that for you?" I asked.

"Well, yeah, but I need an LA agent. And there are supposed to be several at this event. That's why I'm here."

"That's really impressive," Gabby said.

Nick didn't say anything, but I got the impression he was not impressed. Our eyes met. He didn't quite roll his eyes, but yeah, his BS detector was going off, same as mine.

"How about you, Nick?" I asked.

"I've been opening at some of the local clubs on Long Island. And open mics in the city. I can't really travel because of my job, so not a lot of road work." His phone buzzed and he looked down.

"Yeah, the day job makes it hard, but it pays the rent right now," I said. "At least you're in close proximity to New York. You can get some visibility. I'm working the Florida circuit." I didn't add that last week I played a hot dog stand. It was actually a great gig, but doesn't look good on the old resume.

"Doing shows at the old folks' parks?" Chad snorted.

"No. Those actually pay well." I passed it off as a joke, but Chad was already wearing on me. Great that he was going somewhere and doing well, but I was always suspicious of people who were eager to cut you down, especially if you've only just met. He screamed insecure male.

Nick was looking down at his phone. "Kasey McCormick. Florida's Funniest Comedian. I thought I knew the name." He looked at me with a smile.

"Oh my God!" Gabby said. "That's so cool!"

"Runner up, actually."

Chad sniffed. "Sort of a popularity contest, isn't it?" His brain hooked on something. "Didn't someone die at one of those contests? Florida is whacked."

"Almost died. Competition is stiff there." I tossed off the line lightly. Nick grinned at me and shook his head. No one else caught the pun.

So, I'd been outed already. Nothing like raising expectations. I figured I'd shift the conversation off me.

"I saw you at baggage claim, Gabby. Did you come in on the Atlanta flight?"

"Everything connects through Atlanta," she said. "I connected there from Dulles."

"I'm from Atlanta," Chad said. "Well, not originally. Otherwise, I'd sound like a hick."

"We must all have been on the same flight," Gabby said.

Nick looked up. "I flew in from JFK. I've been at the airport for an hour and a half trying to locate my bag."

"Maybe Gabby could loan you an outfit. She brought enough baggage for a month," Chad said.

Gabby blushed. "I wasn't sure what to bring. I mean, is it going to be casual? We've got our showcase spot, so I brought a couple of choices depending on how everyone is dressing for that. And then, there's a pool and maybe we'll have some free time..." She trailed off, embarrassed. "I brought too much stuff." I saw her clench and unclench her right hand twice.

"You need my friend, Ali," I said. "She helped me put together outfits and pack. Now if I'm missing anything, I can blame her."

"Outfits," Chad rolled his eyes.

"Yeah, well, we all can't get away with jeans and t-shirts like you guys do."

"Dress for the job you want," Nick said.

"I guess that's why we're all here," I said. "Moving to the next level."

"I'm just trying to get to the first step," Gabby said. "I've done some open mics and I've bought some more material, but I need help putting everything together."

"You bought material?" Chad asked.

"I'm more of an actress than a writer, so yeah." She looked concerned. "Is there something wrong with buying material?"

"No," Chad said. "I can probably supply some top material for you, depending on what you're paying."

"That would be so good," Gabby almost gushed. "Let's talk while we're here."

"The trick to having good material is that it is personal to you, Gabby. It has to sound right coming out of your mouth," I said. Not that I was any expert, but I had learned that much. Somehow, I didn't think Chad's personality was a good match for Gabby.

"So, I shouldn't buy material?"

"There's nothing wrong with buying material. You just don't want it to be generic. If you're paying people to write material for you, make sure it's tailored to you." Then of course, I had to put the icing on the cake. I don't know why I don't just stop myself. "I'm sure Chad has a process where he gets to know you, goes over topics and your perspective, and then writes the material. He's not going to just sell you jokes that anyone could tell." I smiled at Chad.

Nick was looking down at his phone but I could tell he was smiling. Chad, on the other hand, did not look happy with me. Selling off his C-level material to Gabby was exactly what he intended to do. He was shooting darts at me with his eyes.

Great work, Kasey. You haven't even gotten to the resort and you've made an enemy. I really needed to keep my nose out of other people's business.

The driver gave a short wave to the security guard as the shuttle van pulled through an entry gate to the resort. We went up a circular drive and the van stopped under a portico in front of the main doors. The side door and back hatch opened simultaneously. The driver stood by the open door as we got out and then went around the back to pull out our luggage. Chad grabbed his pack and walked in. Nick wrangled a luggage cart for Gabby. We tipped the driver. I noticed Gabby was especially generous, but then, she had a lot more bags than I did.

Chad was already checking in at the counter. We waited our turns, Nick graciously waving Gabby and me to go ahead of him, and a second clerk came out to help. Chad left with a "See you later" and I walked up to the counter.

In slightly accented English, the clerk said, "Welcome to The Santa Ana Winds Resort. I am Stavon." Chad had been blocking a delicious view. Stavon gave me a charming smile.

I already had my license and credit card pulled out ready to hand to him. I stopped in mid-air. "You look like a young Keanu Reeves."

"Ha, yes. Many people tell me that. It is good, yes?"

I handed him my license and card. "It's very good." I returned the smile. "Are you an actor?" It was a safe bet. Half of southern California was in the industry or wanted to be.

He looked confused. "No. I am a desk clerk. I am real."

"Real is a rare trait."

He took care of my paperwork, gave me a map of the resort and two room key cards, and then directed me to the elevators. Gabby was finishing up about the same time. A bellman was ready to help with her luggage. There was just enough room in the elevator for the three of us, her cart and my suitcase. The bellman hit the button for the fourth floor and looked at me.

"I'm on four, too."

He nodded and we rode up in silence. I felt a bit claustrophobic, jammed into the corner. I don't like to be in spaces where I don't have a clear path out. I watched the floors tick by on the digital readout. The bellman pushed the cart out on the fourth floor and we all trooped down the hall in the same direction. My room was the one just beyond Gabby's.

"Hey, we're neighbors!"

"They must have us all in the same section of the resort," I said. "I need a shower to wash the airplane grunge off me. See you later."

"Hey, Kasey?"

I looked over.

"The mixer is at six, right?"

"Yeah."

"Do you want to go down to lunch in a bit? After your shower?"

"Sure. About 45 minutes okay?"

She smiled and some of the tension went out of her shoulders. "Yeah. Just knock on the door when you're ready."

I could hear the bellman lifting the suitcases off the cart and Gabby talking to him. There was a connecting door between our rooms which was anything but soundproof. Luckily, I wouldn't need any privacy. I hoped Gabby wouldn't either. I heard the bell cart rattle down the hallway.

I just had my one suitcase and carry-on. I haven't done a lot of overnight traveling for comedy, but I had already worked out a system. Unpacking took all of five minutes. I use those packing cubes so I just lifted them out and put them in the dresser drawers. My cosmetic bag and toiletries went in the bathroom. I hung up the clothes that needed hanging, happy to have a hotel that supplied enough hangers for a change. A quick shower and I'd be good to go.

Chapter 2: Blurters' Anonymous

CLOSE TO AN HOUR later, Gabby and I walked into the dining room. It was fairly empty; we had missed the lunch rush, if there was one. She had showered and changed into linen slacks and a silk tank top with heels. She'd even changed her jewelry to go with the outfit. She didn't need my friend Ali to put her outfits together. She had reapplied her makeup expertly. I wondered if she used one of those airbrush thingies. I had managed to apply a little eyeliner and mascara. I finished off my look with tinted Burt's Bees instead of lipstick. Did everyone in California look perfect all the time? I was going to have to up my makeup game.

I looked over the menu and tried not to cringe at the prices. I reminded myself that I had budgeted for this. Still, if this was the lunch menu, dinner prices would be astronomical. At least breakfast was included. The server took our orders and we settled into our seats.

"Have you figured out what sessions you're going to attend?" Gabby asked.

"For the most part, yeah. I'm not sure about some of them. I mean, Dolphin Cold Auditioning? What do dolphins have to do with auditions?"

Gabby shrugged. "I don't know but I'm going to find out. I figure at some point I'll be auditioning for something and anything I know about the process will help."

"Good point." I sipped my water. "Do you think Flipper had to audition?"

Gabby laughed. "Flipper was a born talent."

"I wonder if Flipper was like Lassie... a series of dolphins all given the same name."

"We could Google it, but really, some things are sacred. They need a little mystery. And Flipper," she paused for effect, "Is one of those sacred things." She had timing.

Our meals came. I looked over at her Caesar salad with grilled chicken breast and felt a bit guilty about my burger and fries. I knew it wasn't a particularly healthy choice, but I was in a strange place. I like my comfort foods. I looked at the little ramekin of ketchup on the plate. It was not going to do.

"Could I get another ketchup, please? Maybe two?"

The server nodded. "No problem."

"I'd love a burger and fries. Father says if I'm going to be an actress, I need to watch my weight. The camera adds ten pounds."

"Glad I'm just a comic," I said. She was eyeballing my fries like a starving mountain lion. "Help yourself."

"Just one." It was a whisper. She took one and ate it slowly, enjoying every bite. It was almost sexual.

I slowed down my chewing. "You can have more, really."

"No. That was enough. Just wanted the taste." She settled into her salad. Between forkfuls she asked, "What are you wearing to the mixer tonight?"

"I hadn't given it much thought. It's kind of casual, yeah?"

"Yeah, but is it California casual? New York casual? Kansas casual?"

"I hadn't even thought about that. In Florida, if it's casual, people show up in anything from a t-shirt and shorts with flip flops to a sundress and strappy sandals." I shrugged. "I was planning on jeans and a nice blouse. I'm pretty basic."

"Do you think the agents will be there tonight?"

Shit. I hadn't thought about that, either. I flashed back to what Nick said in the shuttle: Dress for the job you want.

"I think they are coming in just for the showcases, but you never know who will be there. Doesn't hurt to impress."

"Yeah, but we don't want to look like we're trying too hard, either. It's a balancing act."

I looked at her.

"Make everything look smooth and easy. Effortless. Don't trip. Don't say the wrong thing. Dress appropriately for the occasion. Order the proper drink for the occasion. Never get drunk in public. All the unspoken rules." She rolled her eyes.

"So, we're not going to be doing tequila shots?"

She laughed and then covered her mouth. "That was too loud."

"There's no one in here. You're allowed to laugh. You're with me. Makes me look good, so thank you."

She shifted in her seat as she looked around the room. Nobody at any of the occupied tables had even looked over, but she was very conscious of them. "Sorry. I overthink everything."

"Then you'll be good for me. I don't think things through. I hadn't even considered that the agents might be there tonight and that I should be thinking about how I present myself. So, thank you for that." I felt so naïve. Maybe I should be more strategic about the sessions I was taking, too.

I looked around the dining room. "I wonder how many people are attending the comedy seminar."

"I don't know. But those people over there are definitely not comics." She pointed out a family of four, with two little kids.

I nodded. "Oh, boy. Little kids mixing with foul-mouthed comics. Probably not what the parents were expecting."

"They're probably going to spend their days over at Disney, though why they didn't book closer to the park, I don't know."

I saw a couple of people sitting at tables alone. I figured they were comics. Comics were almost always alone. I was glad to have Gabby to hang with.

"There's Nick," Gabby said.

He was at the hostess stand, waiting patiently. He saw us and Gabby waved him over.

"Sit with us," she offered.

"You're just about done with your meals."

"We're in no rush," I said. "And I'm definitely going to need coffee after this."

He sat down and the hostess hurried over with a menu.

"Any luck on getting your bag earlier than tomorrow morning?" I asked.

He shook his head. "No. I'm going to have to outfit myself at the gift shop. Hoping there's something besides Hawaiian shirts. Not quite my style."

"You'd rock a Hawaiian shirt," Gabby said. "It could be a whole new you."

He laughed. "Maybe I'll reinvent myself out here."

The server came by and took his order and picked up my empty plate. Gabby was still delicately eating her salad. I'm a fast eater. With four brothers, if you don't eat fast, you don't have a chance at seconds. I was thinking about dessert but ordered coffee instead. I had a feeling Gabby didn't get dessert very often and I suspected I'd be tormenting her.

"Has anyone seen the actual schedule for the sessions?" Nick asked.

"I was just wishing for one. I think we're supposed to get them at the orientation mixer thing tonight."

"Doesn't give us a lot of time to figure things out."

"Well, I know I'm going to take the auditioning and performing track. But I need some of the business stuff, too," Gabby said.

"I definitely need the business stuff, but I'm leaning more towards the writing. I guess that's both my comfort zone and the place I need to work on the most. Well, I need to work on performing, too. Crap. Okay. At this stage, I need everything." I threw my hands up in the air.

They laughed. "I think we all do," Nick said.

"Not Chad," Gabby put in. "He seems to know where he is going."

"And yet, he's here." Nick had picked up on the same thing I did. Chad was all talk so far. It would be interesting to see his set during the showcases.

"Don't let him intimidate you, Gabby. Not everyone is who they say they are."

Gabby looked at Nick. "You think he was lying?"

"Well, he may have been stretching the truth." Nick was being kind.

"Yeah. My Spidey-sense tingled." I stirred sugar into my coffee.

"Most of us aren't who we say we are," Nick said. "I mean, face it. We all want to present our best selves."

"That's exactly what Gabby was getting at about the mixer tonight. We don't know if the agents are going to be there or who else might be in the room. First impressions."

Nick sighed. "I really hope they have something other than Hawaiian shirts in the gift shop."

We laughed.

"Don't worry, you can carry it off."

We spent the remainder of lunch chatting about what we had done so far with our comedy careers. Nick and I were at about the same level, but I definitely had more stage time. Gabby was a bit newer but eager to learn. She'd been to several seminars and had taken acting classes. She'd been taking dance and voice and piano lessons since she was little. I felt awkward next to her. With six kids, our money was spent on necessities, not extras. We didn't really go without, but our after-school activities were usually school sports or Scouts. You got one activity a year, not three. Or more.

"What made you decide to go into comedy, Nick?" I asked.

"You mean at my age?"

"Actually no, I didn't. Are you older than you look?"

"Sorry. I feel a little ridiculous getting into comedy at this age. I'm in my thirties and it seems like all the new comics are teenagers. I feel like I'm having an early mid-life crisis."

"It's good to get it out of the way early. Though most men just get a red convertible. And a much younger wife."

He cringed. "Yeah, well, I'll save the sports car for my forties."

I noticed he didn't say anything about a wife, in spite of the wedding band.

He paused, thinking. "I've got my career established and for the most part, I have time at night. Stand-up is something I always wanted to do, but it's also something that's frivolous. I have too much overhead to make a living at it. I'd have to start at superstar pay and I just don't see that happening."

"My friend Ken would like to do comedy full-time but he has a really good job. Hard to give up the paycheck. And at a certain level, it's stupid to give up a steady paycheck."

"More so if you have responsibilities like a mortgage and car payments. People counting on you." His dark brown eyes clouded over and he looked down at his food for a second or two. Then he looked up and shrugged. "So, I do it for fun but I'm a Type A. If I do anything, I want to do it well."

"Father says I'll make a hash of this like I do with everything else in my life," Gabby volunteered. "A hash of things. That's how he speaks."

I was starting to not like Gabby's father. "You're too young to have screwed anything up beyond repair."

"Well, I was supposed to be a dancer, but I fell off my horse and broke my leg and that was the end of that. I was good at piano, but not world-class." She brightened. "I can sing fairly well."

"And you're funny," I said.

"Let's hope so. I really need to make this work."

"Or?" Nick asked.

"I don't know." She shook her head and repeated quietly, "I don't know."

She seemed to have a lot of pressure on her. "How old are you?"

"I'm twenty-two which is old for LA. I really should have been out here three years ago, putting in the time, going to auditions, meeting the right people..."

"Well, if you're too old, I'm ancient," I said. "I'm almost twenty-five."

"Oh yeah, that's too old." Gabby said matter-of-factly. Then she caught herself. "Oh, God! I am so sorry! I stuck my foot in it, didn't I? Father always tells me to think before I say anything."

I laughed. "It's okay. I'm a blurter, too."

"I didn't mean that you were too old. And really, you could pass for 20 or 21. You should shave your age if you want to get acting work out here. Everyone does. Agents really want you to be young. It's a whole thing."

"I think I'll stick to comedy, then." But now I was worried. Was there an age ceiling in comedy? "Wait, what about all the guy comics who get TV shows? They're in their thirties and forties."

"And usually overweight," Nick added.

"The age rule doesn't apply to guys. At least not as much," Gabby said. "But look at the actresses who play their wives. Even when they try to make them look like normal middle-class wives, they're all much younger."

"Good point," Nick said. "Face it. In real life, guys who look and act like that never get the young, hot wife."

"Yeah, the women are all gorgeous with size zero bodies and the men are incredibly average-looking."

"I hate that they're all portrayed as bumbling idiots," Nick said.

"Or jerks if they're successful at their jobs," I added. "But it's TV. They need conflict to make it interesting."

"Are you taking the screenwriting classes?" Nick asked.

"Yeah. I'm looking forward to those the most actually."

"Me, too. I figure anything that helps with my comedy writing is a bonus."

We sat talking for another half hour. Nick left to check out the offerings at the gift shop. Gabby and I headed back to our rooms. She was probably going to hit the pool... or maybe not. She wasn't sure. I was going to go through the course offerings again, this time more strategically.

I was on the bed halfway dozing, when I felt the computer slip off my lap. I made a reflexive grab at it. I must have been more than halfway dozing because I could clearly hear voices in Gabby's room. She was in the middle of a conversation with another woman.

"Listen, Gabby, I know that you're ambitious and you don't play small..."

"Well, I'm grateful you're telling me about this," Gabby said.

I shook my head. What did I just hear? Was Gabby being offered a special opportunity or was she being given bad news? I set the computer aside and moved closer to the door. I'm nosy. What can I say?

I didn't know who was talking to Gabby, but it was obviously someone with the event.

"We don't offer this upgrade to everyone, Gabby, but we noticed the professionalism of your package—the headshot, the resume—and we feel that you are someone who is going places. There's an elite, limited showcase that will be held Saturday night for only a select, few people."

"So, not everyone will know about this?"

"As a matter of fact, we want to keep this strictly confidential. No one wants to be told they don't have what it takes, but let's face it—there are over one hundred comics here. It's going to be tough to stand out in that sea of showcases, no matter how good you are. Take it from me, after going through a day of auditions, all the candidates just blur into one."

"That makes sense."

"So, the elite showcase is open to only ten comics. You've been shortlisted. For an additional $1,000, you can have a private audition with Sollie Vincenzo, owner of Comedy Concepts and Ross Zieff, the agent from Pro Casting Creative. You and I both know what that could mean for your career."

"Oh my gosh, yes. Can I give you a credit card?"

"No problem. But remember, don't mention this to anyone else. People will be hurt that they didn't get selected."

"I understand. Let me get my card."

It was a little quiet and I heard a bit of mumbling.

"I just need your email address to send the receipt." Gabby gave it to her.

"And there you go. You are in. You'll get a special invitation with all the information you need. Prepare your best ten minutes of material. And bring two copies of your headshot and resume with you."

"I am so excited! Thank you!"

I grabbed the ice bucket and started down the hall, heading for the ice machine as Gabby's door opened. Juliet Hartwell, America's Comedy Sweetheart, stepped out and looked straight at me.

"Wow! Hi!" I hoped I appeared cheery and clueless. I continued down the hall.

I didn't bother looking at Gabby but she must have felt a need to cover.

"Well, uh, thanks for that information. It wasn't in my packet."

I hoped Gabby had signed up for the improv class. She needed it.

"You're welcome. I'll see you later." Juliet was about twenty feet behind me, heading for the elevator. I took the left into the little side area that had the ice and snack machines. I forced myself not to look up as she went by. Juliet didn't stop. I guessed I wasn't on her special invitee list. Not that I had an extra $1,000 to fork over.

I got the ice that I didn't need and headed back to my room. I put it on the desk and plunked down on my bed, feeling deflated.

So, there was a special upper level going on. "Elite" Juliet had said. I sighed. Why would comedy, and especially the Los Angeles scene, be any different from everything else in life? Everything seemed to be pay to play. I wondered if I had wasted my money putting in for the regular showcase. Probably.

I squared my shoulders. All it meant was that I wouldn't get there as fast as some people, wherever there was. I'd just have to make it on talent and hard work. Because that works out so well for people.

Chapter 3: It's Nice to Be Asked

GABBY AND I WENT down to the mixer together. I am used to walking into a room alone, but it doesn't mean I like it. I sensed that it was harder for Gabby so I made the offer. Two assistants were at the registration table, one man and one woman. The woman, Pamela according to her name tag, checked off our names on a print out. I glanced at the list: It was alphabetized by last name. About half the names were already checked off. The young man, Trystan, handed us two drink coupons each from a big roll of numbered tickets.

"The most important part," he said, flashing a smile at Gabby.

At least I wouldn't be blowing my budget on alcohol the first night. We thanked them and went through the door. We were about ten minutes late and already small knots of people huddled near the two bar carts in the private event room.

Heads turned when we walked in. I was pretty sure it was Gabby causing the stir. Not that I couldn't turn a few heads myself, but she had an upscale glamour going on that made me feel like the poor relation in a Jane Austen novel. She had chosen a cobalt blue dress that hugged her body without being too tight or revealing. She was wearing matching heels, higher than I could walk in for sure. The outfit was appropriate for a New York or LA cocktail party. I had gone with the outfit Ali had picked out for me—the little black cocktail dress with emerald accents. I had added the cuff bracelet, matching necklace, and dangly earrings. Heels of course, but not as high as Gabby's. Whenever I felt intimidated, I liked to go on the offensive. My heels made me as tall or taller than most men. The emerald green accents, Ali had said, would make my hair and face stand out. She seemed to think that was a good thing and I deferred to her judgment. Most of the women were dressed for a cocktail party. They understood the game.

I scanned the room. The assemblage was about one-third women, two-thirds men. Comedy is very much a man's game. But I was happy to see more women entering the field. Maybe someday having three women on the bill wouldn't be listed as "Girls' Night Out." I could dream, couldn't I?

Most of the guys were in jeans and the popular untucked, long-sleeve dress shirt. A few were in t-shirts. I had long ago learned to check people's shoes and watches to see if they were doing as well as they said. Most were not. Harder to do with comedians because most of the guys defaulted to running shoes and watches were almost a thing of the past. There was a certain homogeneity that they fell into. Same clothing, same haircuts, same material. They were killing their opportunities and didn't know it. You can get work being like everyone else, as long as you're dependable and not a jerk. But you're not going to rise to the top. You've got to stand out in a good way.

And there he was, coming through the door, a definite stand-out.

"Hey, Luke!" I waved at him and he headed right over and grabbed me up in a hug. "I didn't know you were going to be here."

"Yeah, I'm stalking you," he grinned.

I felt Gabby elbow me. I couldn't blame her. Luke belonged in Hollywood. Tall, with dirty blonde hair, blue eyes and cheekbones that screamed for a camera. I could sense the other men in the room hating him on sight.

"Oh, sorry. Luke, I'd like you to meet Gabby... What is your last name?"

"Leigh. Gabby Leigh."

"Luke Hallidade. Nice to meet you."

They shook hands and Luke turned back to me. "Did you just get in?"

"Yeah, around noon. How about you?"

"I've been here for a few days. Well, not here. I was in LA. Had some meetings."

"You mean auditions?"

"Yeah, I read for a couple of things. Don't know how I did."

"You're an actor?" Gabby asked.

"Yeah. Or working on it."

"Gabby's an actress," I said. "She reminded me of you right away. Working her way in through the comedy angle. Maybe you can give her some tips."

"I'd be happy to, for what it's worth. I'm not exactly breaking down doors."

She smiled up at him. "I'd appreciate it."

"May I join you or is this only for the beautiful people?" Nick slid in beside me. He was wearing a fresh, light blue, long-sleeve shirt with the resort's logo on it. Not as much fun as a Hawaiian shirt, but it did the job.

"I think you make the cut," I said. I introduced Nick and Luke. They shook hands with smiles on their faces but they both eyed each other territorially. I figured Gabby was bringing out their testosterone.

We drifted towards one of the service bars. The first two drinks were free and it looked like some of the comics were afraid the liquor was going to run out before they got their second freebie. The guys ordered beer; Gabby and I got wine. She went with something white, I defaulted to a cabernet. There were high cocktail tables to stand around—no seats—but we found one and set down our drinks. We all looked around the room. People were standing around awkwardly for the most part, not quite sure what to say.

"It's like a junior high dance," I said.

"They'll loosen up once the second drink gets in them," Nick replied.

Gabby took the conversational lead. "So, how do you and Luke know each other?"

"We started out together," Luke said. "Same comedy class."

"Then, of course, we did Florida's Funniest Comedians."

"You did it. I was out cold for most of that weekend."

"You're the guy!" Nick said. "Are you doing okay?"

"Let's just say that I no longer date comics," Luke rolled his eyes. Nick brightened at that.

"How do you feel about actresses?" Gabby asked.

Luke laughed. "I proceed with caution." But he gave her a smile.

I felt a pang of jealousy. There was no reason for it—Luke and I were never a thing, but there it was. We seemed to be a series of missed opportunities. We didn't see each other often enough for our relationship to settle into a real friendship. We bumped into each other a few times a year and it was always like this. Friendly on the surface, with a dangerous electrical charge just beneath. He was my third rail.

"Does anyone know anyone else here?" I asked, to change the subject more than anything.

"Well, there's Chad over there," Nick said. We followed his gaze. Chad was standing with a few other guys, and had definitely established himself as the alpha in the group. He was talking, they were listening.

"Looks like they're buying his BS," I said.

Gabby turned to me. "What?"

Shit. I had blurted out inside thoughts. Again.

Nick came to my rescue. "You picked up on that, too?"

"Didn't sit right with me or maybe I'm just a skeptic."

"I take it you've all met that guy," Luke said. "Fill me in."

"He's a headliner and he's out here looking to get a new agent," Gabby explained.

"Except he's really not a headliner. Well, not a full-time headliner anyway," Nick said.

"You Googled him, too? I thought I was being bitchy but I did it anyway."

Nick laughed. "Well, I'm a bitch, too then."

Gabby looked confused.

"He's not quite as good as he says," Nick explained. "He's getting some headliner slots at lesser clubs but he's mostly a feature. He was stretching the truth a bit."

Gabby nodded. "Yeah. Well, he was kind of arrogant."

"Looks like he is building a posse," I said, taking a sip of my wine.

"We'll see how long that lasts. People tend to give themselves away over time." Nick's eyes had narrowed.

"It's very hard to stay in character 24/7 once you've created it," Luke said.

"You've got to be very good." I smiled at him.

The background music faded down and a microphone clicked on. People stopped talking and looked around. Juliet Hartwell had entered from a side door and people turned to face her.

"Good evening and welcome everyone." She paused. "I'm Juliet Hartwell."

People started applauding. I joined in because why not?

She nodded and then did a humble little bow to us.

"First and most important, did everyone get some drinks?" People laughed and there was scattered applause. "You're welcome. Second, thank you all for being here. I love to do this conference because when

I was coming up in the business, there was no one to guide me along. I was clueless. I knew that comics needed to learn about the business side of comedy, to help them get ahead and to learn the ropes. And, frankly, not to be taken advantage of."

She pivoted. "Tomorrow, we'll all meet in this room for our welcome session. Tonight, before you leave, please pick up your orientation packet with the conference schedule and bring it with you tomorrow. The packets were a little late in getting here, but Pamela and Trystan now have them available for you." She indicated the registration table and Pamela, the woman who had checked us in, held up a folder, so we could all see what it looked like.

"In there, you will find the conference schedule. I'll go over the two tracks tomorrow. I'll also introduce you to your instructors and session leaders. We start at 9:00 am tomorrow, but if you could get there by 8:15 or 8:30, we can check you in, give you your conference badges, and yes, there will be coffee." She waited for the expected laugh and got it.

"I'll be wandering around tonight, so don't be shy about saying hi. Some of our other instructors have arrived already," she pointed to a couple of women and man huddled near a side door. They put friendly smiles on their faces and waved. "Okay. Don't forget, your breakfast is included. The breakfast buffet is in the dining room and opens at 6:30. We have three days of intensive sessions planned for you. Drink up tonight, because we're gonna fill your heads with information and make you work for the next three days."

She paused for a second, looked down at the floor, then looked out at us.

"There is so much talent in this room, so much talent. I want to see you all succeed. That is our goal here at this conference—to give you the tools and knowledge you need to succeed in this crazy business. Again, thank you for coming. And... party on!"

She turned the microphone off and handed it to one of the bartenders. People immediately surrounded her. I figured she would work her way through the crowd and eventually get to us.

"Well, that was nice," Gabby said.

I was silent. She'd like to see us all succeed, but some were getting a bit of a push up the ladder. "America's comedy sweetheart." I looked at my glass; It was close to empty. "Anyone else ready for a refill?"

We all were. Or close enough. "Give me your drink tickets and I'll get us another round," I offered. I needed to adjust my attitude a bit. I could feel myself bristling at Juliet already and I needed to get past that if I was going to get the most out of the conference.

"I'll help you carry," Nick offered. We moved off to wait in the short line at the bar.

I watched Juliet chatting people up as we waited.

"I can see the gears in your brain cranking," Nick said.

"My face gives everything away. I hate that."

"So, what is it?"

I lowered my voice. "So, you know how she said she wants everyone to succeed?"

He nodded.

"She has offered private showcases to some people. For an extra $1,000."

"Yeah, I know."

I looked up at him, surprised. "You do? God, I'm such a loser. Did she make the offer to everyone but me?"

"I doubt it. I think she looked at who could afford the fee. Remember the questionnaire we all filled out?"

I nodded and we shuffled closer to the bar.

"She probably looked at the occupations listed and went off that. And maybe a social media search since that was on the questionnaire, too."

"You've got a really logical mind. I work as a copywriter at an ad agency. I guess she could tell I'm not hauling down the big bucks."

He laughed. "Yeah."

"So, did you take her up on the offer?"

"No. Comedy won't be my bread and butter for a long time, if ever. I can put that money to better use. This conference is more about self-indulgence for me than trying to make it in comedy."

We gave our orders to the bartender.

"Your day job is that good?"

"It's a career. Went to school and everything. I'd have to make it very big in comedy to replace my income."

The bartender handed us our drinks. We put several dollars in the tip jar. Nick picked up the beers and I took the wines.

"Well, good. Since you saved yourself a thousand bucks, you can buy the next round."

"See, already it's being put to a better use."

My attitude was adjusted. We set the drinks down on the table and Juliet walked over. Our turn for a personal chat.

We all introduced ourselves. Juliet asked what we wanted to get out of the conference, what our special interests were. Nick and I leaned more towards writing; Gabby and Luke were heading for all the performance stuff, naturally. Juliet was warm and friendly and in the short time she spent with us, I think we all came away feeling a bit special. I gave her the benefit of the doubt.

"Well, there's our six degrees of Kevin Bacon," Luke said.

Gabby looked at him. "Huh?"

"There's a game that says most of us are only six people—degrees away from knowing Kevin Bacon. He's done so many movies that he's worked with just about everyone in Hollywood. Even average people, non-showbiz, probably know someone who knows someone who knows someone..." Luke left it at that.

"And now we know Juliet," I said. "And she worked on a TV show with Jane Curtin who worked with John Belushi on *Saturday Night Live*, who worked with Kevin Bacon on *National Lampoon's Animal House*. So does that make us two degrees or three?"

"Doesn't matter. We are in the presence of greatness," Nick said, raising his beer. "To greatness."

"Or presence," I said. We clinked glasses.

"Well, we're almost famous, then," Gabby joked.

"Some closer than others," I said. I figured I'd put it out on the table. "You're doing the private showcase."

Poor Gabby almost choked on her wine.

"How do you know about that?"

"We've got adjoining rooms and that door is not soundproof. Something to think about before you bring anyone back to your room."

"Same goes for you," Luke put in quickly.

"Not a worry. I'm here to work." A thought occurred to me. "Are you doing the private showcase, Luke?"

"Yeah. I ponied up."

"I didn't even get the offer."

"There were only ten slots," Luke said. "She may have filled them before getting to you. I can't imagine too many people turned a chance like that down."

"Nick did."

Gabby and Luke looked at him. He shrugged.

"I've been informed that the thousand dollars I saved will be put towards buying us drinks over the weekend."

It broke the tension. Maybe the slots did fill up that quickly. My mind drifted while they talked. A little voice inside me wondered if I just wasn't pretty enough. I mean, Luke and Gabby were Hollywood gorgeous. There was just no two ways about it. I'm okay pretty. It's a different level. Nick was definitely handsome and could be a "type."

But he was older and LA liked young people. Or those who look young. So maybe Nick was right: It was about who was most likely to have an extra thousand dollars. And that, I definitely did not have. In a way I felt better but not much. Then again, maybe Juliet had just gone alphabetically and all the slots were filled before she hit the Ms.

"I don't know why we couldn't get a schedule in advance," Gabby was saying. "I really need time to go over everything so I can make the best choice of sessions. I mean, the descriptions all sounded good, but what if I can't get into a session I need? What if everyone decides to go to one session and not the other that's scheduled for the same time? Will there be enough seats for everyone? And how will the other session leader feel if nobody shows up for their session?"

"You may be overthinking this," Nick said.

"Yeah. Yeah. You're right. It will be fine." She nodded to herself. The hand that wasn't holding her drink clenched and unclenched twice. I wondered if she knew that she did it.

A thirty-ish woman came up to our table. "Hi, I'm Amber. Do you mind if I hang with you guys for a bit? Some guy is telling me how wonderful he is."

"Been there," Gabby said.

"I don't even have to look," I said. "Chad?"

"How did you know?"

"We've met."

Luke said, "Gee. I've got some catching up to do."

"Maybe he's just nervous," Gabby said.

"You are so much nicer than I am," I said. We all introduced ourselves. I raised my glass to Amber. "You get to tell us how wonderful you are. And... go!"

"Oh, crap." She looked around the room and then shrugged her shoulders. "I'm a feature act out of Michigan. What can I tell you? I want to move up."

"That's how you knew Chad was bullshitting you," I said.

"Yeah, well, if he's headlining, he's doing it in toilets." She looked up. "Sorry, that was rude."

"I think you nailed it," Nick said.

"I'm not a snob, but I don't know... I just wasn't buying it."

"Yeah, he's stretching," I said. "We'll just leave it at that."

"I guess that's why we're here," Luke said. "Trying to get to the next level."

"Have you picked up your packets yet?" Amber asked. She pulled one from her bag. "I don't know why they didn't publish the schedule earlier. That would have been helpful."

"I know, right?" Gabby looked towards the door. "I'm going to get packets for everyone."

Nick watched her go, a look of concern on his face.

"What else is in there?" Luke asked.

"Let's see... a sample resume, a speaking one sheet, resources... looks like a lot of web stuff like lists of clubs, website information, something on mailing lists. I need a mailing list?"

"What? You don't have a fan club yet?" Luke asked.

"Unfortunately, no. Who'd want to be on my mailing list? I have three fans. And one is my mom."

"Maybe we'll learn that in one of the sessions?" I wasn't sure why we would need a mailing list either.

Gabby returned and handed out packets. We all started leafing through.

"We can get our headshots done if we need them. Maybe I need new headshots." She frowned.

"Six hundred dollars for a one-hour headshot session? We must be in California," Nick shook his head.

"Hell, it must be just as bad in New York," I said.

"Lots of actors, lots of photographers. And everyone is building a portfolio."

"I'm wondering if there's a different set of headshots for television work than for comedy," Amber said. "I guess we'll learn that, too."

"You've been out here doing auditions, Luke. What have you seen?" I asked.

"I honestly hadn't thought too much about it. I've only read for a few things. No one spit on my headshot, so I guess it was okay. And, I've got my modeling portfolio. But jeez, now I'm wondering, too."

"Well, if we weren't insecure before we got here, we are now," Amber said. We laughed.

"That is something, though," Nick said.

"What?"

"People are going to tell us that we need to do certain things and that will include spending more dollars. Not just here, but probably throughout our careers. Things we need to do that will get us ahead. We need to evaluate each offer as it comes and ask what the person's motivation is."

"Like the private showcases," I said. He nodded.

"What private showcases?" Amber asked.

We all looked a bit guilty.

"Some of the attendees are being offered a private audition with the club owner and booking agent." I paused. "For an extra $1,000."

"Yikes. Well, I'm out. I'm a feature act. It was a stretch to come here in the first place." Amber looked around the table. "Are you guys doing it?"

"I don't see anything wrong with doing it," Nick said. "If it really is a decent agent. But it was a no for me."

"I'm doing it," Luke said. "The thousand dollars was a bit stiff, but I'm trying to break in out here. I need to be seen so to me, it's just another business expense."

Amber turned to me. "Are you doing a showcase?"

"Hell, I wasn't even asked. But like you, too rich for my blood. Luke here makes big bucks as a model."

Luke played it off. "My face is my fortune."

Gabby was looking down at the table. "Maybe I should have said no."

"Is it a financial stretch for you?" I asked. "I'm sorry. That's a personal question. But it would have been for me."

Now she looked more embarrassed. "No. Finances are not a problem. I just don't want to hear my father complain that I wasted money because I got sucked into another scam."

I was about to ask about what other scams but Nick caught my eye and shook his head. I changed tack.

"If I had the money, I would do it. I think it will be okay."

"You'd do it?"

"Sure. Are you kidding me?"

I could see the relief pass through her body. Out of the corner of my eye, I could see Nick nod. Our Gabby was pretty high strung. I was already feeling protective.

We chatted in our little group, but for a mixer, most of us weren't really mixing. Comedy seems to have more than a fair share of awkward introverts. That was fine by me; it was nice not to be the only uncomfortable person in a room.

The mixer was scheduled to go to 9:00 pm. My stomach started growling at 8:30.

"I'm starving and the hors d'oeuvres went in the first ten minutes. Anyone up for a real meal?" I am not shy when it comes to eating.

"Great idea."

We trooped over to the restaurant but Gabby split off at the elevators. "I'm a little tired. Jet lag, I guess. I'll see you in the morning."

I was more hungry than tired. Once the hunger was taken care of, tiredness took over. I signed my check with my room number and prepared to leave.

"I'm ready to turn in, too. Long day," Nick said. "I'll head up with you."

"Not me," Amber looked at Luke. "I'm up for a night cap. How about you?"

"Um, sure. Why not?" he said, looking at me.

"See you tomorrow," I said.

Nick and I rode the elevator up to the fourth floor. His room was off the other hallway.

We said our good nights and headed to our rooms.

Chapter 4: Style Level: Cramped

My alarm went off at 6:30 and I resisted the urge to ignore it. I did ignore the hotel room coffee, which is rarely good and even if the coffee is decent, I like real cream in my coffee. Powdered crap, flavored or not, will not cut it.

I showered and dressed in my usual 45 minutes, but spent an additional ten on makeup today. This was southern California and the "natural look" was on a whole different level. I was at the breakfast buffet by 7:30. Most of the hotel guests were there, too. Who got up early on vacation? I filled my tray and was looking for a table.

"Kasey."

I turned towards the voice. Luke was at a table with a woman who looked vaguely familiar and he waved me over.

"Hey, Luke. Glad you have a table. Crowded in here." I took the food off my tray, placing the plates and cup on the table and put the tray on a nearby stand. I leaned over to shake hands with the woman before I sat down. She didn't look too happy to have me joining them. I went full-on puppy-dog friendly.

"Kasey McCormick."

"Patti Minette," she responded.

"Great to meet you." I sat and started fixing my coffee. There was a bowl of individual creamer choices. I went for the unflavored Half and Halfs.

"How do you two know each other?" Patti asked, which was the obvious question.

Luke shot me a look. The look. "We started in comedy together and, well, what can I say. I knew Kasey was the girl for me from the start."

I played along. "Well, I'd say we had a rocky start..."

"Yet, here we are," He gazed into my eyes with a look that said *you've got me for life*.

"He's such a romantic mush," I said, touching his hand.

It was enough for Patti. "That's so sweet. Oh, look at the time. I better be going."

"So cool to meet you, Patti. I'm looking forward to running into you over the next few days," I said.

Luke stood up about halfway as Patti left the table, but she didn't notice. I shook my head at him.

"Dude."

"I'm sorry. She was hitting on me and there you were..."

"Yeah, well, how do you explain us being in separate rooms?"

"I'll tell everyone you snore." He didn't hesitate.

"You couldn't channel your inner asshole?"

"I think I will leave that behind me."

"Good place for an asshole."

We laughed. "So, that was why you gave me the look when Amber suggested a night cap."

"It worked out alright. I was more worried about you heading off with a married man."

"Not an issue. Off-limits for me. And he wasn't asking anyway." Luke nodded.

"So, I guess I'm hitched to you for the next few days," I said. "Not for nuthin' but you're kind of cramping my style."

"I've seen your style. It's permanently cramped." He said it with a smile to show he was kidding, but he wasn't wrong. I am not good at picking up on signals. "Besides, you don't date comics."

"The desk clerk kinda looks like Keanu Reeves," I said.

He nodded. "Plus he probably has access to the vending machines."

"It's a very attractive feature."

I worked through my eggs and breakfast potatoes and toast. I love breakfast foods. I could probably eat breakfast three times a day.

Luke looked at my coffee cup. "Need more?"

"Yes, please. More than oxygen."

He took our two cups and went for refills. I looked around the room. I didn't see Gabby. Nick was at a table in the corner with a couple of guys. I saw Amber sitting with another woman. Chad was in a booth with three other guys, holding court and chowing down as if this was the only meal he'd get for the day.

I watched Nick. He was watching Luke come back from the coffee area with the two cups. Luke leaned over to put the coffee cup in front of me and went around to his side of the table. Nick turned to one of the men next to him and said something.

Then Luke said something.

"I'm sorry, what?"

"What floor are you on?"

"Fourth. East Wing, with a fabulous view of not much. How about you?"

"West Wing, fifth, pool view. Do you know what sessions you're attending today?"

"Well, first session is easy since we're all in it. Then I guess the Build Your Fanbase thing. It seems like a lot of computer stuff, but I can handle that. How about you?"

"Physical Comedy and Body Language."

"Well, I expect you're going to see a lot of body language over the next few days. Think you can handle it?" I couldn't resist teasing him.

"Sorry. I didn't have enough coffee in me and I panicked."

"Don't worry. I'll protect you from all the scary women." A thought occurred to me. "Unless you have one that you have your eye on. Then I'll butt out."

"I'll let you know."

There was a pause. "And you'll do the same for me?" I said, making it more of a question than statement.

"Kasey, really? Not a chance. I'm going to scare off every skeevy comic who dares to go near you."

"Thanks, tons."

"What about this afternoon? Which sessions?"

"I'm definitely doing the cookie break," I said. "Improv Techniques or Dolphin Cold Auditions. Neither one really appeals to me."

"Come to Cold Auditions with me."

"Gabby is doing that one, too. Sure, why not? We can do Flipper impressions afterwards."

"Where is Gabby this morning?" Luke asked.

"She was up—I heard her blow dryer going. I'm betting she's not a breakfast girl."

"Actresses. Have to be impossibly thin. And, I'm learning, actors too."

"You're in great shape. You're a model for Pete's sake."

"It's not quite as bad for the guys, but before a shoot, I have to work down my body fat and make sure I'm lean enough for the muscles to stand out. It's very..."

"Sterile? Mechanical?"

"Mechanical is closer. You drop weight, dehydrate, do the shoot turning this way and that way, waiting for lighting. You're very much a product."

"Sounds unhealthy. Is it worth it?"

"Well, they pay me a ridiculous amount of money. So yeah, right now it's worth it. But I'll be happy to leave the modeling gigs behind."

"Well, then, you better pay attention in Dolphin Audition class so you can get some acting gigs."

"With my luck, I'll be cast in a remake of Flipper, have to run around shirtless, and still have to train constantly."

"Here's hoping that private showcase works its magic. Is it tomorrow night?"

"Yeah. I think it's the worst kept secret here."

That brought me up a bit. "Other people know?"

"I overheard some grumbling when I was working out this morning. People weren't real happy to know there was a private track, but when I told them it was $1,000, they all said it was too steep for them anyway."

"Did you mention you were doing it?"

"No, didn't bring that up." He looked away. "But they knew only ten people were selected. I guess word got around last night. As I said, worst kept secret."

"Yeah. I think there's bound to be some resentment because, well, it's just another reminder that the playing field is different for different people. You can afford the $1,000. A lot of people can't. That gives you an unfair advantage."

Luke nodded. "It is an unfair advantage. My looks are an unfair advantage in acting and modeling, not so much in comedy. Your looks give you an advantage; so does your height. It gives you a presence that other comics have to work for. Most people have some sort of unfair advantage in some area."

There was loud laughter coming from Chad's table. We looked over.

"What do you think his unfair advantage is?"

Luke shrugged. "I don't know, but the fact that nobody has punched him out yet tells me he has one."

We laughed. I looked at the clock on the restaurant wall.

"Crap. Five after." I swigged down the remainder of my coffee.

We rode the elevator together.

"See you down there," Luke said as I got off on four.

"Yep." I hustled to my room. Gabby was just coming out of hers.

"Heading down?" I asked. Another Captain Obvious moment. I really needed to work on my small talk.

"Yes, I want to be on time." She seemed a little anxious about it.

"You'll be right on time. I'm about five minutes behind you."

I went to the bathroom, brushed my teeth, and put my laptop in the room safe. I had brought my leather portfolio that holds a pad of paper, has places for my pens, and a slot for loose papers. It also had a zip pocket for money and credit cards so I didn't need to carry a handbag. I put my bag in the safe, too. There was nothing of value in it, but it's not good to leave stuff out. I've stayed in enough hotel rooms in the last few years to pick up a few good habits. People are basically honest, but tempting them is just plain stupid. I checked my back pocket to make sure I had the hotel key cards there, and headed down to the main room.

Chapter 5: First Instinct Is the Best Instinct

I GOT TO THE registration table at 8:20 and there were about forty people milling about, forming two messy lines, one for A-M, the other for N-Z. The N-Z looked shorter. Of course. The two assistants were behind laptops, checking people in. I sighed. No sign of Gabby. She was probably already inside. I wondered if I should have waited another half hour for the first rush to be over. I saw Nick heading into the meeting room. He must have been one of the early ones, too.

I shuffled forward, listening in on a couple of conversations. People were excited—I could feel the buzz of energy in the lobby. I was feeling kind of excited, too. I was hoping to come out of this event with some kind of plan of attack to get myself steady feature work. I still wouldn't be able to quit my day job, and that limited me a little bit. I could use my paltry two weeks' vacation for two week-long gigs per year, though I was using up three days for this seminar. Obviously, vacation days weren't going to work in the long run. So, it would have to be local work and a lot of driving back and forth to gigs so I could be at work by 8:30 every morning. Luke's modeling work was perfect for him: big money and flexible hours. I wondered what Gabby did for a living and then I flashed back on the Louis Vuitton matched luggage. Light dawned on Marblehead, as we say in Boston. Gabby's job was to become an actress. She obviously came from money. She could spend her days taking classes, improving her skills, flying to events like this. Talk about an unfair advantage: Money, looks, years of training. Well, the years of training weren't really an unfair advantage; she had done the work on that. I don't think she took her advantages for granted, either. She mostly seemed afraid that she was going to screw up somehow. I guess if people had unfair advantages, they might also have unfair disadvantages.

I finally reached the registration table, got my event name tag and lanyard, and went into the main room. It had seating for about one hundred and fifty people. There was a microphone on the stage, along with five tall directors' chairs. I looked around the room, hoping to see someone I knew. At least I saw something I knew: coffee. There were three coffee stations set up: one large one in the back of the room and two on each side of the room. The one on the far side had the least amount of people at it. I made a beeline.

This resort had good coffee. I was grateful for that. I filled my cup, added cream (real cream-yay!) and sugar, and stood against the wall, sipping and people-watching. A redheaded guy was juggling his notebook and cup of coffee. He joined me at the wall to get out of the fray.

"Mind another ginger sharing your wall?"

"Nah. We have to stick together. I'm Kasey McCormick."

"Roger Weathersby."

"Nice to meet you." Our hands were full so we bumped elbows. "Where are you from?"

"Originally? Oregon. I'm out on Long Island now. Went east for school and stayed."

"I met another guy from Long Island—Nick Hill. Do you know him?"

"Yeah, we hit a lot of the same clubs. He's pretty good. Didn't know he'd be here. Random."

"One hundred people and we both know someone at the event. Got to be less random than we think."

He looked at me.

"One of the guys I started out with is here. Good guy." I was scanning the room and I saw Luke come through the door at that exact moment. "Speak of the devil."

"That guy? He was working out this morning."

"So, you're one of the early birds."

"When you're a redheaded guy, you have to work a little harder. Face it, everyone looks at me and thinks Ron Weasley. My initials don't help."

"Tell me about it. My whole family is redheaded."

"It's a recessive gene fest," he said.

"Don't forget, Ron got the girl at the end of the series."

"True," Roger nodded. "It's the only thing that keeps me going." His timing was great. I cracked up.

We looked around the room some more. I wasn't ready to sit down yet. I figured we'd be doing enough sitting during the day.

"There's Nick," Roger said, pointing with his cup hand. Nick was talking to Amber. He was wearing a different shirt with the same dress pants. Luggage hadn't come yet. He seemed to be taking it well. Most everyone was in jeans and running shoes. I had gone for my fallback black jeans and white starched shirt with a black blazer. I had on medium-heeled black ankle boots that put me up to five foot eleven. The room was pretty loud with all the conversations going on. It seemed that just about everyone was on time. People were starting to find seats. I looked at the front row and saw Gabby was already front and center, with her notebook and pen ready. She was chatting with a woman who wore big round glasses and had a mass of dark curls held back with a colorful scarf. Gabby was in a tailored suit with a short skirt, looking sexy and businesslike at the same time. I wondered if she would relax her style over the next few days. I suspected this level was her baseline.

I put my cup on a tray set up to collect the dirties. I was tempted to get another cup, but I didn't want to have to go to the bathroom in the middle of the orientation and miss something.

"Are you sitting with anyone?" Roger asked.

"No. I usually sit in the back so I can stand if I need to stretch a bit."

"I sit in the back so I can watch the whole room." He paused. "Is that creepy?"

"No. I like to see everything that's going on, too. I hate to have people behind me."

"So, we're probably both paranoid freaks."

"Just because you're paranoid..." I started.

"Doesn't mean they're not out to get you."

We walked toward the back and chose a spot in the last row. The room was set up in two sections, twelve rows deep, twelve seats across. There was a wide aisle down the center and an aisle up either side between the chairs and the walls. There was a sound and video booth in the back of the room on one side of the main entrance. The video crew had been working their way through the room, taking crowd shots but now had their cameras set on tripods. The lights flickered twice, a not-so-subtle signal to find seats. We waited expectantly.

The female assistant from last night entered from a side door. "Good morning, everyone!" She was holding a wireless mic and it worked perfectly. None of the "Is this thing on?" that you get at business meetings. At least the tech side of things would be professional. I had paid an extra $250 for a video of my showcase and I had been afraid it would be poor quality. I wasn't thinking I would be in California, the land where people know what they're doing when it comes to sound and video. It was a bit reassuring.

"We still have people checking in, so we're going to give them a couple more minutes to find their seats and then we'll get started. Sound good?"

People were vocally agreeable.

"Okay, see you soon!" She disappeared back through the side door.

"Are you buying a video of your showcase?" I asked Roger.

"Yeah. I'm just doing the regular showcase." He looked at me to see if I understood.

"Me, too. I don't have an extra thousand bucks lying around."

"I wonder if the private showcase includes the cost of the video. You've heard about it, right?"

"Yeah. I wasn't invited." I made a face.

"Me, either."

"I am comforting myself with the thought that there were only ten slots and people probably jumped on them."

"Is your friend doing it?"

"Yeah, but he's going into acting. So, it's more of an investment for him."

"He's also got the LA look." Roger sounded a bit intimidated.

"Yeah. It's not just the Brad Pitt hair. But we think he was asked because he has disposable income. Or maybe a combination of his looks and income."

"How would they know how much money we make?" Roger was incredulous.

"Well, it was Nick who brought it up. He reminded me that they asked for our occupations on the registration form. From there, it's just a quick social media check."

"They asked Nick to do the private showcase?"

"Yeah. He pointed out that he was older and not as good-looking as what the agent was probably looking for. He figures they asked him because he could afford it."

"Sounds like he turned it down."

"He did. He said that comedy wasn't his main career."

Roger laughed. "Yeah, that's an understatement."

I looked at him, waiting for an explanation.

"He's a cardiologist. Actually, cardiac surgeon. One of the best in New York. He probably gets helicoptered to some bigshot's operating room twice a week."

"Wow. What's he doing in comedy?"

"Likes it, I think. Hey, don't tell him I told you about what he does. He doesn't talk about it. Just wants to hang out with comics."

"I'll keep it under my hat." Now I understood why he wouldn't be quitting his day job any time soon.

The lights dimmed and people quieted down expectantly.

A deep, professional male voice came over the sound system. "Ladies and gentlemen, please welcome America's Comedy Sweetheart, Ms. Juliet Hartwell."

We broke into applause and after a second or two, Juliet came out at a fast walk, clipboard in hand. She mounted the two steps to the low stage and gave a big wave.

"Welcome! Welcome everyone! I can tell you've all had your coffee. Ready to hit the ground running?"

Her question was answered by more applause and a few whoops. It was nice to see comics excited by something. We usually try very hard not to appear impressed. This weekend might end up being more fun than I expected.

She ran through some housekeeping items and the basic schedule for each day. Two sessions in the morning, two in the afternoon, a coffee break and a cookie break. Then evening activities. She didn't mention the private showcase, but then, I didn't expect she would.

"I'd like to introduce you to your session leaders. Would you like that?"

More applause. The rhetorical questions worked. I made a note of it. I didn't know if I would ever use it, but when you see something work on stage, you pay attention.

"Before I bring them out here, let me get a feel for the room. By applause, how many of you are here primarily for the performance track?"

There was a loud round of applause. It seemed like more than half the room wanted to hone their performance skills. I wondered if I should be concentrating on that instead of the writing side of comedy. I wasn't locked into anything at this point. I hated when I second-guessed myself. Writing track. First instinct is the best instinct.

"Please welcome one of LA's leading audition coaches, nationally touring comic, and working actress, Darlana DeLuz. Give her a round of applause."

Darlana walked out from the side entrance, gave a theatrical bow to the crowd, and seated herself gracefully in one of the tall director's chairs. She was wearing a flowy gauze dress with a long scarf that wrapped around her neck. Her hair was a cascade of golden-brown ringlets. I thought her eye makeup was a bit heavy for daytime, but this was southern California. What did I know?

Roger leaned over to me and whispered, "I'm getting a definite Stevie Nicks vibe here. You?"

"Circa 1980. The Cold Auditions class should be interesting."

Roger nodded.

Juliet was speaking again. "How many of you are here for the writing track? By applause."

About a fifth of the room clapped. Well, my seminar sessions prob-ably wouldn't be overcrowded. Maybe that meant I could get some questions answered.

"You're in for a treat. We have Rob Tolland, who many of you may remember from *All Hands on Deck* and *No Rest for the Weird*. Rob is now a staff writer on the hit show, *Luck Be a Lady*, starring Jackie Leani. Please welcome, Rob Tolland!"

The applause was warm for Rob. Even if people weren't here for the writing track, they recognized one of their own. Rob was lanky, with dark hair that could have used a trim, wearing a grey cashmere V-neck sweater and jeans. Loafers, no socks. He was wearing round, horn-rimmed glasses that had a slight tint to them. He gave a short, almost embarrassed wave and took a seat next to Darlana. She leaned forward to say something to him. He nodded, but didn't turn to look at her.

"Now I know you are all here for the business aspects of this crazy comedy world. I would not be where I am today without the man I'm about to introduce you to. Danny Schillingford is an online marketing genius. He has been responsible for building not just my online presence, but the platforms of many of LA's top actors and comedians. This is the man you'll want to track down this weekend. Please welcome, Danny Schillingford!"

Danny came out to a nice round of applause, gave a quick bow and a wave. He gave Darlana a hug and shook Rob's hand, before taking his seat. His Oxford button-down shirt was tucked into designer blue jeans. He pushed back a flop of his blond hair, shifted in his seat, crossed and uncrossed his legs, before finally settling on hooking his feet on the chair's cross bar.

"Last, but not least, a founding member of Maxx City Improv and current cast member of the hit show *Comedic Rumblings*, please welcome Maureen "Mo" Thompson!"

We applauded and there were a few whoops. I'm not a big fan of improv, but Maureen definitely was the real deal. In fact, she was the only other "name" on the list of instructors besides Juliet that I had recognized. Her auburn hair was held back in a ponytail that fell out of the back of her black baseball cap. She was dressed in black yoga pants and a grey zip hoodie sweatshirt, over a black tee. A pair of black and white checked Vanns completed the look. She was ready to work.

"Now, you're all going to have a chance to meet and hang out with our instructors over the next few days. And we'll be doing a Q and A panel at 3:45 this afternoon on how we all got our big breaks in the industry, so have your questions ready."

"We're going to take a few minutes and have each of our instructors introduce themselves and talk about what they'll be covering in their sessions. Let's start with Darlana."

Each of the instructors went through a short synopsis of the sessions. It was little more than what had been stated in the package, but it gave us a taste of their personalities. I was tempted to take Mo's improv class but it conflicted with the Cold Auditions session. I wasn't sure how useful either one would be for me, but Gabby and Luke would be in Cold Auditions. And, to be honest, I wasn't really comfortable with the thought of doing improv. Which meant that I should probably take it, but I knew I wouldn't. Some days I'm just not up for a challenge and I figured I was going to be taking in enough new information that I didn't need to add any stress to my load. Also, I'm a chicken.

Mo finished up her pitch and took her seat again. Juliet came back out to center stage.

"I can see you're all scribbling on your schedules now. Don't worry. No matter what sessions you're in, you're going to collect some great information that will move you forward faster." She looked at the clock on the wall. "It's 9:35. We're almost running on time. So, let's start right in on what you came here for, the Business of Comedy."

Chapter 6: Know Your Pastries

The Business of Comedy session was worth the entire seminar fee, at least to me. Juliet didn't hold back on anything—the way club owners thought, what they were looking for as far as talent (people who could put butts in seats, mainly), and most important to me, how to shift from one level to another. She reminded us that there was a "Booked Solid" session later in the weekend and I put a huge circle around that on my schedule, even though I had already highlighted it.

"We have a few minutes for people to ask questions. Are the mic runners ready?" She looked around the room. Two of the AV guys waved handheld mics at her.

"Okay, great. If you'd like to ask a question, stand up and one of the runners will come to you. We'll see how many questions we can get through before we hit the coffee break."

At least 15 people stood up. I noticed Gabby was one of them. Juliet pointed at a woman who had received the mic from one of the runners.

"Okay, give us your name, where you're from, what level you're at—headliner, feature, opener, or just starting out—and then ask your question. One question per, people. We have a lot of folks to get through."

"Hi, Arly Trayton, feature from the Dallas area. At what point should I think about setting up a corporation for tax purposes and do club owners have a problem paying a corporation rather than a person?"

"First, I'd like to say I love the way you snuck two questions in there." Juliet paused for the laugh that followed. "That's really one for your accountant. I will say that I shifted into a corporate structure when my earnings went over... gosh, maybe over $50,000 a year? My accountant set me up with a retirement account and some health account that covers expenses that my health plan doesn't. And I've had no problem getting checks made out to my LLC. If the check is in my name, I just endorse it over to the LLC. Does that help?"

Arly nodded and handed the mic back to the runner.

"Okay, this side of the room. Yes, you," Juliet pointed. It was a question that was very specific to the person so I pulled out my map of the resort. Roger leaned over.

"What are you looking for?"

"The restaurant is going to be a zoo with one hundred people hitting it all at once. I wonder if there's a snack bar or something."

"You're already thinking about lunch? We haven't even had the coffee break yet."

"Priorities."

Roger nodded and pointed at the pool. A little icon with food and drinks was next to it. "I had lunch there yesterday. I don't think a lot of people know about it yet."

"That could work. Worse comes to worse, I'll get chips at the gift shop or from a vending machine." With the exception of a pound of

Twizzlers, I didn't have my regular road food with me. I was going to have to stock up. I made a mental note to hit the gift shop later on.

Juliet finished up with the person and looked around for the next person. She broke into a smile. "Gabby! What's your question? Introduce yourself."

"Hi, I'm Gabby Leigh from Alexandria, Virginia. I'm an opening act, really just breaking in."

I heard Roger say, "Helloooo, Gabby," under his breath.

I laughed. He blushed a bit. One of the drawbacks of our coloring.

"If you're real nice to me, I'll introduce you."

"Oh my God, you know her?"

"She's in the room next to mine."

"I am your slave. Until I am hers."

Gabby was asking a question about material, both quality and quantity.

"Well, more is always better and I have to confess that I was stretching when I made the jump from opener to feature. I barely had thirty minutes of material. And it wasn't killer, that's for sure." She did an eye roll.

The audience laughed.

"A lot of clubs have you do twenty to twenty-five minutes but what you don't want is to be in the position where they need you to stretch and you've got nuthin'. I mean at that point, the only thing you can do is talk reaalllly slooowly."

She waited for the laugh to die down and went on, "As far as numbers, I don't know about other people, but I like to over-prepare. If I need thirty to be a feature in my area, I want to have at least forty to forty-five minutes of solid material. It doesn't have to be genius, but it needs to be solid."

People were groaning. Juliet nodded. "I feel your pain. When you're starting out, every minute of material seems to take forever to write. But I'm going to promise you this: It's cumulative. Eventually you've just written so much stuff and added little tweaks here and there that one day you realize you have an hour. And then ninety minutes. And so on. I'll tell you the part that sucks, though. Singers can do the same songs forever. Everybody wants to hear the old hits. But comedy bits? You've got to keep writing. When you get a national spot, like on a late-night show, you need new material for that show. And a 90-minute HBO special? If you are lucky enough to be asked to do another one, it needs to be all new. So, if you're not into writing, you need to learn to love it. Or start dating a writer."

Gabby nodded and handed off her mic to the runner.

"Okay, we have time for one more," Juliet moved to the other side of the stage.

"Chad Warder, headliner from Atlanta."

Roger snorted at the way Chad emphasized the word headliner. I looked over to that side of the room.

"Hi Chad, what's your question?"

"So, Juliet, why did some people get invited to a private showcase with the agent and not others? Was it only the good-looking people like Gabby here or Luke who were chosen?"

Apparently, the showcase wasn't the worst kept secret. From the reactions in the crowd, I'd say more than half the attendees didn't know about it.

Juliet looked like a deer in the headlights, but she recovered quickly.

"There were some private showcase slots available but I assure you they were not based on looks. This is comedy, after all." People were grumbling. I heard someone say, "What the hell?"

"So, people were asked based on their ability?" Chad continued. "Because Gabby here is a rank beginner and I certainly have a lot more experience than Luscious Luke Hallidade." He gestured at Luke who was sitting with Amber. "It sure looks like you were going with the most photogenic."

I winced at his reference to Luke's old persona. It was one Luke was happy to leave behind.

Juliet looked apprehensive. I wondered how she was going to handle the question without pointing to someone and holding them up as an example of an unattractive person. Or admitting she had done a cursory check of people's finances.

She was saved by the heavyset woman with glasses next to Gabby. She stood up and gave a little wave. "Well, I'm doing the private showcase, so yeah, *obviously* it's based on looks. Who wouldn't want more of this?"

She said it for a laugh and she got it. It helped break the tension. But people were still waiting for an explanation. And Chad wouldn't let it go.

"So, how did you choose the people to invite? Was it money? Because I'm more than happy to pony up a Gee to get a private audition and I bet others here are, too."

He looked around the room for support. He got some head nods and a few "yeahs" but the thousand-dollar price tag was unrealistic for many of us. I didn't feel so bad now.

Juliet looked at the floor and took a beat. Then she faced us. "I owe you all an apology. We had this opportunity come up at the last minute and decided to offer it on a first come, first served basis. We only had ten slots and once those were taken, that was it."

People seemed to accept this. Not Chad.

"Well, I came in on the same shuttle as Gabby. And I didn't get asked."

Someone near me said, "Maybe because you're an asshole," and they didn't bother to whisper. Our little section cracked up.

"You might not have been in your room when I knocked," Juliet ventured. "Did you hit the pool or the restaurant?"

She had him. How many people check into a hotel midday and sit in their room?

"Well, maybe," Chad shrugged. "But if anyone drops out, I'm available."

I whispered to Roger, "That's not lame and desperate."

"Sad Chad."

"Oooh, good one!"

Juliet looked towards the back of the room. "Chad, if you go see Pamela after this session, she'll be at the registration table in the lobby, right Pam? She'll tell you the particulars and we can wait list you in case anyone drops out. And, if anyone else is interested, talk to Pamela. For the rest of us, they've just brought out fresh coffee and there are lots of yummy pastries waiting for you. Your next session starts in 15 minutes, so grab coffee and a pastry and we'll see you in a few."

"Poor Pam, she's going to be swamped."

"I think the thousand-dollar price tag will keep the numbers down," Roger said. "Think about it. Do you think Chad has the extra thousand dollars for the showcase if a spot opened up?"

"Doubtful."

There was a brief round of applause but there had been some damage done. People were talking as they made their way to the coffee stations and I was sure every conversation at lunch would be about the private showcase. I wondered if this was going to taint the atmosphere for the entire weekend. I hoped not.

I looked at Roger. "Which session are you hitting next?"

"That physical comedy thing with Mo Thompson. You?"

"Danny's talk on websites. I don't have one yet and I guess it's time to learn."

"Well, if you need any help, let me know." He paused. "Do you want to meet up for lunch? I don't really know anyone, except maybe Nick."

"Sure. Pool restaurant?"

"Yeah. Thanks."

We swapped phone numbers in case we missed connecting. I grabbed another cup of coffee and skipped the pastries. They were going fast but I know a disappointing pastry when I see one. I hoped the cookies for the afternoon break would be better. I leaned against the wall and just watched the activity for a minute. Some people were talking in groups of two or three, but there were plenty of loners, standing around just a bit awkwardly. We were all people who talk for a living and half of us couldn't make small talk. I looked around the room. I saw Luke talking to the heavyset woman who was also doing the showcase. I didn't see Gabby or Nick. I finished up my coffee and set the empty on the tray. The meeting room for the next session was just a few doors down.

There seemed to be as many people milling in the lobby as in the big meeting room. I glanced over at the registration table. Chad was off to the side with a little knot of people around him. One or two people were talking to Pamela. Roger had read it right—the thousand-dollar price tag was a bit much for most of us. It made me feel a bit better.

Chapter 7: Haters Gonna Hate

I WAS PREPARED FOR a snooze-fest or at least a lot of technical jargon about websites and all the Internet stuff that goes along with them. My goal was to figure out what I needed and how soon I needed it. Or at least not be more lost after the session than I was when I walked in.

Danny Shillingford broke the IT nerdy guy stereotype. He was outgoing, engaging, funny, and absolutely passionate about marketing. Even better, he broke down all the tech language for us. It was still a lot to absorb but he made it seem easy to get on top of the whole website/mailing list thing. While I didn't understand how to set up a website, I understood the mechanics of having an email sign-up and why I should have a mailing list. Now all I needed was fans. Apparently, I wasn't the only one.

"How do we get someone to go to our website and sign up for the list?" someone behind me asked. I saw other people nod their heads.

"That brings us to the second part of our session: Marketing. The question you have to answer is *why* would anyone sign up for your mailing list."

We were silent. Someone ventured, "To know where we're going to be performing?"

"Yes. Absolutely. That's one reason. Anyone else?"

"Maybe see some videos of our stand-up routines?"

"Sure, why not?" Danny let us off the hook. "You need to give people something of value, something worth trading their contact information for. So, maybe it's a newsletter that updates people on what you're doing. Or a calendar of who is performing at the local clubs each week. Or even a special video that you make only for the people on your mailing list."

"Why would anyone want a newsletter about what I'm doing? It seems sort of self-centered," I recognized Amber's voice. I caught her eye and gave her a nod.

"Mostly I eat, sleep, do comedy, and watch TV," a guy said. "Riveting stuff."

"Ah. I know you're all boring as hell," Danny said. He got a good laugh. "But your fans don't. They think you are living the coolest life out there."

"So, we lie?"

"No. That would be..." he waited for us.

"Bad," most of the group filled in for him.

"Right. But the things we think are boring are new to them or at least different from their lives. What's it like driving to a gig? What's it like coming home at two in the morning? What comics did you work with? What movie did you see that stars a famous comedian? Or even that has a not-yet-famous comedian in a smaller role that you can tell them to look for?"

People were scribbling notes.

"But how are we going to fill a whole newsletter?"

"You're not writing a newspaper or magazine. Just a little friendly update, an email with some interesting stuff about what's going on in your world. You're entertainers. Can you entertain people once a month?"

"I'm not really a writer," one guy said.

"Yeah, my spelling sucks. Always has," another added.

"Have someone who can spell go over it for you." He paused. "Look, I get that there's resistance to this idea. It's work and honestly, most of you will never do it. But then, most of you will never build a fanbase."

"Shit got real," someone muttered.

"Yeah, harsh, right? This is what this seminar is all about. Comedy is a business and you need to treat it like a business. You're the product. That means you have to package yourself in such a way that people like you and will pay to see you. You have to deliver quality performances and put people in the seats so that club owners will hire you."

We were all pretty quiet, absorbing this. I looked around the room. More than a few people had that deer-in-the-headlights look. It was uncomfortable. So of course, me and my big mouth.

"Okay. I'll bite. You've given us some ideas for what we should write about. Do you suggest any sort of format or order for the information?"

Danny smiled. "I'm so glad you asked. I just happen to have a sample newsletter for you on my website and 100 ideas for your newsletter. You can get it by going to it..." he clicked his PowerPoint presentation and his website address was on the screen "and filling in your name and email address in the opt-in form here. You'll be sent a pdf of the newsletter sample."

We all laughed.

"That's how it works. I have something that you think is worth giving me your name and email address. And now, you're on my newsletter list. I'll send you a newsletter every month that talks about how to market yourself as a comic and build your fanbase."

"Why would you do that?"

"What do I do for a living?"

"Help Juliet with her website."

"Not just Juliet. I work with comics who don't want to mess with the technical side of building and maintaining their websites. I also create an online presence for them. My clients are stand-up comics who have reached a level of success that allows them to afford me."

"So, like headliners," someone said. "Not me."

"Build your fanbase and you have a better chance of making it to headliner," Danny shot back.

"How much would it cost for you to build a website for someone?" Amber asked.

"I do have packages available and yes, I have a handout for that, but I don't want to get ahead of ourselves. I'm here to give you the information you need to get your marketing going. So yes, I will hand that out and if anyone wants to discuss it further, I'm here all weekend and happy to talk. Just so you won't be distracted for the rest of the session, please know that I am affordable, but not cheap. I am, however, easy."

We laughed and people seemed to relax a bit.

He spent the remaining twenty minutes going through some marketing ideas we could put into play, what to use for social media posts, and encouraged us to make short video clips from any good videos we had of ourselves performing. You can't just stand up in front of a camera all by yourself and do comedy; you need audience reaction. I was glad I opted to get the video of my showcase this weekend. I had some good video from doing Florida's Funniest Comedians, but I had added stronger material since then. I just hoped an audience full of comics would laugh. The showcases weren't a competition per se, but there would be an agent in the house and I didn't know if people would hold back laughing in order to skew the perceived funniness of each comic. Were people that petty? Maybe. I had a lightbulb moment. I needed to become Miss Congeniality. Maybe I could get the sympathy laughs.

The session was just about over. Danny handed out his business info. It was a list of his services and prices started at $1,500 for a basic website. I sighed. Priced out of the market again. I flipped it over and there was a checklist of what you needed to set up your website and mailing list, so that was helpful at least. I added it to my collection of handouts. I thought about what Nick had said about people trying to sell you things along the way. He called that one. Well, maybe Roger would have some ideas for a less expensive way to get this done. People were filing out but there were at least a dozen people talking to Danny at the front of the room. As I stood up, my text notification rang in. It was Luke.

Lunch?

Meet us at the pool bar. They have food.

I joined the others leaving the room and headed through the lobby towards the pool. I saw Roger's red hair and the ladies' room at the same time.

"Roger!"

He stopped and waited for me.

"Can you hang tight a minute? Too much coffee." I indicated the ladies' room.

"I hear you." He looked over at the men's room sign. "Bet I beat you."

"No shit."

Someone was in one of the stalls. I chose one a little bit away. I could hear sniffling while I sat there. I quickly finished up and went to wash my hands. As I grabbed a paper towel, I heard a sob.

Girls' Rule: If someone is crying in the ladies' room, you gotta help them.

"Are you okay?"

There was an intake of breath. "I'm fine."

I knew the voice so I waited. I heard toilet paper tearing and then she blew her nose. A few seconds later the door opened.

"Gabby, sweetie, what's the matter?" I gave her a hug.

"Everyone is gonna hate me because I got chosen for the showcase and they didn't."

"Well, they're gonna hate Luke, too" I teased her.

She laughed and started crying all over again.

"Why did he have to point me out?"

"Because he's a jealous piece of shit, that's why. Look, it will be okay. Most of the people here couldn't afford it anyway."

"That's just another reason to hate me."

"Did someone else say something to you?"

"A couple of the women in the physical comedy class asked me about it. I told them the truth—Juliet came to my room, told me about the showcase and I jumped on it."

"So, they should be mad at Juliet, not you."

"They're not about to hate on America's Comedy Sweetheart. That leaves me."

"Well, I don't hate you and I can't imagine anyone who has actually met you would hate you. So come on, fix your face."

She nodded and pulled a makeup cleansing pad out of a pack and mopped up the bits of smudge under her eyes. Her nose was red but that would take care of itself.

"I think you need a drink and we are heading to exactly the right place," I took her arm.

Roger was leaning against the wall waiting patiently. He snapped to when he saw Gabby.

I introduced them. If Roger could tell she had been crying, he didn't say anything. We went through the door to the pool restaurant and were immediately hit with the sun's glare. At least it wasn't the wet Florida heat. There were about twenty tables, a few already occupied.

I was glad to see that Luke had staked out a table with an umbrella for us.

Luke stood up as we arrived at the table. "Smart call, coming here. The restaurant was mobbed."

"Roger's idea," I said and introduced them. "Let's get our orders in now, though. People will give up on the restaurant and this place will fill up fast." As I was talking, another group came through the door and found a table.

Luke handed the menus around and I scanned it. I decided a grilled chicken sandwich with fries might be a bit healthier than a burger. Gabby barely looked at the menu. I had a feeling her diet was an endless string of grilled chicken salads.

The server arrived. "May I take your drink orders?"

"Would it be okay to order our food, too? You're about to get swamped." I smiled up at her.

"Definitely. Separate checks?"

She was obviously used to handling seminar attendees. She took our orders and we handed over the menus. There was a bit of silence. Roger broke it.

"So, I guess I'm having lunch with the chosen ones."

"Oh God, people already hate us!" Gabby looked on the verge of tears again.

Roger was immediately apologetic. "No, no. I'm teasing you. No one hates you."

"Oh, I hate her. Look at her—she's gorgeous," I said.

Luke jumped in. "Probably funny and talented, too. Blech."

It worked; Gabby laughed.

"Yep, haters gonna hate whether you do anything or nothing so you might as well do something." I nudged her arm. "Might as well be a chosen one."

"Yeah, I guess. I just felt so called out."

"That's because we were called out. I mean, there I am, minding my own business and the whole Luscious Luke thing comes up."

"Yeah, what was that about?" Roger asked.

"It was a persona I used for a while. It, uh... didn't work." Luke looked uncomfortable.

"Well, it worked until it didn't," I said. "But Luke 3.0 is a much better version." We smiled at each other.

The server arrived with our drinks and scurried off again. As predicted, the place was filling up.

"Well, it's good that I'm having lunch with you," Roger said. "Give you some 'I hang with average guys' street cred."

"Not so average. I saw you working out this morning. Those are quite the guns you're hiding," Luke said.

Gabby and I shared a look. Roger caught it.

"You two are undressing me with your minds right now, aren't you?"

We giggled.

"Guilty as charged," I said.

"Well, I want you to know that I am more than a sex object. I have a mind, too." He sniffed with false indignance.

"Oh, absolutely," I said.

"Actually, you could probably do some modeling," Luke said.

"Me?"

"Yeah. You've got the physique. And your face is angular. It will photograph well."

"I hate to say this in front of the ladies, but I'm really not good-looking."

"Actually, you are," Gabby said, assessing his face.

Roger turned a bright red.

"Who told you that you weren't good-looking?" I asked.

"Oh, I don't know. Twelve years of school yard bullies. Practically no dates in high school. I started working out because I got tired of being beat up."

"And that's where you developed the whole comedy thing, too. Right?" I asked.

"Make them laugh and you've got a fifty-fifty chance they won't hit you."

"High school is brutal," Gabby said.

"You were probably a cheerleader, prom queen..." Luke teased her.

"Cheerleading is mostly dance and gymnastics, and every girl at my school had taken lessons for years. But it was an all-girls boarding school, so we didn't have cheerleaders." She thought for a moment. "We had a really bad-ass field hockey team. Those girls were vicious."

"An all-girls boarding school?" Luke said. "I guess you didn't date much in high school."

We laughed.

"You'd be surprised," Gabby said. "Let's say an all-girls school works better for some people than others. We were also paired with an all-boys' school so we had dances together and socials. We'd sometimes go to their games. But yeah, the administrators worked hard to keep us all pure. That was probably the main thing our parents were paying for."

"And then you go into comedy, which is about as low as you can go," I said.

"Well, acting really. Which is also low, but as long as I don't release a sex tape, my dad will back me. Or maybe he is just happy to have me occupied with something until he gets me married off to some Wall Street exec or a friend's trust-fund son."

"He probably just wants to make sure you're taken care of," Roger said.

"It's more that he thinks I'll never be able to take care of myself." There was a bitterness to her voice that I hadn't heard before. She was sweet, but she wasn't stupid.

"Well, then. We're just going to have to make sure you're a success at this whole comedy-acting thing," Luke said.

"That's exactly what I intend to do."

All of our phones dinged at once.

"That's not weird at all," Roger said.

We automatically checked our texts. Gabby gasped.

"Aw, jeez," Luke said.

It was a picture of a hand-written list of about twenty names, checkmarks next to the ten people who had booked the private showcase, a few names that were crossed out, and a few that were on the list to be asked but seemingly weren't. Well, Juliet had been honest about that part: first come, first served.

"Surprisingly enough, Chad's name is not on the list anywhere." Luke grinned.

"Sad, so sad." Roger shook his head.

"Someone is stirring the pot," I said.

"Someone with access to everyone's phone numbers." Roger pointedly looked around at the other tables. Everyone had their phones out.

"Who would do a thing like that?" Gabby asked.

"Someone who wasn't offered the showcase." Luke raised an eyebrow.

"Gee, thanks. Well, that narrows it down to about ninety people here." I shrugged.

"They also have to have some hacking skills. How did they get our phone numbers?" Roger asked.

That set us back a bit.

"Well, there's a list of attendees on the site," Gabby said.

"Yeah, but not email addresses or phone numbers," Luke was thinking out loud.

"Could have used a scraper program to get the names and then done searches. We don't know that everyone got a text." Roger looked around again. "Though it seems like it."

"Scraper program?" Gabby asked.

"Yeah, it's used to go through websites and get certain pieces of data. Like, say you wanted to get all the clubs in the Boston area and you find a site for that, but you don't want to have to copy and paste everything to a spreadsheet. Tedious, right?"

We nodded. I had done the copy and paste technique, making lists of clubs to call. There was a faster way?

"So, you send a scraper program through the site, and it compiles a list of things like club name, location, a contact name if there is one, the phone number, into one neat spreadsheet that you can download."

"How do you get a scraper program like that?" Gabby asked.

"You can hire someone to do it or there are some ready-made if you know what to ask for. It's really pretty simple coding," Roger said.

"Let me guess, you're a programmer in real life?" I asked.

"Just an IT nerd. But this was probably a hack, not a scrape. Our names are on the site, but none of our information. Someone got into Juliet's database."

"Is that hard to do?" Gabby leaned forward, interested. Roger blushed a bit.

"Depends on how good her site security is. Probably not very. Most people's sites aren't very secure. Hackers are always finding flaws in coding, whether it's the site template or a plugin or most of the time, easy passwords."

"I was just in Danny's session about websites and building a fan-base. I don't even have a website," I said. "Do you all have websites?"

Luke, Gabby and Roger nodded. Crap. I really needed to up my game. Well, that was why I was here—to figure out what I needed to do for the business side of things. I looked at Roger. "I'm probably going to need to grab you for some advice on that."

He nodded. "Happy to help."

"Juliet might need some help, too, if someone hacked her," Gabby said.

"She's got Danny," Roger said. "He'll figure it out."

"At least we're not the only ones outed," Luke said. He smiled at Gabby.

"There's that." Gabby looked around. "Somehow, I don't feel better."

People were starting the exodus back to the event. More than a few glanced our way. They didn't look happy.

Roger leaned down to pick up his notebook. "Time to head back. I've got Improv I. Anyone else?"

"Dolphin Cold Auditions," Gabby said. "But I have to go back to my room first."

"Improv scares me," I said. "I'm hitting the dolphin thing with them."

"Chicken."

"Absolutely."

Gabby peeled away at the elevator bank and we turned towards the meeting rooms. Roger looked around at the groups of attendees all heading in the same direction. "I wonder how this is going to play out."

"I hope it will all blow over by the cookie break," Luke said.

"We'll see," I said, but I didn't feel all that hopeful.

Chapter 8: Would You Like the Meat or Fish?

LUKE AND I WAITED in line to check off our names on a registration list, then walked into the meeting room and sat down. I put my portfolio on the seat next to me for Gabby. Even though there was a tech guy in the room, Darlana was fussing with her laptop and notes. She had changed from her morning outfit and was now wearing a vibrant purple, gauzy dress with long bell sleeves that practically covered her hands. A lavalier mic was clipped near her collar and the battery pack must have been hidden by the purple and gold shawl. Every few seconds she'd raise an arm to get the sleeve out of her way, revealing an overflow of silver bangle bracelets. She had added a top hat, with a sun and moon medallion on it. She was wearing feather earrings that brushed her shoulders. I remembered Roger's comment from the morning intros. I waited til Luke was in the middle of swallowing some water.

I whispered to Luke, "Stevie Nicks lives."

He snorted water out his nose. Victory.

"You couldn't have waited?" he said, choking a bit.

"Not a chance. Timing in life is everything. But I gotta give credit to Roger. He made the connection."

We watched Darlana fuss some more.

"Do you think her audition techniques will work anywhere besides Southern California?"

Luke shook his head. "Do they need to work anywhere other than here? Are you heading to Broadway?"

"Hell, no. But I don't know if I am heading for LA either. It was this session or Improv Techniques and I figured this one wouldn't require me to actually do anything."

"Do you think you might do some acting at some point?" Luke asked.

"Never say never, but doubtful. I might be able to pick up some performance techniques. And you never know. Every comic wants to have their own sitcom." I shrugged. I had thought it was far too early to be thinking about that, but maybe I was wrong. "This session should be helpful for you, though."

Luke nodded. "Cold readings are tough. I hope to pick up some tricks."

"Dolphin Technique. I'm thinking if we do a good job, she might throw us a fish."

We heard the hum of the sound system. Darlana huffed into her mic, testing it. It was, of course, working perfectly.

"Welcome, everyone. I am Darlana DeLuz, acting coach and working actress, and creator of the Dolphin Cold Audition Technique. Today, I am going to show you how to excel at cold readings and nail that audition."

Her voice was over-modulated and she fluttered her hands theatrically around her.

I leaned over to Luke. "Five bucks says she worked as a magician or magician's assistant at some point."

"No," he whispered back. "You think?"

"I know."

"You're on."

"First, a little bit about my background and how I came to develop the Dolphin Technique." She advanced a slide and a picture of her at about ten or twelve filled the screen. She was wearing a top hat, cute tuxedo suit with shorts, fishnets and tap shoes, holding a dance cane. Apparently, a top hat was not a new addition to her wardrobe.

"I started out as a dancer and singer," she flipped to the next slide, a shot of her standing at a mic singing her heart out and looking very much like Stevie Nicks. "And it wasn't long before I started doing commercials." Another picture, this time of her dressed as a young mother, spoon-feeding a baby. There was a little stir in the room as people remembered the commercial. She smiled at the recognition and moved her hands as if asking us to hold any applause. Not that there was going to be any.

Luke leaned over to me and whispered, "She kind of went right past the ingénue stage to young mother."

"She'd be the quirky, weird best friend. Pretty, but not pretty enough for the lead."

She clicked to the next slide. Another commercial, this one a Public Service Announcement about sexually transmitted diseases.

"Not sure I'd put that on my resume," I said.

"You're so repressed."

"In this particular case, I'm good with repressed."

She continued through more slides of her in various roles, mostly commercials, but, as I reminded myself, some commercials paid incredibly well. She was doing more than I was so I wasn't going to knock her. Too much. The greatest hits of Darlana montage was thankfully short. I was pretty sure it wasn't due to modesty. The slide changed to bullet point text as she moved into the meat of her presentation.

"You very rarely get a script before an audition. That only happens after you've worked your way up the ladder and your agent is forwarding scripts to you. Until then, you show up to audition and someone puts a script in your hand. You have a minute or so to read it, they'll give you a little background, and then you go. There's no time to prepare once you're in the room."

She clicked to forward the presentation again and I was expecting more text and bullet points. Instead, it was yet another picture of her. This time she shared the screen with a magician and the two were posed in front of a box of some sort. The magician held up his wand with one hand, while assisting her into the box with the other.

"You've got to bring your own magic into the room."

I looked at Luke with a shit-eating grin on my face. "I'll take that five bucks in alcohol."

"Unbelievable," he whispered.

"She's little and a dancer. They fold up nicely."

He gave me a puzzled look.

"They have to scrunch up in the boxes and trunks. You know, like when a magician saws a body in half."

"I never thought about it. Where did you learn that?"

I shrugged. I honestly had no idea. Little useless pieces of information stick in my brain for no apparent reason. It wasn't always a good thing.

Her next slide had a picture of her in the water with a mask and snorkel pushed up on her head and a dolphin beside her. She had obviously gone to one of the "swim with dolphins" attractions at some resort. Maybe at Sea World. She said in an overly-rehearsed tone, "I don't know which one of us has the bigger smile."

"She does know that that's just the way their beak is formed, right? That they're not really smiling?"

Luke snorted. "I have a feeling this talk was not peer-reviewed by marine biologists."

She was going on about how amazing the experience was, shifting between various shots of her in her bikini with the dolphins, and yeah, I get it. It's a once in a lifetime type of thing. But I didn't pay to watch her vacation slides. She flipped to the next slide, another shot of her, this time with a dolphin on either side of her, all facing the camera. The dolphins were well-trained, at least.

This," she paused dramatically, "is where the Dolphin Cold Reading technique was born."

"At last, some meat," Luke said.

"Then why am I still looking at fish?" I had a suspicion there was no meat to be had.

"Swimming with dolphins was both a freeing and transformational event for me. Connecting with nature in its raw beauty created a connection within me, to my true self. Just as dolphins are totally present in the moment, just as they are every bit themselves with no apologies, that's what I knew I needed to bring to every audition from there on out. Over the years, I have refined the technique into a process that never fails, at the very least, to get you a call back."

There seemed to be a lot of talk about being in a "Flow State." I had already partially tuned out and at first, I thought she was talking about floating, the whole swimming with dolphins thing. But no. I guess it was about being "present in the moment" and I really was regretting being present in that particular moment. Turns out, I'm not a Zen kind of gal.

We were thirty minutes deep in the session when Luke leaned over to me. "Gabby still hasn't shown up. Do you think she blew it off?"

"No, she was really firm about coming to this. Auditioning is important to her."

"Maybe someone tipped her off that this would be a total waste of time." Luke sounded disgusted.

"She's just setting the premise. I'm sure she'll get to the good stuff soon." I don't know why I was defending Darlana. Luke was right: So far this session was a bust.

Darlana went through a few more slides but now it was all about her insight and transformation.

"Really, I just want one good tip to make this worthwhile," Luke whispered.

She finally started going through the actual process and frankly, since I don't know anything about acting, it was kind of going past me. I was done. I whispered to Luke, "I'm going to check Gabby's room. If Darlana says anything worthwhile, write it down for me, will ya?"

"Gosh, gee. I hope I have enough paper."

I gathered up my papers as quietly as I could and made for the door. From the looks I was getting, I suspected I was about to start a walk out. It hadn't occurred to anyone that they could just leave.

The halls and lobby by the meeting rooms were empty. No one was at the registration table. I took the elevator up to our floor and knocked on Gabby's door. There was no answer so I knocked again, a little louder this time.

"Gabby, are you in there?"

The door opened immediately.

"Thank God, it's you. Come in." She stood aside, then checked the hallway before closing and double locking the door after me. "Did you see anyone in the hall?"

"Uh, no. What's going on? Why aren't you in the Cold Auditions session?"

She was flustered and unintentionally looked over at an envelope and folded piece of paper on her bed.

"Bad news?"

"I'm not supposed to tell anyone."

"Well, how about if I read it? Then you won't have told me." She made a noncommittal moan, which I took as a yes. I scooped up the paper.

DROP OUT OF THE PRIVATE SHOWCASE.
OR ELSE.
TELL NO ONE ABOUT THIS MESSAGE.

Well, that's to the point," I said.

"I don't know how to tell Juliet that I'm backing out of the show-case."

"You're dropping out? Really? Just because some anonymous note told you to?"

"It says 'or else'."

"That's pretty nonspecific. Someone wants your spot is all. I bet they sent one to everyone who is in the private showcase. It has to be the same person who sent the text to everyone. I doubt anyone else could have looked at the list and gotten a note out that fast."

"Well, people knew about me and Luke and that other woman after the first session. So, they had a couple of hours. Did Luke get one?"

"Not that I know of, but he didn't go back to his room after lunch. I'll text him to check his room between sessions. We could see if we can find the woman who said she was doing it. Maybe during the cookie break."

Gabby shrugged. "I don't know…"

"At the very least, we need to find Juliet and let her know about this."

I sent a quick text to Luke: *Gabby got a threatening note telling her to drop out of the showcase. We're heading down to the lobby, looking for Juliet.*

I looked at the envelope. It had Gabby's name written in the same handwriting, but no room number.

"How was this delivered?" I tried to sound casual.

"They slid it under the door."

"So, it was right inside the door when you got back to the room."

"No. I went to the bathroom and I was fixing my face. When I got out of the bathroom, it was there."

I thought for a minute. A bellman would have knocked. The housekeeper would have propped it on the bureau or on the pillows to make sure it would be noticed.

"They may have followed you to your room. Did you notice anyone in the elevator or the hallway?"

"There were a couple of people in the elevator, but I was the only one who got off on this floor." She thought back. "I didn't see anyone in the hallway, but then, I wasn't looking around either."

"Most of us are in a special block of rooms on the fourth and fifth floors. It wouldn't take much to hang out by the vending machine to see who goes to which room."

"That's creepy. Like being stalked," Gabby said. "Or it could be that Juliet's information included people's room numbers."

I nodded. It made me realize how easy it would have been to get to Gabby. Or me. Or any one of us for that matter. I didn't want her thinking about that.

"Well, if whoever did this sent more than one note, then they won't know if you backed out or not. They just need one person to drop."

"Do you think it was Chad?"

"Definitely a Chad move. But did they actually start a waiting list? That's a question for Juliet. Let's see if we can find her. Give me a minute to text Luke again and ask him to check his room on the break."

I sent another quick text to Luke while Gabby gathered her things. I held onto the note.

"Are you sure we should tell Juliet?"

"This person only has power if you don't speak up. Who knows if he sent it to someone else? If you speak up, maybe someone else will come forward. At the very least, Juliet can contact everyone who is in the private showcase and make sure they're not being threatened."

Gabby was silent. There was something else.

"What?"

"He knows my room number."

My normal reaction to things like this was to get angry and take action. I forgot that most people would be scared. I gave her a long hug.

"We can switch rooms. And no one needs to know because we can just use the door between the rooms."

Gabby took a gulp of air and nodded. I looked around her room. It was going to take her a lot longer to shift her stuff than it would take me. "Let's go track down Juliet."

We stepped out of the elevator on the ground floor. Luke was just getting to the lobby.

"Hey, are you guys okay?"

"We're fine." I showed him the note and filled him in.

"Or else. Sounds like a little kid's threat."

"We figure it's probably Chad."

"It's about his level. I'm going to check my room real quick and then I'll try to catch up with you."

"Sorry you had to leave the class early," Gabby said.

Luke snorted. "Believe me, I'm not missing a thing."

"No meat?"

"Not even fish. Mark me down as dolphin safe." He pressed the elevator button and the doors opened up immediately. Most everyone was still in a session.

"Where do you suppose they hang out when they're not doing something with us?" Gabby asked.

"Usually there's a staff meeting room of some sort. Or Juliet might be up in her room but on the first day, I think she'll be checking on things. Let's ask at the front desk."

Stavon was on duty again and he welcomed us with a big smile. "How may I help you?"

"We're attending the Business of Comedy seminar with Juliet Hartwell. Do you know if there's a kind of break room for the staff to hang out in? Sort of like a backstage?"

A worried look crossed his face. "There is a private room but I'm not allowed to tell you where it is. I would get in trouble. I am very sorry."

"We understand." I sighed.

"I did see Juliet with one of her assistants about half an hour ago, heading out towards the pool. But you didn't hear it from me."

"Stavon, you are a prince."

He looked alarmed. "Who told you that?"

"It's a figure of speech."

"Ah. Of course."

"Thanks so much."

We headed down the corridor that led to the pool. I texted Luke on the fly to meet us there.

We went out to the pool restaurant and found Juliet at a table with her two assistants, finishing up a late lunch. Gabby hesitated. I didn't. I walked up to the table.

"I'm sorry to interrupt your lunch, but something has happened that you need to know about."

Juliet's neutral expression changed to concern. "Okay. Um, I know Gabby. I'm sorry, I don't remember your name."

"Kasey. Kasey McCormick. This actually concerns Gabby more than me." I handed Juliet the note and didn't exactly push Gabby forward but I stepped back so she was no longer behind me. "Someone slid this under Gabby's door about an hour ago."

Juliet read the note. "Shit. Sorry. Actually no. Shit." She read it again. Then she handed the note to Pamela and the assistants read it together. Trystan gasped.

"We're not sure if anyone else got a note like this."

"It was pushed under your door?" Juliet asked, looking at the envelope.

Gabby nodded. "I wasn't sure if I should tell you…"

"I am so glad you did. We'll see if we can nip this in the bud."

Gabby looked relieved.

"Is there a waiting list for the private showcase? If so, whoever did this is probably on that list."

Juliet turned her attention to me. "You're thinking it's the guy from the Q and A session?"

"Chad Warder. It's a douche move and well…"

She laughed. "Yeah, if the shoe fits. But we didn't actually start a list." She looked at her assistants. "Did we?"

Pamela spoke up. "No. A couple of people asked about it, but really weren't interested in being put on the list. That Chad guy came up to us, but when we told him we'd need his credit card number, he said he didn't have it with him and he'd stop by later."

"So, he just wanted to make a stink. He wasn't actually going to pony up," I said. "Nice."

I saw Luke walk through the door and waved him over. He had an envelope in his hand.

Juliet saw it. "Shit. Another one?"

"Sorry to say." Luke handed it to her.

She held the two notes side by side. "Same as Gabby's. Hotel stationary." She looked at Pamela. "We need to get in touch with the other people doing the private showcases and see if they got notes. Tell them it's just a stupid prank."

The assistants left and we sat down. A waiter came over, immediately cleared the dishes, and asked if we needed anything. We passed.

Gabby spoke first. "But it's not a stupid prank, is it? The person knows who's in the showcase and they know our room numbers." Her right hand clenched and unclenched a couple of times.

"How do you figure that?" Juliet asked.

"The room block for the seminar is all on the fourth and fifth floors," I said. "We thought someone was waiting on the fourth floor to see which room Gabby was in. Or anyone who was in the showcase, really."

"Except I didn't go back to my room after lunch. The person knew my room number," Luke said slowly.

"Which means the person has a list of the people doing the private showcase and their room numbers." I looked at Juliet. "Any idea how they could have accessed them?"

Juliet shook her head. "After the group text, I asked Danny to check my website for a breach. I haven't heard back from him yet."

"I went by the registration table during your business of comedy talk," Luke said. The two laptops were unattended and the registration sheets were out. Maybe it was only for that minute, but someone could have downloaded the information or just picked up a registration sheet."

"You have the information online and printed out?" I asked.

"The printouts were in case the laptops or the wifi glitched," Juliet said. "Danny laughs at me, but I like to have back up. Old school, I guess." She picked up her phone and started texting. "I'll have them check to see if any copies of the printouts are missing, but the truth is there were plenty of copies. There's a registration list for each class—we're tracking to see which sessions are the most popular. That's why we have you sign in at the door for each session. And, there were two at the registration desk, one for each station. One last night for the mixer..." She trailed off.

"So, the person could have gotten the list with names and room numbers either electronically or printed. But what about the list of people doing the showcase? Was that printed out anywhere? The list we saw was handwritten."

Juliet looked at me in surprise. "Not really. I hadn't put the final list into the computer yet."

"But it was a larger list, wasn't it?" I pushed. "Some of your candidates for the showcase said no. Nick Hill for instance."

"Yes. When they said no, I just crossed them off the list."

"So was the handwritten paper that we all saw the total list?" Luke looked at his phone, checking for the text.

"That was the semi-final list. I had twenty or so. I didn't get to all of them. Not too many said no."

"Semi-final list. Did you start with more people and cut it down?" She nodded.

"Do you have the original with you?"

Juliet shuffled through her file folder and came up with a handwritten list. My name was on it. Chad's was not. I felt a bit smug. "Out of curiosity, how did you come up with who to ask?"

Juliet blushed. "It was a combination of factors. Professionalism. Have they done any acting? Do they already have head shots? Credits? A website?" She looked at me and something clicked. "Florida's Funniest Comedians. You were a finalist."

I nodded. So, there was some merit involved. Nice to know.

Juliet continued. "A lot of people want to be comics but don't invest in the things they need to have in place to succeed. Or they're not yet at the point where it makes sense to invest a chunk of money into their business. So, sort of a judgment call on who looked like they were ready to take it to the next level."

And who could afford to do it, I thought. Nick had nailed it.

Luke glanced at the list. "I wonder if anyone who didn't get asked knew they were on the list."

"Not likely. I mean, when the opportunity opened up, I basically Googled people's names, checked for websites, took a look at what they had going on as far as experience and marketing, and made my list."

Gabby spoke up. "But your assistants knew there was a list." It wasn't really a question.

"Yes. And Danny because he does my webwork. He helped me filter through the database of people. Anyone without a headshot was automatically out."

"People don't have headshots?" Gabby sounded shocked. "That was one of the first things I did."

"You'd be amazed," Juliet shook her head. "But that's the reason I do this seminar. Because so many new comics don't know they need things like that."

"And it's unlikely that anyone saw this list," I said.

"Unlikely. Not impossible."

"Did you leave this folder laying around anywhere? There seems to be a room behind the main meeting room where the staff meets." It was a shot in the dark, but I didn't think they all stood around in a hallway in between sessions.

"Yes, there's a staff room. We keep the computers in there, paperwork."

"So, everyone was in the main meeting room for the introductions. Someone could have gone in then," Luke said.

"If someone had gone through my files wouldn't they have taken the list?"

Gabby held up her phone. "No need. We all carry cameras these days. They could have taken photos of the printouts with everyone's names and room numbers as well as your handwritten list."

She nodded. "So, it could have been anybody."

"It could have been someone who wanted a list of the participants for themselves for whatever reasons – to sell material, to start their network, and they just stumbled across the private showcase list. They may not have even known about it until they found the list." I was thinking out loud.

"Well, it wasn't the best kept secret," Luke said.

"But it seemed like about half the room didn't know about it until Chad brought it up," I countered. "We knew about it because you two were invited. But not everyone did."

"Do you think Chad is behind this then?" Gabby asked.

"The note sounds like him," Luke said.

"He's my favorite candidate right now, but that's only because I don't like him. It could be anyone at this point."

"How do you really feel?" Luke grinned at me then got down to business. "The real question is, what are we going to do about it?"

Juliet picked up the papers and put them back into her file folder. "You don't need to do anything. My staff and I will handle it from here. I'm sure it's more of a prank than a truly malicious threat."

"Well, Kasey has some experience with this kind of stuff," Luke volunteered. I kicked him.

"Really, I am sorry this happened. But you're here to learn and I don't want this to ruin the experience for you." She glanced at her watch. "It's almost time for the cookie break. Why don't you relax, get some cookies, and leave it to us."

Luke started to protest but I shot him a look. He switched gears. "Sounds good to me. Thanks, Juliet."

We all stood up, gave our thanks, and Juliet walked up to the bar where the server was to sign for her check. At least she wasn't wasting any time.

As we were walking away, Luke said loudly, "I took a few notes during Darlana's class if you two want copies of them."

I played along. "I do. Thanks, Luke."

We went off to an area on the other side of the bar. Luke set his pack in a chair and pulled out his notebook. We huddled around the table, taking pictures of his notes, which were pretty slim. I saw Juliet leave.

"I take it you're not happy leaving this to Juliet?" I said in a low voice.

"Why would I when I've got my own private investigator right here?"

"What is he talking about?" Gabby asked.

"I've uh, I'm sometimes good at figuring things out."

"Kasey's being modest. She figured out who tried to kill me at Florida's Funniest Comedians. And you found the script."

"Someone tried to kill you?" Gabby squeaked.

"And nearly succeeded. Then Kasey almost got killed…"

"Well, those things just happened." I looked at Gabby. "I'm not a private investigator."

"You said it yourself," Luke persisted. "You're good at figuring things out."

"Enough." I broke in. I didn't want to think about it. Remembering how close I came to being killed made me nauseous, even now. "I'm here to learn about the business of comedy. I do not want to get involved in anything. Let's just leave it to Juliet. It's her problem."

I could tell that Gabby had a dozen questions ready to go. I looked at her. "Please, Gabby. I don't like to talk about it." I turned to Luke. "And you are damn lucky to be alive. Don't press that luck."

"Yes, ma'am."

I saw a look pass between Gabby and him. If they wanted to talk about it when I wasn't around, that was fine with me. Frankly, it was something I never wanted to relive.

Chapter 9: Been There, Done That, Got the T-Shirts

THE DOORS TO THE main conference auditorium hadn't opened up yet for the cookie break, but no one seemed interested in going in anyway. The showcase schedule was posted near the registration table and people were jostling to get a look.

"Jeez, they're like sharks circling," I said.

"Yeah, obviously I can wait," Luke indicated a spot slightly away from the crowd and we shifted in that direction.

I saw Roger coming out of the crowd and waved him over.

"Can't believe you braved that crush. Are you going up tonight or tomorrow night?"

"I'm up tonight. So is Nick." He scrolled on his phone. "I'm not sure when you're up."

"You took pictures?"

"Of course. I'll send them to you." He looked down to forward the pictures and then laughed to himself.

Ten seconds later, our phone notifications went off. So did all the others in the lobby.

"What the hell?" Luke asked.

"The hacker's not so smart after all. I just did a reply all to the hacker's text. I figured it might keep someone from getting crushed over there."

"Reply all?" Gabby asked.

"He sent the private showcase list to everyone. Hitting reply all sends it to everyone on his list. I bet he didn't really think about that."

Roger's text seemed to have worked. The crush around the lists eased a bit.

"I wonder how many other people will figure that out and start sending out their own spam emails," Luke said. He tilted his head and looked at me. "Maybe people using his hack will piss him off enough to make him do something stupid."

"Not my circus, not my monkeys. You heard what Juliet said."

"What Juliet said about what?" Roger asked.

Gabby and Luke brought him up to speed. I made a conscious decision to ignore the chatter. Instead, I went through the list for tomorrow night. I was mid-pack. I saw a few names I recognized including Chad's. Joy. Luke and Gabby's names weren't on either list. I caught myself. Of course not. They were doing the private showcase.

I interrupted their talk about the threatening notes. "When's the private showcase then?"

Luke rolled his eyes. "Tomorrow night, between 5:00 and 7:00."

That was going to be a long night for the judges.

He gave it another try. "Kasey, you know we can figure this out."

"There's nothing to figure out. Someone's pissed. They're making idle threats. Danny will trace whoever it was. End of story."

"What if they're not idle threats, though?" Gabby's voice was small. "And now I've gone and told Juliet when he said not to tell anyone."

"It will be okay, Gabby. It's probably just Chad being an ass. He does it so well."

"And I'll be your personal body guard," Roger volunteered. "I have three sisters. I am very good at waiting outside ladies' rooms."

Gabby laughed and I shot Roger a knowing look.

The elevator dinged and the doors opened to the conference room at the same time. We hung back, letting people crowd through the door. Nick, walked up to us in fresh clothes and smelling of expensive soap. It was not the room soap.

"Got your luggage?" Gabby asked.

"Yes, and I feel so much better."

"Too bad. I was wondering if you could actually carry off a Hawaiian shirt," I teased.

"Not quite my style."

"Oh, I would have liked a picture of that to flash around. Nick's the best dressed comic on Long Island." Roger took a beat. "I'm the funniest."

Nick made a small bow in Roger's direction. "Of course. But, no pictures. What happens in Orange County stays in Orange County." He held up his hand and pointed to his wedding band. "And for me, not much will be happening in Orange County. I'm focusing on the important stuff, learning as much as possible."

"Right now, I'm focusing on cookies. Let's get in there before they're all gone." I may have sounded a bit more anxious than I should have.

Luke nodded. "Priorities."

I was very glad to see Juliet didn't stint on the cookies. I led our group over to the farthest station. I was hoping people wouldn't figure out that it always had the least amount of people at it. I grabbed several cookies and debated between a bottled water and more coffee.

Nick reached for a bottled water, of course. "Afraid the coffee will keep you awake tonight?"

"Not at all. I'm wondering if my stomach can handle more acid. I think the cookies will balance it out, don't you?"

Nick shook his head. "Get coffee and a water. You can at least dilute it."

We found a row towards the back with half a dozen free seats and made ourselves comfortable. The stage was set with the directors' chairs, ready for the panel discussion. There was a low table with half a dozen bottled waters in a clear plastic ice bin. A bit stark, but that's comedy.

"How was Cold Auditions?" Roger asked me.

"I left early. I felt like a fish out of water." I got a round of groans.

Luke stepped in. "It was pretty lame. It was all about her and how wonderful dolphins are and really, not much on how to handle a cold audition. Or at least not much that was useful."

"What about the improv? Was it fun?"

"It was really cool. Mo talked about the improv games that they play to loosen up and the ones they do in shows. Then we got to do some." Roger looked at Nick. "You were pretty good."

"I've had a lot of practice thinking on my feet."

"Of course, with improv, if you don't think fast, you're dead in the water. It was surprising how many people choked."

I couldn't resist. "Was Chad in there?"

"Yeah. He sucked. It was great."

Nick didn't say anything but I saw the corners of his eyes crinkle up.

"I'm not going to throw stones," Gabby said. "At least he was brave enough to try it." She paused. "Okay. I'm really glad he sucked. Serves him right for outing us on the private showcase."

"Go, Gabby!" Luke said.

"Oh, that was mean. I shouldn't have said that. Sorry."

"No takesies-backsies," Roger said. "I just wished more people saw him suck."

"Well, he's going up tomorrow night so we can see if he's any better at stand-up," I said.

"Unless someone drops out because of the notes," Gabby said. "Then he can do the private showcase."

"Only if he ponies up $1,000 and I'm pretty sure he won't."

"What notes?" Nick asked.

Luke reached into his shirt pocket and handed his note to Nick, who read it at a glance.

"Or else," he huffed.

"That was our favorite part, too." I said brightly.

He looked at Gabby. "Did you get one, too?"

She nodded.

"And, you've told Juliet, I assume?"

"I didn't want to, but Kasey said we should. Then Luke checked his room and he had one."

"We're assuming all the private showcase people got one," Luke put in. "We haven't checked with everyone yet."

"Juliet's handling that. It's probably just a prank."

Nick didn't say anything, just handed the note back to Luke.

"Luke says we should do our own investigation. Kasey solves crimes." Gabby looked at me like I was her new idol.

"I don't solve crimes."

"Yeah, you do." Luke pinned me down with a look.

"Well, this isn't much of a crime and it's not my problem. I'm here to learn how to get work. And, Juliet told us to butt out." I could feel my face heating up. Sometimes I hated being a redhead. I could blush faster than a nun at a strip club. Though why a nun would be in a strip joint, I had no idea.

Nick started to say something but the lights flickered three times and a voice came over the speakers. "Ladies and Gentlemen, Ms. Juliet Hartwell."

We all applauded as Juliet walked out and took the stage. I noticed the applause was not quite as enthusiastic as it had been this morning. I wondered if anyone else noticed. Probably. Comics are human applause meters when they're watching someone else. Accuracy seems to be off when they evaluate themselves.

"Thank you. How are the cookies? Good?"

People whooped a bit and applauded.

"Thank you. I made them myself."

Good laugh on that one. She waited for the laugh to die and then launched into some background on what was about to be discussed.

"We all hear about that mythical big break that performers get, that one time they are finally seen by someone who can advance their career. For those of you doing the showcases, you're getting a chance to be seen by some important people here in LA. So, yeah, you want to do a smokin' hot set. No pressure."

There were nervous laughs.

"And it's good to be seen. The more you're seen, the more likely you are to get work. I will tell you in all honesty, that most of us worked for a decade or more before we started landing even small television roles. That goes for actors, too. For comics, most of us aren't focused on getting acting gigs at first. We're just trying to work our way up the rungs, opener, feature, headliner. But making it up to headliner doesn't guaranty anything. There are very talented guys," she paused, "and women who never get a chance at TV and some of them never wanted it. So, if you're not on the rich and famous, HBO-sitcom-feature movie track, that's okay."

She took a sip of water. "But you're here. And that tells me that you think bigger than most comics, yes?" She got nods and "yeahs" in agreement. "And you want more than just playing local dive clubs. Been there. Done that. Got 1,400 freaking t-shirts that didn't sell."

We laughed.

"We have a session about merch this weekend. A session I could have used *before* I bought the t-shirts. I make these mistakes so you won't have to. You're welcome."

"So, the mythical big break, as you're about to find out, comes after a lot of years of hard work. There are very few overnight successes in any business. And comedy is one of those fields where you really can't fake it. Either you're funny or you're not. You have timing or you don't. You know how to read an audience or you're tone deaf. How many of you remember a few years back when a rather famous headliner sent out her sister, who looked exactly like her, to do her act?"

"Oh yeah," I muttered. Gabby looked confused. "Renee Everest. She was pregnant, didn't want to be on the road, so she taught her sister the act." Gabby nodded.

Juliet continued. "The sister memorized the act, even the pauses and the physical bits. But she couldn't read or work an audience. Now as a headliner and a woman, you don't get heckled a whole lot. But it was pretty obvious that the sister couldn't handle even side comments from the audience. It's the type of thing you only learn from doing stage time. As you know, club owners figured it out, big scandal, the fees had to be paid back and, well, not good all around."

People shifted in their seats.

"So, working your way up the ladder gives you something the overnight successes don't have and sorely need: Chops. And when that break finally does come, you're ready for it. You won't blow it. I'm going to bring out our panel and you're going to see that the big break takes different forms. And sometimes, it might not seem like a big break at the time. It can be small, like an introduction that gets you steady work or a commercial that gets you seen. Today, we're going to tell you how we all got our quote, unquote big breaks. Give our session leaders a round of applause so they know to stop drinking back there and get their butts out here. Come on, guys!"

She called off their names and one by one they jogged up to the stage and took a seat.

"But... before we get started with our panel discussion," Juliet paused. "So THAT happened."

It finally broke the ice. She got a big laugh. I thought it was interesting that she brought the session leaders out before addressing the elephant in the room. Strength in numbers?

"First, I'd like to apologize again. The private showcases were very limited, as you all know." She paused. "And if you don't know, check your texts."

Another laugh. Juliet was a pro.

"After this morning, I'm a little hesitant to open up the floor for Q and A..." There were nervous laughs. "I don't want to spend a whole lot of time on it, but I also want to answer questions that anyone has about the private showcases."

A guy with dark, curly hair stood up. "Hi, Tim Norris from Cincinnati. For the record, I'm not upset about the private showcases." He gave Juliet a reassuring smile. "But, how did the person get our phone numbers to text us all?"

"That's the question that Danny is working on right now. We're not sure if he got into the database on the website or if he just managed to steal an attendee list."

Danny stood up and came to the front of the stage. "We don't know how the information was obtained, but we do want you to know that the only information the person could obtain was a list of attendee names, and if you signed up for the SMS alerts, your cell phone numbers. There was no other personal information involved."

"Except our room numbers," Gabby whispered.

"Do you think he's doing damage control or just not releasing that information yet?" I asked.

Gabby and Nick shrugged.

Tim still had the mic. "What about our credit card information?"

"All your financial information is handled by a secure third-party merchant account. We don't have that information. In fact, we never see it. We just get an email notification that you registered and paid."

"Thanks, Danny," Juliet said. "Anyone else?"

Chad didn't wait for a microphone this time. He stood up and positioned himself to face the room.

"Well, I just want to be clear on one thing. You lied to me when you said I was on the list and it was a matter of first come, first serve. And I want to know why."

"He's actually sneering," Roger whispered to me.

"I think that's his natural expression."

Juliet nodded. "I did lie." She let it sit for a few seconds. "The agent is looking for certain types. You didn't fit the parameters."

"Well, what the hell are they looking for?" Chad asked.

"Not you," a woman near me muttered.

Rob stepped up and bailed Juliet out. "Look, in LA, it's all about types. If you're doing an ensemble sitcom, you've got a hot lead guy, hot lead girl, sometimes sweet and innocent, sometimes sharp. You've got the tough guy with the soft center. Every sitcom has a wacky neighbor or a dumb character. Yes?" He looked out over the audience. People were nodding their heads.

"You'll notice people are paired off. The ingénue and the leading man, the B character love story or journey if you will, parallels their story."

Juliet broke in. "So, when you asked earlier if the choices for the showcase were based on looks, the answer is yes, in a way. Producers want a certain look. But it isn't always traditional beauty. Sometimes they want a certain ethnic look or—forgive me but this is really what they say—the fat best friend. And please know that in Hollywood, fat is a size eight or ten."

I sighed. My size six days were over unless I wanted to starve myself. I dug out the cookie I had saved from the break. In for a penny...

The heavyset woman spoke up. "Well, obviously, I'm the hot in-génue." She got the laugh. I made a mental note to get to know her better. She seemed like my kind of people.

Juliet was right there. "Absolutely. No contest."

Chad wasn't having it. "So, you flat out lied to me."

"To spare your feelings," Juliet came back.

"I'm not some snowflake. Tell me why I didn't make the cut."

I watched Juliet straighten up. I had a feeling Chad was about to be sorry he asked.

"Okay. I'll give it to you straight. First, we were looking at people who already had some acting background. You don't. Second, and more important, and I'll say this to everyone, half of you in here—guys and gals—are interchangeable. Your looks, your material, the way you dress. Some of you have figured that out and that's why you're here: You want to up your game and you're willing to do the work to get there. I'm going to give you two recommendations. First, I'm going to change out the schedule tomorrow and move the Honing Your Persona session to this room so that everyone can take part in it. Second, if you want to get TV and movie work, you should sit in on Rob's screenwriting session to learn what the character types are and see if you fit into one or more of them. Now, does that mean sacrificing your individuality? Absolutely not. But it might mean expanding your persona to include a type or two. The beauty of stand-up is that you act out your bits. So, if you have a bit where you are acting out a wacky neighbor type of character or your mother or an asshole boss, that shows you've got some range. That's what agents and producers want to see." She turned to face Chad directly.

"I didn't want to hurt your feelings or embarrass you in front of everyone. But since you asked, it wasn't just that you lacked any acting experience."

"Ooh, nice. Now if he's embarrassed it's his own fault. Sweet," I whispered.

"Suicidal tendencies," Nick said.

Juliet continued. "I know club owners in the Atlanta area. You've got a reputation for being more than a little drunk on stage and frankly, a pain in the ass to work with. One owner summed it up by saying," she glanced down at her clipboard, "*thinks he's better than he is. He's not bad, but he's not headliner material.*" She looked at him. "So not exactly a high recommendation."

A stir went through the audience.

"BURN!" someone said in a voice loud enough to carry to the back. People snickered and whispered.

"Who the hell said I was drunk on stage? That's libel!" Chad was incensed.

"I'd be more worried about not being funny," the heavyset woman said.

"Slander, actually. If it's not true. But more than one owner said you liked to have a few before your set. As for me, I'm just telling you what was said." Juliet smiled sweetly. "Anyone else?"

"This girl don't play," Roger whispered.

"She was armed for bear," I agreed.

Chad was clearly pissed. He strode towards the exit and hit the door bar as hard as he could. The sound echoed around the room as the door swung wide, hitting the wall on the other side. Chad sent an explicitly instructive invective over his shoulder as he left.

"That was kind of redundant," I said.

"I would NOT have gotten that from context," Luke deadpanned.

There was an uncomfortable silence in the room as everyone looked at the now-closing door and then back to Juliet.

"Well, um... now that we've got the big question out of the way..."

A few people giggled, but mostly people shifted uncomfortably in their seats.

I stood up and gave a little wave.

"Yes," Juliet looked relieved.

A runner handed me a mic. "For those of us doing the regular showcases, do you recommend any sort of, I don't know... dress code? I mean, should we dress up?" I handed back the mic and sat down again.

"You are such a girl," Luke said.

"Awww, you noticed."

"A long time ago," he said it quietly but he made sure he made eye contact.

I blushed. "Shut up."

Juliet was happy to answer my softball question. I already knew what I was wearing—the suit I had worn for the final night of Florida's Funniest Comedians. But I wanted to give her something easy to bring the room back together.

"Dress for the level up from where you are now. If you've been wearing nice jeans and a good shirt or blouse, you might want to level up. If you've been getting onstage in ratty jeans, a t-shirt, and running shoes, stop that right now. You're a performer, an entertainer. Respect your audience. Now, I know you're thinking, half the guys working the local circuit dress like that. You're not here because you want to spend your life working the local circuit. Upgrade your look. Ladies, a little sexy goes a long way. You're comics, not strippers."

She got a good laugh on that.

"Most important, make sure you're wearing something you're comfortable in, something you can move in. If you're not used to wearing heels, then wear your flats, gentlemen."

Bigger laugh that time. People were coming back together.

"Any more questions about the showcases?" Juliet looked around the room. "Okay then, let's get the panel started. We're going to be talking about how we got our big breaks in comedy and you're going to see that we put in a lot of foundational work; luck had very little to do with it. Are you ready?"

She got a nice response from the audience. The members of the panel took turns talking about how they got started. It seemed fairly Hollywood-based and I have to admit, I tuned out a bit. Could have been a slight sugar coma from the cookies. I was glad my showcase was set for tomorrow night. I needed a nap before sitting through the showcases tonight. I wondered if there would be time.

As Juliet had said, most of the panel had worked the club circuit for years. It turned out that Danny had a lucrative business as a voice-over actor. I hadn't even thought about that. Darlana had been doing bit parts and commercials since she was a kid. Her big break was getting a national commercial. It didn't sound like much, but it had been shown for over five years and made her a tidy sum of money from royalties.

I leaned over to Luke. "Think it was the STD commercial?"

He grinned. "It was an amazing performance."

Juliet, of course had won a nationwide televised talent competition. It was one of the forerunners to the Funniest Comedians franchise that Luke and I had been in. She had lost out to a singer/dancer with the improbable name of Tawny Tanager. Tawny was still touring with the other winners from that show, doing lesser concert halls and the occasional TV appearance. Juliet had done better.

"Because of that show, even though I didn't win..."

"You wuz robbed!" someone shouted. We all laughed.

She pretended to be indignant: "Yes, I was! But it still worked out. Part of the deal was the finalists were signed by an agency. Rupert Himes, who developed the hit show *GlitterTatti* saw me and I was invited to audition for that. That was a one-shot role, but it led to being cast in a recurring role on *That's Just Nallely*. Now, I still really haven't hit it huge. I get regular work on TV. I have done the rounds of the late-night shows. And I tour nationally. The TV recognition helps me pull people into clubs and that means club owners want to book me. I can get steady work on the road, but if I leave LA for too long, the

TV roles will dry up. You have to be here and actively putting yourself out for work. So, it's a balancing act. Everything feeds into everything else."

The panel broke up a little after five. Showcases didn't start until 8:00 and that gave us all time to eat, change if we wanted to, or in my case, take a nap. People stood up, gathering their things and looking around as if they were just a little bit lost. I heard people mention going to one or the other bar. It was too early to eat. We looked at each other expectantly.

"Drink?" Luke asked.

"I'm tempted, but I am giving serious consideration to a nap," I said.

Gabby said, "I have stuff to do in my room. Kasey, is it okay if we do that thing now?"

God. I had forgotten we were going to switch rooms. I was about to lose at least part of my nap time. I forced a smile.

"Sure. Of course."

"That thing?" Nick asked.

"Girl stuff," I said quickly. The men all nodded, pretending not to be clueless.

"I'm up for a beer," Roger said. "Nick?"

"Sure. We'll let them do girl things while we drink beer and do manly things."

Chapter 10: The Fickle Finger of Fame

GABBY AND I HEADED back to our rooms. I went in my door, she in hers. We unlocked the door between the rooms so we could go back and forth.

"Why don't we swap the closets first, since everything is on hangers."

I could carry all my closet stuff in one trip. I laid my clothes on one of the beds in Gabby's room. She had hangers in both hands.

"Is that all you have? I'm going to need a couple of trips."

I grabbed the rest of her clothes out of the closet and carried them through. I handed them off to her and she rehung everything in the closet. Then we went back into her room and I had my stuff in the closet in two seconds flat.

I went back to my room to pack up my stuff. The bathroom was fairly easy. I just threw everything back into my toiletry bag. Then I pulled all the packing cubes out of the drawers, zipped them up, and put them back in my suitcase. Easier to fit everything in because half my wardrobe was on hangers. I had a feeling Gabby was going to need more help.

"Hey, Gabby, I've emptied the drawers, so if you just want to bring your stuff over drawer by drawer, it's probably easier than repacking and unpacking everything."

"That sounds good. I've almost got the bathroom packed up." She sounded kind of proud.

I looked around my room. Everything was packed, including my computer bag and all my snackie-snacks. I did a last recon of the room and cleared out the safe. I'm always afraid I'll leave something behind. I brought my stuff into her room and piled it on the little chair—after I had picked up a sweater that was strewn on it. It was super-soft. If I believed in angels, I'd say it was made with angels' wings. I glanced over at the bathroom to make sure Gabby was still occupied and then checked the label of the sweater. One hundred percent "cachemire" under the name Brunello Cucinelli. I'd never even heard of that label, but I liked it. I needed to make more money; this sweater was incredible. I laid it gently on one of the beds. I could hear her packing things in the bathroom. My nap was not going to happen.

"I'm all set here. I'll give you some space... unless you want some help?"

"Oh, no. It's enough that you're switching with me. I'm sorry to cause such inconvenience."

"No trouble at all. I'm just really good at packing. I'm going to run down to the gift shop. Do you need anything?"

"No, I'm good." She had the two smaller Louis Vuitton cases in her hands. Two cases for toiletries? I mentally shrugged. There's a reason why she looks so good.

"Take your time switching stuff over. I need to stretch my legs a bit, too." I checked my back pocket to make sure I had my room key and started for her door. I stopped.

"Listen, we need to keep going in and out of our assigned room doors. If anyone is in the hall, I don't want them to know what room you're really in."

"Makes sense. And we lock the door in between when we're not here?"

"Probably. Maybe we each need a key for both rooms. We'll figure it out." I took one of the cases from her and she followed me into my old room. I put the case in the bathroom, waved a goodbye and headed out the door, making sure the lock clicked behind me.

I took the elevator to the lobby. I wanted to know if all of the private showcase people had received the same threatening note that Luke and Gabby had. I headed down the back hallway behind the main room. The speakers' "green room" was most likely back there. The hall had a number of doors, all on the left-hand side. I was going to have to open each door a bit to check every room. My stomach did a little flip, letting me know it was not okay with this plan. I started to open the first door when I heard raised voices coming from a room near the end of the hall. I walked towards the room, then stopped, mostly because I didn't want to walk in on an uncomfortable situation.

"You had no right to do that, Juliet."

I recognized Darlana's voice. I decided not to turn around and come back later. What can I say? I have an inquiring mind.

"Of course, I did; it's my event. But I didn't do it to take anything away from you. It just seemed like it was necessary to open that session up to everyone."

"Well, I should be leading it then, not you. I've got my PowerPoint all set to go and I spent a lot of time on this."

"Darlana, I appreciate that you did and you'll be paid the same amount we agreed on..."

"It's not about the money. You're undermining my authority."

"I don't need to undermine your authority. It's my event!" Juliet paused for a moment. "Look, I wasn't going to bring this up, but the feedback we got from your Cold Auditions session was not positive. People said it was more about you than actual auditioning techniques."

Good to know that Luke and I weren't the only ones who thought that session was a waste of time. Juliet must have her sources out there, checking on the instructors.

"I'm the creator of the technique. I'm an innovator. You can't learn the process without learning about me. The Dolphin Cold Technique is going to change the way people audition, that's a certainty!"

"That may well be, but tomorrow's session on Honing Your On-stage Persona is not something you developed. And frankly, I'm better qualified to lead that session."

"You just can't stand sharing the spotlight with anyone."

"And when you organize your own event and take on the financial risk of that, you can have your own spotlight."

I unconsciously nodded my head. Juliet had her there. Apparently, Darlana had come prepared for battle.

"You need to watch your step, Juliet. I've known you since college and I know your secret. America's Comedy Sweetheart! If people knew what you really were, you wouldn't be so high and mighty."

"So, it's you! You're the one who's been blackmailing me!"

"What are you talking about?"

"Don't play the innocent with me. You were always jealous of me. Well, you've cost me enough money. Congratulations. I'm broke. You've bled me dry."

"What are you talking about? And you better not be too broke to pay me!"

"You're telling me you haven't been blackmailing me over the accident?"

"Wish I had thought of it. But now I know it's an option..."

"Just try it. I am so done with you."

"You can bet your ass I'll be on that stage with you tomorrow morning. Just make sure the check doesn't bounce or we'll be talking about a lot more than honing your persona. Or maybe we'll talk about how you invented yours... Joanne."

"Don't ever call me that again. You'll get your money. Once this weekend is over, we are done. It was a mistake inviting you to teach. I just felt sorry for you because your career is in the toilet. So much for old friends."

"Try to get through the weekend without killing anybody else. Because I know exactly who you are, Joanne."

"If I kill anyone this weekend, it will be you, you ungrateful bitch. Get out of here. And if one word about that accident comes out, I'll know who to look for."

This was followed by Darlana shouting the same instructional expletive Chad had used and America's Comedy Sweetheart responding in kind. Darlana flew through the door and rushed past me so quickly that I'm not sure I even registered on her radar. She was definitely not connected to her Zen Flow.

What had Darlana meant by "Try to get through the weekend without killing anybody else." I debated giving Juliet time to recover for all of three seconds. It would be better to catch her when she was off-balance. Obviously, there was more going on than she told us. I don't mind butting out when something doesn't concern me, but if Juliet was being blackmailed by someone, then the threatening notes to Gabby and Luke might be tied to that.

I walked in the room. Juliet was in a chair, slumped over a table, crying. Sobbing, in fact.

She looked up at me and I'm not sure she realized who I was.

"It wasn't my fault. It was an accident. I am so sorry." She buried her face in her arms again, sobbing harder. I grabbed napkins from the coffee setup and waited for the sobbing to subside. It seemed endless. I wanted to cry just listening to her.

Gradually, the sobs turned to hiccups and she raised her head again. I handed her the napkins. She blew her nose in a wad of napkins and found a clean one to wipe her face. She was still sniffling and I handed her more napkins. Her breathing slowed.

"It was college. Twenty years ago," she said without preamble.

"What happened?"

"Driving home from a party. I was the designated driver so I hadn't been drinking, thank God. But everyone else in the car had. I went through a green light and a kid on a motorcycle shot the red. Ted Armitage. Theodore Scott Armitage. Nineteen years old and never got older." She was crying again, but not at the level of the previous racking sobs.

"It really wasn't your fault."

"I should have been paying more attention. We were having fun, laughing, joking. If I'd been paying better attention, maybe I would have reacted faster. Maybe I would have seen him run the red and slammed on my brakes in time."

"And maybe there was nothing you could do. He sealed his fate when he ran the light."

She shook her head. "But I timed it, you see." She looked up at me, eyes appealing. "I wasn't very good with a stick shift yet, so I hated to start from a dead stop. I had a habit of slowing down for red lights that were about to change. I'd time it so I could hit the green without having to go down to first or stop and start again."

I nodded. I've done that a hundred times at least.

"He caught the light when it went red. It was maybe a second past the red. His light was red. My light went green." The way she said it made me realize that she had probably repeated this phrase to herself every day for twenty years.

"Darlana knows about it."

She nodded, miserable.

"And someone has been blackmailing you over this."

"Well, Darlana, I guess."

"I don't think so." She looked up at me and I vaguely waved towards the door. "I overheard the exchange. Who else knows about the accident?"

"Danny and Darlana were in the car with me. Some of my friends from that university, but I'm not in touch with most of them anymore. The cops, I guess. Ted's family. My family."

My heart sank further with each addition to the list.

"That's a lot of people. I'm surprised this hasn't come out before."

"I changed my name. I went home for the summer. I couldn't go back to that school. Everyone knew I was the girl who killed Ted, accident or not. I switched schools, cut my hair. Colored it. Even worked to get rid of my southern accent. I left Joanne Preston behind and I became Juliet Hartwell."

"How many people know you changed your name?"

"My family. A few close friends. But I left a lot of people behind when I left that university. I went home. I couldn't really function for a year."

"Did people in your home town know?"

"No. My parents were embarrassed and ashamed. Wanted to sweep it all under the rug. Kept telling me I needed to put it behind me. I wanted to, but it's something you never really forget. That accident is always with me."

My mind was weighing various options. At least two people knew Juliet's secret and either of them could be sabotaging the event. I asked the obvious question.

"Does anyone else here know about this? Know that Juliet Hartwell isn't your real name?"

"Well, really, most people in the business expect that the name you use isn't your real name. Club owners don't care. Neither do agents for that matter. They just want to make sure you have a tax ID number.

Rob and Mo probably know. Pamela and Trystan probably don't know."

"So, if someone suspected that Juliet Hartwell wasn't your real name and wanted to find out what it was…"

"It would take some searching. I changed it almost twenty years ago, legally. Before I started doing stand-up. I suppose if someone had really good computer skills they could find me."

"But they would have to know to look for a name change in the first place." I was thinking out loud. I wondered how strong Chad's Internet search skills were. "You told Darlana you've been bled dry by the blackmailer. When did the blackmail start?"

"A little over a year ago."

That probably took Chad out of contention, at least for the blackmail part of it. Maybe the threatening notes and the blackmail were two separate issues.

"Do you really think Darlana could be your blackmailer?"

"I wouldn't put it past her." She thought it over for a few seconds. "But no, she really didn't seem to know what I was talking about when I accused her. And she's not that good of an actress."

"What about Danny?"

"No, he's solid. He was in the car that night and he's been my support from the beginning. In fact, he loaned me the money for the last payment to the blackmailer. That's why I need this event to be successful. The private showcases will help me pay off Danny and get my finances back to stable. Until the next payment is demanded."

I nodded. "It was an accident that happened twenty years ago. Why not let it come out?"

"Because I'm America's Comedy Sweetheart. I'm pretty sure killing someone is not going to look good on my resume. Fame is fickle."

"This secret has kept you looking over your shoulder for years. It's cost you what? Thousands of dollars?"

She nodded. "Tens of thousands."

"The only way out of this is for you to tell the truth. It's better for you to control the narrative than for the blackmailer to put his slant on it."

She was quiet, but she shook her head no.

"Just think about it. You don't have to do anything about it yet. We just have to get through this weekend."

"Will you help me?"

"Of course."

I knew I'd be kicking myself for that, but what could I say? At least I had the opening I was looking for. "Did all the private showcase people receive the same note that Luke and Gabby did?"

She nodded. "That was another mess I was straightening out this afternoon. I talked to all the showcase people and reassured them that it was just someone trying to stir up trouble."

"Do you think that threat is tied in with your blackmailer?"

"I don't see it. I was getting blackmailed before the event was announced."

"But you hold this event every year."

"Yes, but the private showcases are a new thing. It was really just an opportunity that came up."

I processed the information. She might not think it was related, but I wasn't so sure. I had more questions, but she was looking kind of shaky. "You probably should head back to your room, take a shower, and wash all this crap away."

She rose out of the chair slowly and checked herself in one of the big mirrors in the room. "God, I'm a mess."

"It's been a rough first day. Let's just take things one step at a time and see what we can find. In the meantime, the show must go on."

She rolled her eyes, but I got a smile out of her. America's Comedy Sweetheart was getting back into gear.

"Thanks, Kasey. We can talk more later. Maybe tomorrow?"

"Absolutely. Now go make yourself gorgeous."

She gave me a quick hug and headed for the door. I took a look around the room, trying to see if there were any file folders or documents lying around, but it looked like Juliet had learned her lesson on that score. I followed her down the hallway and we went our separate ways.

The truth was I couldn't really do much more than keep my eyes and ears open. I could get the others to help, too, so that at least increased our chances of finding something out. But at this point, my whole strategy depended on luck. I was ready for a drink.

Maybe the guys were still in the bar. I looked in the lounge. There were a lot of people from the seminar, but I didn't see Nick or Luke. I went to the pool bar, since it was near the gift shop. Nick, Luke, and Roger were at a table close to the pool. I looked at the assortment of empty and partially full beer bottles on the table.

"Am I in time for a beer?"

Nick stood up. "Absolutely. I'll grab one for you."

"I can get it for her," Luke said, pushing his chair back.

"You can get the next one." He held up his bottle. "This okay?"

"Great, thanks."

Nick picked up a few of the empties and carried them back to the bar. I took the fourth seat at the table. The day was warm and the sun was bright but not blinding. I took a minute just to soak up some sun and recover from the always-too-cold air conditioning.

"Nice."

"Doesn't suck," Roger said.

"Are you ready to go up tonight?"

"It's six minutes. So, yeah."

"Ah, nerves of steel."

"Check back with me in a couple of hours. I'm assuming we go in the order we were listed. That would be the most obvious."

"What's obvious?" Nick asked, setting a beer down in front of me.

"Our order tonight. Probably exactly the way it was listed in the notice, right?"

"Audience should be pretty tired by the time they get to us," Nick said.

"You'll be the bright spots in their night," I put in.

"We'll be yelling for you," Luke said. "We'll be your fan club."

"But payback's a bitch." Luke and I looked at each other and clinked bottles.

"Ain't it though."

"Did you and Gabby get your girl stuff done?" Nick asked, changing the subject.

"My girl stuff doesn't take nearly as long as her girl stuff. But then, she does girl a whole lot better than I do."

"I wouldn't say that," Nick started.

"You're just different kinds of girls," Roger said. "Women, I mean. She is LA-Hollywood and you're..." He hesitated.

"Oh, I do want to hear this," I teased.

Nick looked amused.

"Well, Kasey you're just different."

"Thanks, Rog, that means a lot." I gave him the side-eye.

"What he means to say is that you are one of a kind," Nick threw Roger a lifeline.

I was feeling kind of saucy. It was fun watching the guys squirm. "Luke, anything to say?"

Luke took his time. He looked away into the distance and looked back at me. "I work with beautiful women all the time. Most of them are two-dimensional. I'm not saying Gabby is; Gabby has a certain electricity about her. She has star power."

Served me right for prodding him. I looked down at my beer.

"But you, Kasey," Luke continued. "Are a different kind of beautiful. Nick is right; you are one of a kind. You are more striking than traditionally pretty—which is superficial, by the way. Looks fade. You're not just funny; you're smart funny. You genuinely care about people. You're inherently kind." He emphasized the word *kind* as if it were a rare quality. I could feel my face getting red.

"And I am sucking up to you like nobody's business, because you are going to be that person who makes it and gives us all jobs."

It broke the tension. I balled up a napkin and tossed it at him. "Damn, Luke. That's why I've been sucking up to you."

"Well, you're missing the boat, because I'm about to blow everybody out of the water tonight with my set," Roger said.

Nick tipped his bottle at Roger in a small salute. "Make sure they're still breathing when I get up."

I looked around the table. "So, tonight. I might need a bit of a favor."

I got three different versions of "sure" back at me immediately.

"I haven't even said what yet!"

"You need something, we've got you covered," Roger said. The other two nodded.

I told them about my encounter with Juliet. I said that Juliet was being blackmailed but I didn't give the details. That was her business and if she didn't want people to know, I wasn't going to tell anyone. I also told them that Gabby and I had switched rooms and I swore them to secrecy on that.

"Do you think Gabby's in physical danger?" Roger asked.

"Probably not. But Gabby seemed worried and if I can take that off her plate, then she'll be in a better frame of mind. Maybe someone is just trying to make the private showcase people blow their sets."

"Do you think one of the private showcase people is psyching out the others?" Nick asked. "That's kind of extreme."

Luke caught my eye. "You'd be surprised what people will do in a competitive situation."

Roger looked at him, a question in his eyes.

"Florida's Funniest New Comedians," I explained. "Luke's girl-friend kind of went all out to make sure she won."

"All out?" Nick exclaimed. "She stabbed him!"

"It was a rough break up," Luke joked.

"Funny now. Not so funny then." My voice was sharper than I intended it to be. "You damn near died. There will be none of that here."

"Yes, ma'am. Same goes for you." Luke met my eyes. I nodded.

"So, while I appreciate your help, I want to set some ground rules. I really just want you to listen to what people are saying about the showcases, about Juliet, whatever seems pertinent. Ask questions if you can without being suspicious. Don't be too interested in anything or anyone. We're just gathering information at this point. And whatever you do, don't go charging off alone on a wild hunch. Let's set up a group text chat and if anyone sees something worth following up on, text."

Roger was busy on his phone. He looked up. "Should I put Gabby on the chat?"

I thought for a second. "Yeah. It's better if she knows what's up."

Roger nodded and about 30 seconds later, our text notifications all went off at the same time. We instinctively checked our phones, even though we knew what the text was. Pavlovian response. I looked at the group name: Juliet's Jesters.

"Jesters?" I did my best Joe Pesci: "Like, I'm a clown? I amuse you?"

I got a better laugh than I deserved.

I looked down and tipped my beer bottle a bit. I had finished my beer.

"Another?" Luke asked.

"Thanks, no. I need to go back to my room and start getting ready for tonight."

"Why? You're not going up," Roger said.

Nick started laughing. "You are so not married."

"What?"

"Guys show up in whatever they're wearing. Women get dressed to go out," Nick explained.

"And since you two are going up tonight, you might want to spiff up a bit," I said. "Good looks will only take you so far."

Luke nodded. "The agent and club owner are going to be there both nights, and maybe we're just faces in the crowd, but if most of the people are going to be very casual because they're not performing, we just need to take it up a notch to stand out." He got a shit-eating grin on his face. "Besides, I'm going to be mingling with the ladies, tonight!"

"Because that works out so well for you," I said. "You can't even have breakfast without turning rabbit."

"What's that?" Nick said. He didn't miss a thing.

Luke started to blush.

"One of the *ladies*," I emphasized the word, "sat with him at breakfast and apparently came on a little strong."

"Yeah, I have that problem all the time," Roger said with just the right amount of snark.

"Me, too." Nick said.

"Well, I'll be there tonight to defend you all."

We stood up, chairs scraping on the pool deck. Nick and I both ended up at the gift shop. I needed a quick snack to put in my stomach before tonight's show. Nick picked up a large water and a protein bar. We walked out together.

"Are you nervous about going up tonight?"

"A little. I always am."

"Me, too." I decided to ask the question that had been bugging me. "So, what does your wife think of your comedy career?"

"Oh, that's a sit-down question." He pointed to a couple of over-stuffed chairs tucked away in a corner. "She thinks I'm at a medical convention, if that's any indication."

"Oof."

"Yeah." Nick twisted his wedding band. "Not what she signed up for."

"Well, it's not like you're going to chuck your practice and go on the road."

"It's undignified." He made little quote marks in the air.

"She's not wrong." We laughed.

"But it's not like doing stand-up is going to hurt my professional reputation. I see it as a stress reliever. Most of my colleagues do, too. I think they're secretly a little jealous."

"But she wants you to play golf."

"And tennis. Which I do. We belong to a country club. We've got the life that she wants. I don't see why she has a problem with this."

"Does she go to your gigs?"

"She came to a few of the early ones when I was doing open mics." He paused. "I was not very good. She was most likely embarrassed that I didn't do well."

I nodded, thinking about some of—most of—my early sets. It's hard to sit through a friend having a bad set. Must be worse to sit through someone you love doing it.

"But she must think you're funny or she wouldn't have married you."

Nick gave me a look. Oops. Foot in mouth. I am so good at that.

"That probably wasn't her main criteria."

"No, I mean, you're good-looking and smart and all that."

"Thank you for noticing." His eyes crinkled a bit at the corners.

"But, I mean, if she didn't think you were funny, she wouldn't enjoy being with you so she wouldn't have married you."

"Not to sound too egotistical, but I was a bit of a catch. A lot of women would put up with bad jokes to marry a successful cardiac surgeon. You don't even have to be good-looking. Not that I think I am, I mean, I'm not stuck on my looks. I'm no Luke Hallidade."

"Very few people are Luke Hallidade."

"You two seem to have a special thing."

"Not a thing." I don't know why I wanted to make that very clear, but I did.

"Are you sure? He is very protective of you."

"Yeah, well, we started out together. In comedy."

"And then you nearly died trying to catch whoever stabbed him."

"You've been Googling." I smiled at him to show I wasn't weirded out. "Just a concussion. And some sore ribs. And stitches. Not fun. But it wasn't exactly a bonding experience. He was in a coma; didn't even know about it 'til later on."

"Still, it's a bond."

I nodded. There was no denying there was something between Luke and me. What, exactly, I didn't know. And nothing had ever come of it. It was pointless to talk about it.

"Why don't you invite your wife to come see you now. You've undoubtedly gotten better."

"I have. She's not interested. As I said, she's embarrassed that I do this. I embarrass her. Apparently." He sighed. Out of nowhere he said, "She's spending this weekend in the city with girlfriends."

"Sounds like fun?" Something in the way he said girlfriends made me finish the sentence with an uptick.

"Except she's not with her girlfriends."

"And you know this how?"

"Private investigator. He's been following her for a couple of months. She's been making noises about separating. I might not be the best husband and I understand I work a lot of hours, but she knew that going in. She accused me of cheating on her." He winced, his dark brown eyes clouding over.

"Do you cheat on her?"

"Of course not. I don't have the time, much less the inclination."

Well, that put me in my place. My face must have reflected this.

"Until this weekend."

"And we're not going there, Mr. Married Man, are we?"

"That's Doctor Married Man and I wouldn't do that to you. Or even her."

"So why does she think you're cheating on her?"

"Psychologically speaking," Nick started, "when someone accuses you of something that is so far out of character for you, it generally means they are doing it themselves. Projection."

"Her accusation tipped you off."

He nodded. "I suggested marriage counseling. She doesn't want to go because I'm the problem. I tried to set up date nights with her, be more attentive. She just wasn't interested in working on the relationship. I've seen how these things play out. And really, I don't mind her getting a settlement. She's pretty successful in her own right, no kids, so, just a division of marital assets. But the accusation bugged me. I talked to a lawyer friend and he recommended having her followed for a few weeks. Sure enough."

"That sucks."

"My attorney thinks it's gold. I'm just sad about it. Love does not last." His voice was flat.

"Sometimes it does. My parents have been married for over 30 years."

"Does your mom appreciate your dad's sense of humor?"

I nodded. "And vice versa. They're both pretty funny. Maybe you just need to find someone who appreciates your sense of humor."

His eyes met mine. "And do you appreciate my sense of humor?"

I broke eye contact and did what I do best: deflected. "We'll find out tonight."

He grimaced. "Great. No pressure. For what it's worth, I'm filing divorce papers when I get back and moving out."

"And then the ring comes off?"

He looked down at his left hand. When he looked up, he had a rueful smile on his face. "Right now, it serves as a very good reminder that I am still married. It keeps me from doing something just out of spite."

"I think that's wise."

There was a kind of sad, awkward silence.

"You'll be great tonight," I said.

"What makes you think that?"

"I'm betting you work best under pressure. Just adding a little to the pot."

"Oh, thanks a lot."

There was nothing to be done about it at this point. We picked up our packages and headed towards the elevators. I stopped at the front desk to make sure there would be some place to eat after the show. Both the main restaurant and the pool bar restaurant served until midnight. I thanked the clerk and we headed up to our very separate rooms.

CHAPTER 11: YODA NEVER HAD TO DO STAND-UP

GABBY AND I WENT down to the showcases together, making sure we each left from the correct room. We were dressed to be seen but I was pretty sure that no one would notice me when I walked in with Gabby. She was in a little black dress with subtle red accents and black, patent leather, slingback pumps. I trailed a little behind her, checking for the tell-tale red soles of Christian Louboutin. I was not disappointed. I looked down at my Nine West pumps. Well, at least I was out of my cowboy boots. I had on a jade green silk blouse tucked into black straight-legged dress pants. The blouse set off my hair color nicely; the pants would cover whatever the hell I would inevitably spill on them. Some people dress for success; I dress to anticipate disaster.

Roger had texted that he and Nick were already there and had a table. I noticed there was no check-in table outside the door. Maybe anyone at the hotel could come in and watch the show. That would be kind of cool. Then I thought about the family with the kids. Maybe not so cool. Comics are fairly foul-mouthed.

The room had been reset from the rows of meeting seats to round tables. Six chairs were arranged at each table close enough together so that no one had their back to the stage. I did a quick count: twenty-four tables set in three offset rows, covered with white tablecloths. Very nice. The room was about half-filled, with some people already seated and the rest milling around. There were no free drink coupons tonight so the two portable bars were active, but not slammed. The room had a busy hum and you could feel the tension in the air. The first night of showcases would give everyone an idea of the level of talent at this event. While it wasn't a competition, people still wanted to do well.

"There they are," Gabby said pointing.

Roger had probably picked the table—he was sitting with Luke and Nick at a table across the room, but towards the back. It was also not too far from one of the portable bar setups. We joined them and Luke let out a whistle.

"Looking good, Ladies."

"You guys clean up pretty well, yourselves," I said. And they had. Nick was wearing a charcoal grey suit with a medium blue shirt, open at the neck. Roger was in dress pants and a blazer. Luke was comfortable in dress jeans and a white cotton shirt that looked both dressy and casual at the same time. I wondered how that worked. I was pretty sure that it was the way he was wearing it, not the shirt itself. They each had a bottled beer in front of them and Nick also had a bottled water. The man drank a lot of water.

I glanced over at the portable bar. I was in no rush to get a drink. I figured the lines would die down once the show started.

"Do you want anything yet?" I asked Gabby.

"I'm good for now. We've got all night."

We settled in and a minute later Amber walked up and we asked her to join us.

Who's going up tonight?" she asked.

Nick and Roger raised their hands.

"How about you?" Nick asked.

"Tomorrow night. I wish I were going up tonight. Get it over with. I figure everyone is going to be so sick of these showcases by tomorrow night, the only people who will show will be the people going up."

"We'll be there to cheer you on," Luke turned on his full mega-watt smile.

"We'll even laugh in all the right places," Gabby said.

"Thank you! I have a feeling we're in for a couple of long nights. What's the sign-up procedure?"

"Same order as we were listed on the sheets. I'm number 11 tonight."

"Number 14," Nick said, reaching for his water bottle. "You just go to the front table, let them know you're here and they tell you what number you are."

I saw the heavyset lady with the curls hesitate as she came through the door. I half-stood and waved her over. She was someone I wanted to meet.

She walked up and looked us over. "I don't know... three of the ten private showcases at one table? Are we being elitist?"

"Water finds its own level," Amber said. "I'm just here to keep it real. I'm Amber." She held out her hand.

"Philipa Carroll."

We went around the table and introduced ourselves. Philipa sat down and put her bag on her lap, digging through it until she fished out her wallet. "How many people are going up tonight?"

"Twenty-five," Gabby said.

"Oh man. It's gonna be a long night."

"Hey, Roger and I are going up tonight!" Nick pretended to be indignant.

"Well, there's the silver lining. Still..."

"Yeah, we've all done the math. Twenty-five people. Six-minute sets. A minute between at best."

"I'm already feeling like I'm throwing my money down the toilet," Roger said. "We're all going to be a blur to the agent."

"Hopefully we'll at least get some decent video," I said.

We all looked over at the table where the agent and club owner were sitting. Mo, Darlana, and Danny were with him. I assumed Juliet was emceeing the show. I bet it had been a while since she emceed anything, but she would move it along. After witnessing the argument earlier, I was surprised Darlana had shown up for this event. She had positioned herself next to the agent, so maybe she was working her own agenda.

Philipa looked over at the portable bar. There was a bit of a line.

"Yeah, I'm thinking of waiting until the show starts and the lines go down. They've been steady."

"Good call." She put her wallet back in her bag and set it on the floor.

I looked at my phone to check the time. Two minutes after the hour. Already running late. Well, that was to be expected. Talk turned to the sessions we had attended. Mo's improv class had been a winner.

"I saw you leave Darlana's session early," Philipa said to me. "I wish I had followed you out the door. That was a waste of time."

Luke jumped in. "I kept waiting for her to tell us something useful."

"But enough about me. How do you feel about me?" Philipa mimicked Darlana's feathery voice to a T. She looked at Luke. "You left early, too. Something going on we should know about?"

"Absolutely," Luke said. "Kasey and I are very close." He held up two fingers and crossed them. "Like that."

Amber shot a calculating look my way. I pretended not to notice. I'd check with Luke later to see if he wanted me to run interference.

"I texted him to check his room. Gabby got a threatening note about doing the showcase. So did Luke." I looked at Philipa. "Did you?"

"Yes, I did. But Juliet asked me not to mention it."

"No secrets here," Nick said.

"You all got threatening notes?" Amber asked.

"Yeah, well, it sounds like all the showcase people did."

"I'd say so. But the threat was pretty non-specific," I said. I didn't want Gabby getting upset again.

"Or else!" Luke snorted.

"Like a ten-year-old wrote it. I suspect Chad," Philipa said.

"He's a definite possibility," I said. "Was the note pushed under your door?"

She nodded.

"So, whoever it is definitely has access to room numbers."

"And phone numbers. Most of us got the text he sent," Roger pointed out.

Juliet had talked to each person in their room. I opened up my phone and looked at the image of the list. It was cut off on the left-hand side. The room numbers could have been on that list. That was a question for Juliet. I clicked my phone off and looked up. Nick was watching me with a questioning look. I gave him a slight shake of my head. He had already put it together.

"Could be a she," Philipa said. "Women can be very competitive."

Luke and I looked at each other and smiled.

"I've heard that," Luke said.

"But if we go with most likely suspect..." I led.

"Chad."

"You don't think it's just because we all don't like him, do you?" Gabby wondered. "Because maybe we're just focused on him because he's a jerk."

"Yeah, but he's been a jerk *about* the showcases..." Roger started.

"And everything else," Amber said. "He's just a first-class jerk."

"On the plus side, because he was such a jerk, Juliet is doing the Persona workshop tomorrow and that means that we'll actually get some good information, not more Life of Darlana," Luke said.

"I'd say the highlight of the day was Chad throwing his hissy fit," Roger said.

"Oh my GOD could you believe that?" Amber rolled her eyes.

"And did Juliet totally shoot him down?"

"Down in flames!"

"Burn baby, burn."

"It felt pretty good," Gabby said quietly. "I know you're not supposed to be happy when another person is being—"

"He had it coming," Nick broke in. His voice was calm and even. "I think just about everyone in the room was pleased. It's only human." He met Gabby's eyes and nodded reassuringly.

She flashed back a smile. "It really did feel good!"

"Go, Gabby," Roger said.

"Is he even here tonight?" I asked, looking around.

We all started craning our necks.

"Yep, there he is. Is he going up tonight?" Amber asked.

"From the way he's dressed, it doesn't look like it."

"No, he's going up tomorrow night," I said. "I get to say I shared the stage with Chad Warder."

"Well, I doubt if he'll dress up tomorrow night, either. It sounds like he doesn't exactly care about how he presents," Luke said.

"He's so funny he doesn't have to," Amber said. She pitched her voice lower and used Chad's bombastic style: "He kills every time he gets on stage, man."

"Oh my God, he actually told you that?" Gabby asked.

"Let's just say I was THRILLED to join up with you guys last night. Saved from the Chad."

The lights flickered a couple of times and then went down. The room quieted a bit and a male voice came over the sound system.

"Ladies and gentleman, America's Comedy Sweetheart, Juliet Hartwell!"

We gave a nice round of applause which Juliet was smart enough not to milk. She plunged right into a welcome and introduced the club owner, Solly Vincenzo and Ross Zieff, the agent. We all gawked at them on cue. Then she did about five minutes of material that was casual enough to not sound like material. Smooth.

I glanced at my phone for the time and mentally set the end time of the evening back ten minutes. The restaurants would still be open—just. I have my priorities.

"I'm hitting the bar," Philipa whispered. Is everyone all set?"

Amber stood up. "I'll go with."

Philipa came back with two glasses of wine. I gave her a thumb's up.

"Two-fisted drinker. Game on," Luke kidded her.

Philipa rolled her eyes. "Saving myself a trip. It's going to be a long night."

The night's showcases—unsurprisingly—proved to be a bit of hit or miss. Most people did fairly well. Gabby and I got up for wine about the third comic in.

I was slow-drinking my wine. Philipa was right about it being a long night and I figured one glass an hour would get me through. It wasn't a matter of budget—I wanted to stay sharp. Too much had already gone on without me getting stupid drunk.

Roger's turn finally came up and the energy at our table switched from lethargic to full attention. It was like we thought we could will him to do a good set. As it turned out, he didn't need our help.

He held up his hand. "For the record, not a Weasley." He paused for the expected laugh. "Just like to get that out of the way up front. However, I am literally—the redheaded stepchild." He paused a beat for the laugh. "They call us a blended family. Red don't blend. They stick me on the side of every family portrait just to make it easier to crop me out. They're too damn lazy to photoshop it. People come over and look at the family pictures, 'Oh, is this your son-in-law?'" He appeared to be exasperated. People were laughing. "Yes, please. Laugh at my pain."

His set went quickly. He was extremely likeable onstage. Not afraid to make fun of himself and he did it without really putting himself down.

"My mom and I lived with my grandmother for several years so we're close. I love my grandma, she's awesome, but there are certain things you just don't want to know about your grandma. I was helping her with her phone because she couldn't get to one of her apps... 'No Grandma, you want Tinder, not Grindr.'" He paused for the laugh. "She says, 'But the guys are hotter on Grindr.'" He paused again for the laugh. He looked out at the audience, as if totally bewildered and horrified at the same time. "What do you say to that? Thanks for the heads up?" He got a huge laugh.

I leaned over to Nick. "You didn't tell us he was this good."

"He's pretty solid. I haven't seen him in a few months. He's getting more comfortable onstage."

I nodded. I wasn't completely comfortable on stage yet, but I have had my moments. It's a level. A lot of comics try to fake it—they pretend to be cool or relaxed but since they're trying... it shows. I thought of Yoda: "Do or do not. There is no try." Yoda never had to do stand-up. I imagined he'd have a pretty dry delivery. My mind was wandering.

"I love my grandma and I'm not ashamed to say it. She's just so cool. Three of my friends asked her to prom." He took the beat. "Like they stood a chance with her." He got a nice laugh. He held up his right hand. "God's honest truth. Four of us were going STAG to the prom and my grandma was like, "'Oh, that will not do.' She got three of her friends and we took them all out for prom."

He got an audible "awwww" from a bunch of cynical comics. "Oh, we had an angle. We had homemade cookies for months!"

Roger came off to a solid round of applause. We added some whoops from our table. This wasn't a competition or anything, but I figured it couldn't hurt if the club owner and agent saw that someone was really liked by the audience. We high-fived him when he got back to the table. Juliet was bringing up the next comic and Nick stood up to position himself closer to the stage. He had a good ten minutes plus before his slot, but things happen. People chicken out or someone runs short. It's good to be in place ahead of time. We wished him luck and he moved towards the side wall where a few comics were standing.

The next guy up was new and nervous. His material wasn't great and the audience started twitching in their seats. The table talk grew a little louder, which made the kid a bit more nervous. It was a long six minutes and he was relieved to get off the stage. I felt for him. Hard enough to do comedy. Doing comedy in front of comics who have heard just about everything is a special ring of hell.

One more comic before Nick. Juliet brought up the second female comic of the night. I checked the list for tomorrow night. There were at least ten women going up. I wasn't sure if that was good or bad. The women tonight were standing out just because of the sheer lack of numbers. I could easily get lost in the sauce tomorrow. I sighed.

Gabby leaned over. "What's wrong?"

"Nothing really. Just so many comics in one night. I think you were smart to do the private showcase. At least you'll make an impression."

She nodded. "I wasn't thinking that strategically, but now that I'm sitting through this, I see your point. My butt is sore already." She giggled. I looked at her glass of wine. It was empty. I was pretty sure she hadn't eaten much all day. She was only a couple inches shorter than me, but she was about 110 pounds soaking wet. I'd make sure our next round included some bottled water. I wished there were snacks but no luck on that count. My stomach was already complaining.

The woman was talking about her date mansplaining football to her. "I grew up in a football town. He's talking to me as if I've never seen a game before: 'Okay honey, it's third and eight and the quarterback, that's the guy who gets the ball at the snap...'" she looked out over the audience. "Ooh, thanks for that clarification." We laughed, the women probably harder than the men. "'and because he needs the yards, he's going to pass.' Ooh, it's like I'm sitting with Bill Belichick." She paused. "I pick up my beer and keep my eyes on the screen. I say, 'Quarterback's going to call an audible, attempt a sneak, and get sacked eight yards back. It'll be fourth and sixteen and they'll have to punt.'" She looked out at the audience and gave a knowing nod. Someone shouted, "You go girl!" She laughed. "So, he's looking at me, misses the snap, sure enough, QB is sacked. They lost seven yards, not eight... so, what do I know?" She got the laugh. "And that, ladies, is how you make sure you never get a second date." She got a nice laugh on that one. She finished her set to a healthy round of applause.

At least the sets were going by quickly. Juliet was moving through the introductions without looking like she was rushing, but she wasn't taking a lot of time, either. I noticed she always thanked the comic by name before reading out the intro to the next comic. I wondered if it was for the benefit of the club owner and agent. They must have had a list in front of them that they could make notes on. But truly, thirteen people in and most everyone who had already gone up was a blur to me.

"From Long Island, please welcome Nick Hill."

There was light applause. People were getting tired. I figured by the time we got to number 20, no one would be applauding.

I would say Nick looked good on stage, but Nick looked good anywhere. His first bit was about growing up in an overachieving family.

"I come from a family of overachievers. My mom is literally a rocket scientist. You can't slide anything past her because she's got that whole logical scientific side *and* women's intuition. Somehow, she always knew I was about to do something stupid before I did. Well, to be fair, teenage boys are always about to do something stupid." He paused for the laugh. "She had a better than fifty-fifty chance of catching me out."

"Whenever I need advice, I call my mom. She's the human equivalent of Google, but faster. Plus, if you ask her for a recipe, you don't have to read through eighteen paragraphs of back story before she gives it to you." There were laughs of recognition from the women in the audience.

"My wife, my mom, and my sister are like this holy trinity of wisdom. They've got so much intelligence and intuition that I sometimes wonder if they're secretly running the world and my dad and I are just here to kill the occasional bug." Another good laugh. He was hitting on those basic truths that people don't think about but everybody knows.

"Women's intuition is a superpower. Some weird, never-before-seen problem comes up and they immediately know how to navigate it. Meanwhile, I'm over here trying to find my glasses while they're on my head."

"Women's logic is a bit like quantum physics. You can't quite understand it, but it's always right. Their logic is so advanced that they can win an argument with a single raised eyebrow. I've learned never to argue with the 'look.'" That line got knowing laughs from the men.

"Women just have a different logic pattern than men. Always jumping to conclusions. The *right* conclusions, but still. Make it look like it's a little hard, will you?"

His style was warm rather than edgy. He had a likeability factor that was noticeable. I imagined his patients loved him. Good bedside manner. My mind drifted a bit with that one. I brought my focus back to Nick. But I was smiling.

And then he went into a bit about his wife and my smile disappeared. Nothing like reality coming at you.

"I met my wife right after grad school and it was love at first sight… well more like love at first 'nice to meet you.' We met, and two weeks later, we were sharing a Netflix account. Our whirlwind romance was so intense that even Shakespeare would've been like, 'Slow down, you two! You're making the balcony scene look like a casual chat.' What can I say, she swept me off my feet."

He got some "awws" from the women in the audience. I pasted a smile on my face and privately wondered if he was going to drop that bit from his act anytime soon.

"Guys, I'm telling you right now, the only thing that is going to save us is to admit they are smarter than we are and to suck up."

Then he moved into a bit on having surgery. Never mentioned he was a surgeon. Just a regular guy up there, observing life. He closed out his set and while the crowd didn't go wild, he was definitely appreciated. I saw the agent make some notes, but I hadn't really been watching him so I wasn't sure if he made notes on everyone.

Nick collected his high-fives at the table and we all whispered back and forth while Juliet brought up the next comic.

"Only eleven more to go and then we can eat," I whispered.

"I guess it would be rude to cut out early," Philipa said.

There were nods all around.

"I'm going to get another." I glanced over at Nick's beer to get the right brand. Everyone else, with the exception of Gabby, looked set for drinks. We had all been going back and forth to the bars during the sets. I went to the portable bar and ordered wines for Gabby and me, a beer for Nick and a couple bottles of water. I figured I would have to make two trips but the bartender pulled a tray out from under his set up.

"Thanks."

"Just bring it back."

"You bet."

I arrived with the tray and put the wines and waters down, then moved around the table to give Nick his beer.

"Hey, you didn't buy me a beer," Roger pretended to complain.

"Tomorrow night. You all have to take turns being my favorite."

I returned the tray and then settled back in at the table. Comic #15 was just finishing. Ten to go. Were people really going to sit through a second night of this?

Gabby leaned over. "Thanks for the water. I think I'm getting trashed on one glass of wine."

"Lightweight," I whispered back. A little closer to the truth than I meant it to be. "We'll get some food in us after this."

She nodded.

We waded through more comics. Luke and Roger got up at some point and brought back wine for Amber and Philipa. It was very chummy and casual, but we all must have felt that we were trapped out of politeness.

When we got to comic 21 or so, it was all we could do to pretend to muster enthusiasm. People had been leaving slowly since about the halfway point. Luke leaned in and whispered, "Hey."

We all leaned in as if we were about to plan a bank robbery. Then we looked at each other. Gabby giggled.

"How about I get us a table at the pool bar before the rest of the mob starts to exit?"

"Great idea."

Amber jumped up. "I'll go with."

Luke looked a little surprised but covered. "We'll see you in a bit."

They left and we all looked around at each other like high school kids.

Roger wiggled his eyebrows.

Nick laughed but I noticed he was watching me. I don't know why. Luke and I weren't a couple. I smiled and took a sip of my wine, then turned my attention back to the stage.

We were up to comic #23, the guy, Tim somebody, who had asked about the text messaging. He'd also been in the Cold Auditions session. I wondered what his take was on Darlana. Apparently, he had decided that doing a set was a lost cause and he was just riffing with people. It was such a relief and really much appreciated.

"I mean really, three hours in and you want to hear another six-minute set? I don't think so." People were laughing and nodding their heads in agreement.

He was totally relaxed up there, like he didn't care if it went well or not. I had to hand it to him; he really knew his audience. I was sure he was working some material in, but just like Juliet's opening warm up, he kept it conversational. Great technique. I stuck it in the back of my mind to think about later. What situations would come up that I might be able to pull out this trick? And now that he had done it, if any of the last comics tomorrow night used that technique, they would just look like they were copying him, no matter how good they were. I sat back and watched with real appreciation. This guy was saving the last twenty minutes of the show. He got a huge round of applause and the final two comics rode his goodwill as the show closed out.

I opened my phone and made some notes. He had changed the whole energy level of the room. That's the type of thing that would get you noticed. I needed to talk to someone better than me about this. Juliet had way too much on her plate to ask her. Maybe I could ask Rob.

We joined the crowd shuffling out of the main room and made a beeline for the pool bar. I could overhear people discussing getting something to eat. I was glad I had checked on the restaurants earlier. I was starving.

About half of the tables at the pool bar were taken. It looked like some of the people who had left early on were finishing their meals. Luke and Amber were at a table near the tiki bar. Gabby sat down next to Amber and Roger quickly positioned himself next to Gabby. Nick pulled out a chair for me. I might not be good at girl, but I knew this trick. Smile, pretend to sit but keep your weight on your toes with your ass hovering. He pushed my chair in and then held a chair for Philipa. He took the open seat between Luke and me.

A server came by and placed a large order of nachos and a couple of plates of fried mozzarella sticks in the center of the table.

"Oh my God, thank you! I'm starving!" I said.

Luke smiled. "I knew that."

The server took our drink orders and we dove into the appetizers. No one was shy in this group.

"Jeez, that was long-ass night," Amber said.

"Yeah, if it wasn't for that guy, I don't think I would have made it." Gabby was cutting a microscopic bite off a mozzarella stick.

"What guy?" Luke asked.

"You left just a little too soon," Roger said. "Number 23."

"He's got a name," Philipa chided.

"Which is?" Roger challenged.

"Crap." She popped a loaded nacho chip in her mouth.

"Tim... Somebody." I searched my brain. "Norris. Cincinnati."

"You're good," Nick smiled at me.

"He was in the Cold Auditions session today."

"I was in that session. I don't remember him." Philipa looked a little disappointed with herself.

"I'm really good with names." I put some nachos on my plate. The server was coming back with our drinks. I hadn't even looked at the menu yet.

"I'm terrible with names," Philipa volunteered. "If I get someone's name wrong at the beginning, that's it. I'm never going to get it right."

We nodded.

"Or sometimes I just rename people."

"Like a nickname?" Gabby asked.

"No, more like I get the wrong name stuck in my head so I decide that this is the name they should really have. Like, I keep wanting to call Juliet Joanne but I don't know why." She shrugged and popped another chip into her mouth. "I wonder if I can make money naming babies."

I felt myself grow cold. Did Philipa know Juliet's real name or was this just some weird coincidence? I thought back. Had I told anyone about her name change? No. I was sure I hadn't.

"Well, whatever his name is, he saved the night," Gabby said.

"What were we, chopped liver?" Roger demanded.

"Oh, no, you were caviar. For sure," Gabby said quickly with just the right amount of insincerity. We all laughed.

It was good getting to know Amber and Philipa. It was just after 1:00 am when we wound up the night and made our way to the elevators. Gabby, Nick, and I got off on the fourth floor. He said good night and took a left. We went right. We walked down the corridor to our rooms, made a show of saying goodnight, then switched rooms once we were inside.

It was late and I should have been tired, but I was too restless to sleep. Unusual for me but not for the circumstances. This whole thing was a mess. After an hour, I gave up on sleep. I do my best thinking when I am walking, and pacing the room wasn't going to cut it. I threw on jeans and a long-sleeved T-shirt and went down to the lobby. Maybe there'd be something better than room coffee available.

I was surprised to find Stavon at the front desk. He looked up as I entered the lobby, and stood to greet me.

"Are you always here, Stavon?"

"Yes."

"You live here? Sweet."

"No suite. Just a room. It's all I need."

I nodded. "I was looking for some coffee."

"You cannot sleep?"

"No."

"Jetlag probably."

"Yes." That and people were being blackmailed, Juliet wasn't Juliet, and I was attracted to a married man.

"This is a very bad thing. Sit right there," he said, indicating one of the lobby sofas. "I will get you my special coffee."

He scooted through the rear door and a few minutes later returned with a cup of coffee on a tray, with cream and sugar on the side. There was a folded napkin, a spoon, and a small orchid blossom.

"Wow. Presentation really is everything."

He shrugged. "How you do one thing is how you do everything."

"You work long hours."

"I pick up extra shifts. I'm here anyway and I can use the money. At night I can study." He walked a few steps back to the desk and retrieved his cup of coffee from behind the counter and sat down on the opposite sofa.

"What are you studying?" I added cream and sugar to my coffee.

"Hospitality Management. I am working on my master's degree."

"Impressive. What's your bachelors in?"

"Culinary Arts. I studied at Atalier Ancienne Allain in Paris."

I took a sip of the coffee. It was several steps up from the already good resort coffee. I closed my eyes and took another sip. "If you can do this to coffee, I can't imagine what you can do with food."

"It's part of my training. I am learning all aspects of resort management. I can do just about anything at this point—turn a room as fast as the housekeepers, food and beverage ordering, bartend, organize events... I learn as much as I possibly can."

"Are you going to have your own resort one day?"

"I am going to have the largest chain of elite resorts in the world." He said it as if it were a vow.

"Really? Sorry. That was rude. You are just so certain."

"I am... determined." He smiled to lighten a bit of his intensity. "I start with one and build from there. But for right now, I learn as much as I can."

I narrowed my eyes at him. "You are not what you first appear to be."

He shrugged. "Very few people are. Or sometimes, you don't really see the other person. You see one or two sides. Maybe the side they want you to see. Maybe they make a mistake and you see the side they don't want you to see."

"People can be false."

"Not always for bad reasons. Sometimes you show someone a side of yourself that they don't want to see; they can't accept it." He thought for a minute. "There are two kinds of people who are as they appear: the very simple and the very evolved. It is difficult to become yourself. And sometimes even more difficult for those closest to you to accept that."

His voice held a trace of sadness.

"It is difficult to become yourself," I repeated, turning the thought around in my head. "Sometimes people who have known you a long time want you to remain who you have always been."

He nodded. "Or stay the way they thought you were. You..." He hesitated, looking for the words. Then he stood, drew himself up and took a step forward. "You step into who you are, yes?"

"Yes." I felt like something was catching in my brain.

"And the people who knew you before don't see you. They've already put you in a box and they don't want to reopen that box."

"Pigeonhole you."

"Pigeonhole you." He let that sit for a minute. I could feel him absorbing the word. His teachers must love him.

But I was chewing on it, too. "To some people, it is easier to accept the role you are given. They go along with it. But, to break out of that pigeonhole, to be seen the way you want to be seen..."

Stavon smiled. "Sometimes you have to go someplace new and start fresh. To live as you really are."

"And here you are."

"Yes."

I had finished my coffee. I set the cup back on the tray.

"Will you serve this coffee at your resorts?"

"Yes, I will."

"Then I will be your first guest."

He smiled. "That will make me very happy."

"But I think your talents are wasted in hotel management."

"No."

"Yes. You should be a philosopher."

He laughed. "Maybe I will put a resort on top of a mountain in Nepal. People will have to climb to get there and ask me questions."

"Make them work for it."

"You cannot sleep, anytime, come and see me."

"Will do. Thanks for the coffee. And the enlightenment."

I walked back to the elevator bank, thinking about people wanting to be seen in a different way. Wasn't that why we were all here? Trying to move to that next level? Maybe trying to step into who we wanted to be. I pressed the button for four and thought about what Stavon said, how people who have known you a long time don't want you to change. You're a known quantity and they don't want to have to relearn you. Known quantity. I thought back to what Rob had said about certain actors being hired because the producer or director was confident in their abilities to do the job. There was something there, but I couldn't connect the dots. Too tired. I really didn't even know if it was important or not.

The elevator dinged at four and I walked towards my room. I started to pass the door to Gabby's room and remembered it was now my room. The door wasn't shut all the way.

CHAPTER 12: THINGS GO BUMP IN THE NIGHT

I STOPPED DEAD IN my tracks. If there is one thing I do without fail, it's make sure I lock my hotel room door. I was stuck. If someone was still in the room, they would know I was out in the hallway. I should have just kept walking. Too late for that now.

There was no way I was going to walk into the room, either. I backed down the hallway to the little cut out where the vending machines were. I could call down to the lobby from there. I got out my cell phone and realized I didn't have the hotel's number in my phone. There was a house phone on the table between the two elevators. I scurried the short distance back to the elevators and picked up the handset and dialed 0. Stavon answered.

"Stavon, it's Kasey. There's someone in my room. Or someone's been in my room."

"Are you there now?"

"No, I'm at the elevators."

"Fourth floor, yes? I am sending Security right now. Stay on the line; I'll be right back."

I heard his muffled voice calling Security. I didn't like standing out in the elevator area, but it seemed to be better than going to my room. Shit. Gabby. The connecting door.

"Stavon, I have to check on Gabby."

"Stay by the elevators. Security is on its way."

"I'll be right back." I heard him protest as I put the handset beside the phone and ran back down the hall. As I got close to my room, a man in a hoodie came out. He came at me from an angle and less than a second later, I was flying sideways. The side of my head connected hard with the wall behind me. I was down on the floor before I realized what was happening. I got to all fours in time to see the guy turn for the stairwell. A second later, the elevator dinged.

To his credit, the security guy came down the hallway at a good clip.

"Are you okay, ma'am?"

I was picking myself up and he helped me the rest of the way.

"Guy in a hoodie. He went into the stairwell."

"Do you know if he went up or down?"

I shook my head. "Sorry."

The security guy was on his walkie-talkie. "Suspect in a hoodie. In the stairwell, but probably out by now." He looked at me. "Color of the hoodie? Pants?"

I resisted the urge to say he had pants on. "Dark green maybe? And dark pants. Probably jeans." I tried to think but really, talk about a fleeting impression. He repeated the description over the walkie-talkie. I gave him zero chance of finding the guy. Not his fault.

I made a move towards my door. The security guy wanted to enter it first and I was very good with that.

He flipped on the lights. The room had been rifled, but my laptop was still on the desk. I really didn't have anything of value. I checked the door to Gabby's room. Locked. I knocked on it fairly loudly. I heard her voice call out "What?"

"Are you okay, Gabby?"

"What time is it?" She sounded like she had been in a deep sleep.

"Sorry. Go back to sleep."

I heard the lock slide back and Gabby opened the door. She was wearing pink satin pajamas with matching slippers. She even wore ensembles to bed. She saw the security guy and blinked.

"I went down to the lobby because I couldn't sleep and someone broke into the room."

The security guy looked up. "Did you hear anything, ma'am?"

Ma'am again. Gabby was younger than me, so I guess we were all ma'ams. I felt marginally better.

"No. I didn't hear a thing."

Gabby's room phone rang. We all jumped.

Gabby picked it up. "Hello?"

"It is Stavon at the front desk. Are you okay, Miss Kasey?"

"It's Gabby. I'll get Kasey. She's okay."

I walked over and she handed me the handset.

"Hi, Stavon. It's okay. I need to check but I don't think anything is missing. Maybe I surprised him and he didn't have enough time."

"I am so sorry this has happened to you, Miss Kasey. I am glad that Miss Gabby is with you. We will have Security keep a special eye in your area."

"Thanks, Stavon."

We clicked off. The security guy was looking around. "I'm going to need your name and contact info for the report."

I gave it to him.

"You'll probably want to do a more thorough check in the morning. If you're missing anything, please contact us. Just go down to the front desk and they'll get you to us. And we'll be keeping an eye on your room tonight. But I doubt he'll be back."

I doubted it, too, but it didn't make me feel any better. "Thanks."

"And ma'am, you might want to get that cut looked at. Looks like you're going to have a shiner, too."

I put my hand to my head. Crap. "Great. Just freakin great."

"I'll get some ice," Gabby offered.

"You're not going for ice alone," I said quickly.

"I'll walk her down and make sure she gets back to you."

Gabby was back in under a minute. She closed and locked the door. I went into the bathroom and wet a washcloth, dabbing at the side of my head. I had hit the wall just at the temple. Must have hit the cheekbone a bit, too. The security guard was right; I could see swelling already.

Gabby wet a second washcloth and wrapped some ice in it.

"Come on. Lie down on the bed and we'll ice this." She set the pillows up against the headboard so I could half sit up. I took the ice pack from her and held it against my temple and cheek. I sucked in my breath. "Ooooch." I started to lift it away.

Gabby moved my hand and the ice back into place. "This will keep the swelling down, and then tomorrow I'll do your makeup. With luck, no one will really notice."

I looked at her.

"Well, it won't look as bad."

"We've got bigger problems than that, Gabby."

"What?"

"We switched rooms. It didn't hit me until Stavon called... my old room. There's a good chance that whoever broke in was after you. Or something you have."

"Oh, Kasey, I'm so sorry. This is my fault!"

"No, no. That's not what I'm saying. Besides, we switched rooms in case of something like this. So, we outsmarted whoever it is."

"Yes, but now you're hurt."

"I have four brothers. This is nothing."

Her eyes widened.

"And he could have been after me. Though we've been careful about going through the right door. Except for when I left tonight.

Duh." I was thinking out loud and I realized that it wasn't helping Gabby's state of mind.

"Maybe it was just someone who wanted to rob me. I'm a pretty obvious target."

I was surprised by Gabby's awareness level of that. She saw my surprise.

"Hell, my father has had kidnapping insurance on me since I was three. Maybe before."

"Kidnapping insurance? What the hell does your father do?"

She ignored the second question. "In case I get kidnapped and they need to pay ransom right away. He's got the money but sometimes it's hard to get large sums fast."

"I feel you." Sometimes it was hard for me to get even small sums fast. "Kidnapping insurance. Sheesh. You live a whole different life."

"I'm sorry."

"Don't be sorry. Be happy. Being broke all the time sucks." I smiled to let her know that I didn't hold her father's money against her.

I could feel the blood trickling down into the washcloth. I held it up to gauge just how much there was.

"Might need another washcloth," I said casually.

Gabby looked at the wound and nodded. She went into the bathroom. "Looks like we've used up your two. Back in a minute."

She headed through the adjoining door. I could hear water running and then a couple of drawers opening and closing. She came back in with the washcloth in one hand and a box of Godivas in the other.

"Oh, baby!"

"Let me make you a new ice pack and then you can have a treat."

She made up a new ice pack, switched it out with the bloody one, and went back into the bathroom. I heard her dump the ice into the sink. The water ran for a minute and she was back.

"OK. The beautiful thing about these is that they are all dark chocolate. It's my personal mix. These are chocolate truffles, these with the single red line are raspberry, and the rest peppermints. Dark chocolate is healthier than milk chocolate."

I popped a truffle into my mouth. "This is almost worth getting hit on the head for. Hey, you were holding out on me!"

"I eat salads so I can have a Godiva or two every day. It's a trade-off."

She handed me a glass of water. "And I brought you Ibuprofen but I'm not sure if you should have it or not. Do you have a concussion?"

My head was throbbing. "I don't think it matters."

There was a knock on the door. Gabby seemed to be expecting it. She gave a quick look through the keyhole but was already unlocking the door.

"Thanks for coming."

Nick walked in, carrying a small kit bag.

"Oh, this isn't necessary."

"She hit her head," Gabby said, like a child blurting a secret.

"You owe me another Godiva for this." I looked at Nick. "It's just a bump. I've had worse."

"Yeah, let me be the judge of that." He sat on the bed next to me while Gabby hovered. "Tell me what happened exactly."

"Someone broke into my room and—"

"Someone broke in here?"

"Yeah. But we think he might have been after Gabby."

He looked at me. "Because...?" Then he remembered. "You switched rooms."

"You, Luke, and Roger are the only ones I told. So, probably, whoever broke in thought it was Gabby's room."

"Okay. We'll get into that. How did you get the bump?"

"I called down to the front desk and they were sending Security, but then I remembered that Gabby and I keep the door between the rooms unlocked sometimes, so I needed to check on her."

I stopped. He was shining a flashlight in my eyes. "Keep going."

"So, I came back down the hallway to go to Gabby's room which is when the guy came out of the room, hit me like a linebacker, and knocked me over."

"You saw the guy?" He took a pair of gloves out of a sterile pack and started pulling them on.

"I saw a guy. He had a hoodie on with the hood tight around his face. And he basically hit me with his shoulder, so I really only saw the side of him."

"And did you lose consciousness at all?"

"No. I watched the bastard run down the hall to the stairs."

"Any vomiting?"

"No." *Even if I did, I wouldn't tell you*, I thought.

Nick tilted my head this way and that, shining the flashlight on the cut. "Hotel room lighting sucks." Gabby flipped on every light in the room.

"Thanks, Gabby. Can you move that desk lamp over here? Take off the shade, please."

"This is good training if you get a role as an ER nurse," I said. She smiled but she looked like she was on the verge of tears. I winked at her.

He tried to move some of my hair out of the way. It was matted from the blood and the wet washcloth. "This is right at the hairline. Too bad. I was wondering what you'd look like with a shaved head." He grinned at me.

"Oh, great bedside manner!"

"To be fair, most of my patients are asleep when I get to them. Kind of fun to have one talk back to me."

"Well then, how does it look?"

"I think we can clean and butterfly this. You're going to have a shiner, though."

"Yeah, that's been the general consensus around here, starting with the security guard."

"Can she have Ibuprofen?" Gabby asked.

"Better to have Acetaminophen. It doesn't look like you're concussed, but I'm a little concerned with the amount of blood here. It's not a deep cut. But Ibuprofen thins the blood. If this reopens, you'll have a mess."

He reached into his bag and brought out some alcohol wipes and steri-strips.

"Okay. This is going to be the tricky, hurty part. Gabby, I'm going to need you to help keep her hair back. Do you have something to pin it?"

Gabby dashed into her room and came back with a case of hair supplies. Three different-sized round brushes, two combs, scrunchies in every color, bobby pins, hair clips... She had more supplies than my hairdresser. She clipped my hair back so Nick could work.

"What were you doing out of your room at this time of night?" His voice was casual. His eyes were not.

"Couldn't sleep. So, I went down to the lobby and had coffee with the desk clerk."

"Coffee. With the desk clerk." He sounded like he didn't believe me. He snipped a few strands of hair and applied the steri-strips. "You thought having coffee would help you sleep?"

"More like, I couldn't sleep and coffee wasn't going to matter one way or the other. Good coffee."

"Hmm."

He balled up the paper that the steri-strips had been wrapped in, stripped off his gloves and threw all the waste in the trash. He repacked his bag and gave one last check of my eyes.

"Do me a favor and don't wander the halls alone in the middle of the night."

"Not a problem."

"Get some sleep." He gave my hand a squeeze and stood up. "Gabby, would you mind staying with her tonight?"

"Are you kidding? I'm so freaked out I was going to be in here anyway."

Nick laughed. "Okay, see you two tomorrow. Kasey, if you start feeling nauseous, if you get light-headed, you call me. Immediately."

"Yes, Doctor."

"No kidding around. Gabby, I'm counting on you."

Gabby nodded. She locked the door behind him.

"He's kind of scary when he gets all serious," she said.

"Yeah."

"Let me go get my stuff and I'll sleep in the other bed."

"That's not necessary, really."

"How about we keep the door open between us and if you need something, just yell."

"Deal."

She turned off most of the lights in my room. "Do you want me to leave this light on?" she asked, indicating the bathroom light.

"Yes. I'll probably keep the light over my bed on, too."

She nodded and said good night, leaving the door between the rooms partly open. I was too wound up to sleep and my head hurt. I grabbed the novel I was currently reading from the bedside table. Five minutes later, the words were blurring and I was asleep.

Chapter 13: Someone Made Sharknado

IF YOU DIDN'T KNOW, you didn't know. I had to hand it to Juliet and Darlana: They were tag-teaming the persona presentation as if they were best friends. Had Juliet backed Darlana down already? That must have been a late-night talk. There were a couple of small digs back and forth at the beginning, but once they got into the presentation, the digs were dropped and they were sincerely enthusiastic about the topic. I noticed Juliet went out of her way to build Darlana up in front of everyone, so maybe there was a type of payment being made after all.

I was sitting with Luke and Roger in the back of the room. Gabby was again in the front row. Nick was a few rows up and over, sitting with Amber and Philipa. The one person I didn't see was probably the person who needed this session the most: Chad. Childish of him to skip it, but not surprising. He probably thought he was making a point. I was betting that few people noticed his absence.

Gabby had done my makeup and the steri-strips were hidden by my hair, but Luke had taken one look at my face and asked what happened. So much for no one being able to tell. I had filled the guys in on the late-night happenings but we didn't really get a chance to discuss it before the presentation started. Luke leaned over and whispered, "We'll get into this later. In the meantime, we're not letting you out of our sight." Roger had agreed.

Juliet started the presentation off by talking about how your persona should be rooted in your "authentic self" and I wondered if she felt a bit hypocritical saying it. Of course, I don't think Darlana could have said it with any less irony. Maybe none of us were who we appeared to be. But what they were saying made sense, finding parts of your personality that you wanted to highlight. The two of them worked together to show us how to choose and build a persona. With the exception of Luke, we were all scribbling notes as fast as we could. I nudged him and gave him a questioning look. He shrugged, then leaned over and whispered, "I think I'm better off staying away from any persona for a while."

I laughed and agreed. "Well, maybe a nicer persona this time. Maybe closer to your real personality?"

He gave me a funny little pleased look and turned his attention back to the presentation. The ninety minutes flew by. Darlana and Juliet got a huge round of applause at the end and they took a couple of bows, arm in arm. Maybe the friendship was mended.

The coffee break was packed since everyone was already in the room. I was not up for standing in line, even with the promise of pastries. I checked my schedule to see where the sitcom class was being held and decided to get there early. Luke walked me to the room. Pamela was set up at a table with the sign-in sheet ready.

"So, now you're my bodyguard, is that it?"

"Kasey, it could have been a lot worse last night."

"Yeah. But I don't think anything is going to happen during the day with all these people around." There were already people signing in and going into the meeting room. "Besides, they may have been after Gabby."

"Roger sacrificed himself and volunteered to keep an eye on Gabby."

"Poor bastard."

"Yeah, I had to talk him into it."

We laughed. Just then, Nick came around the corner.

"How are you feeling this morning, Kasey?"

"Fine, thanks to you."

He put his hand to my chin and tilted my head a couple of times, looking into my eyes, then lifted my hair to check the steri-strips. My eyes slid to the side; I could see Luke watching him in a less-than-friendly way.

"Looks good. Gabby did a good job with the makeup. If you didn't know…"

"Luke knew right away," I complained. "I was totally busted."

Nick looked over at Luke. "Good eye."

"The makeup was the tip off. Kasey doesn't usually wear that much." He shrugged. "I've got to get to the Getting an Agent Session. I'll leave her in your capable hands. Would you mind walking her to lunch after this? We can meet up at the pool restaurant."

"I don't need to be watched like I'm helpless," I protested.

"It would be my pleasure," Nick said. "Let's get signed in."

The sitcom writing class was the best session so far.

I was surprised and happy that the class wasn't overcrowded. I guess more people wanted to be in front of the cameras than behind the scenes. Nick and I took seats at one of the tables. I saw Philipa sitting with Tim, aka #23. Interesting that she was on the writers' track, not the performance track. There were only about thirty of us in the room, plus, of course, Rob Tolland who worked on *Luck Be a Lady*, a sitcom that had been running for several years. The session blurb in the program said that Rob would discuss how to get a job as a staff writer, what the work was like, and basically, behind the scenes information.

Rob had an extra-large coffee in front of him. His eyes were blood-shot and he seemed grumpy. It was a little too late in the morning to be nursing a hangover. People were settling into seats and getting out notebooks and tablets to write on. I leaned over to Nick.

"He looks kind of rough. Hung over?"

Nick shook his head. "He looks exhausted. He needs water more than that coffee."

I looked at Rob more closely. I could see it in the way he held himself. His eyelids drooped. I wondered how much sugar he had put in his coffee, hoping to get some energy. He gulped down several mouthfuls and took a deep breath, as if summoning whatever strength he needed to get through this.

"Thanks for coming. I'm Rob Tolland and I'm a staff writer on the sitcom, *Luck Be a Lady*. This is a smaller group, for which I am grateful," he paused and there were muffled laughs. "That said, I'm also glad I'm not getting paid per head."

Bigger laugh this time.

"But since I'm getting the big bucks, let's see how you want to do this. Do you want to ask me questions or do you want my canned speech?"

"How did you get your job on *Luck Be a Lady*?" one of the guys asked.

"Questions it is," Rob said. "I knew someone. Next."

We must have all looked stunned. He laughed.

"Kidding. But not. I started out doing stand-up, just like all of you. And along the way, I made friends, so everyone should be nice to everyone. You never know who is going to make it. Outside of the fact that you should just be nice anyway." He kind of said the last sentence to himself. Then he sighed and took another gulp of coffee.

"You knock around long enough, you're going to know someone who gets a show or maybe you'll get a show. And a show needs writers. Not that there aren't more than enough writers to go around in Hollywood, but the truth is, when someone gets big enough to call the shots on their own show, a lot of times they want to have people around them that they trust. And sometimes those writers know you and call you in. I didn't know Jackie Leani, but one of my buddies is a lead writer on the show and when they had an opening, he called me."

I wrote, "Know someone" on my pad of paper. Then underlined it even though I knew that writing it down wasn't necessary. I guess I just wanted something to write. Nick's hand came over onto my pad. He added "funny" after the "someone." I nodded. Sage advice so far.

Rob put his head down for a few seconds. Then he looked up. Apparently, he had made a decision.

"Do you want to know what it's really like working on a sitcom?"

"Yes!"

He took a deep breath.

"You work your balls off trying to get a decent storyline together and you're always behind schedule. So that means you come in early and work late. For the first year or two you usually don't even get to sit at the main table. You're taking notes on your lap. It's a big deal when you get to sit at the table." He rolled his eyes to indicate that he knew how ridiculous the system was.

"You finally get a workable script that the producer is happy with, or he is happy with the rewrites that he has done because most of the time the producer does a lot of the writing. Then it goes to the cast for the table read and the first thing the actors do is count how many lines they have. And God help you if one of the actors doesn't have the minimum number of lines that they are guaranteed in their contract."

"They have the number of lines they get written into their contracts?" a woman asked.

"Oh, it gets better. We start the read and there are some laughs and things are going as smoothly as they ever go, when someone hits a line with a big laugh. So now, Jackie is pissed off because someone got a funnier line than she did and since she's the star, she wants the line, even though it makes no sense for her to say it. Which pisses off Rick or Mariana or whoever just got the line taken away from them. Or someone doesn't want to say a particular line or joke so they screw it up and it gets cut."

I looked around the room. People's eyes were wide open. In more than one sense.

He continued, "Which means we're going to have to rewrite that section and we all dutifully make notes. And of course, we're only about four minutes into a 21-minute script. Let's take stock: We have another hour of pissed off actors worried about their motivation, Jackie not happy whenever someone else gets a laugh, any new people looking around while trying not to look around and ignoring the tension, and a director who is trying to keep everyone civil."

He paused. "Sound like fun yet?"

"The director calls a break, we go back to the closet that passes for the writers' room, and quickly make adjustments to the script. And that's how it goes every week."

The room was quiet for a few seconds while we absorbed that.

"How funny do you have to be to get a job as a writer?" Philipa asked.

"You don't find me amusing?"

"No, you're hysterical, really," Philipa responded insincerely. Then she softened. "But um… it doesn't sound like much fun."

"Sometimes it's fun. Right now, it's not fun because we're working fifteen hours a day and nobody's happy. How funny do you have to be..." he trailed off. "Well, there are lots of not-very-funny people writing sitcoms. Someone else, like me, comes in and saves their asses by making it funny."

He looked around at us. "Does that sound egotistical? It is. But here's the deal. You need someone to come up with solid story lines and someone to make it funny and if you're really good, you can do both. But it's really hard to do both day in and day out. Which is why there's a team of writers. Someone comes up with something mildly funny and maybe someone else can tweak it and make it funnier. Make sense?"

I spoke up. "Kind of like when another comic gives you a stronger punchline or a tag for one of your jokes."

"Exactly. Just so you know, when you do that on the regular for other comics and one of them gets a TV show or an HBO special or just a gig writing, there's a good chance they're going to remember you. That's kind of what I meant when I said you had to know someone. It's really that someone has to know you. Part of your job as you're working your way up as comics is to help each other."

"I thought you were the jaded, cynical, seen-it-all writer," Nick said with a smile.

"Yeah, well. You're hitting me on a bad day. I'm too tired to be cynical today."

We all laughed and I felt the comfort level in the room rise.

He seemed to get some energy from the laughter. He stood up. "Do you want to go through a script the way we do in the writers' room?"

We must have looked like kids at Christmas.

"Okay, let's all shift these tables together so it's like a big conference room table."

Chairs started scraping and people started talking as they maneuvered furniture into place. Rob handed out copies of a shooting script for the show. I had seen a shooting script up close and personal before, back when I was taking my first comedy class but I hadn't really had a chance to do much more than flip through it.

"Sitcoms are mini three-act plays. The first act sets up the situation and a subplot. Let's take a look at the second act, first scene. This is the act that is mostly shenanigans that will, hopefully, keep the audience amused until the third act where we tie the whole thing together and bring the show to the conclusion that anyone with half a brain knew was coming."

He looked around at us to make sure we were following.

"So, our job is to go through this script, line by line asking several questions: Is this line necessary? If it's not necessary, is it funny enough to keep in? That's one. Well, two." He took another swig of coffee. "Slightly different from the first question, if the line isn't funny, does it serve a purpose, either setting up a joke or moving the action forward? So, every line in a script serves a purpose. The best lines move the action forward *and* get a laugh. The good news is that you all have a seat at the table, so congratulations."

We started working through the script. Rob would ask, "What does this line do?" and we'd say if it was a laugh line or an action line or a set up. He'd ask "Keep it or lose it?" and we'd give our opinions. Sometimes he'd agree, sometimes not and he'd tell us why, either way.

He read out the next line. "What about this line? What's wrong with it?"

There was silence around the table. People had their heads down, looking at the script. I looked up and shrugged.

"There's nothing wrong with that line. It's a solid laugh and it moves the action forward." People seemed relieved that someone had spoken up.

Rob laughed. "Thank you. I wrote that line." He paused. "It got cut."

"Well, it shouldn't have," I said, giving him a grin. "It's pure gold."

"I wouldn't go that far, but Jackie was pissy about it and away it went."

He took on a serious tone. "Listen, you have to be okay with criticism, deserved or not. You have to have really thick skin because every last one of your words is going to get picked apart. And sometimes something you wrote gets tossed for no other reason than the star doesn't want to say it or the director just ran out of time in the final edit. That's the reality of writing for TV and movies. Actors always complain that their best work gets left on the cutting room floor. Well, our best words sometimes end up there, too. It's the nature of the beast."

"So, Rob." We shifted our attention to a soft-spoken guy with glasses. "What about writing a movie? What are the odds of getting a movie script sold?"

"Well, I'm covering that in the screenwriting class tomorrow. But I'll give you a preview: If you're very, very lucky, you will get a script optioned. That's the first step. Well, the first step is getting it to an agent who will put it in front of someone who might option it. Once optioned, your script might never get green-lighted. The option term might run out and then you can try to sell it again. Or it might get some interest and it will look like something is going to happen with it. I don't want to discourage you. In fact," he looked at the door, "I'm not supposed to discourage you. But it's a rare thing to get your script even in front of the right people, much less optioned."

We all looked discouraged.

"But here's the good thing. There's a ton of streaming services like Netflix and Hulu and Prime and they are all hungry for new material to feed to their audiences. So, absolute crap is getting green-lighted. My best advice?"

We all leaned forward.

"Write one of those ridiculously stupid Christmas romance scripts. Hit all the tropes. Give them their happily-ever-after."

"So, you're telling us to sell out? Not that I have a problem with that," Philipa said.

"Absolutely. Hey, it's LA. We've all sold our souls. Why should you be any different?"

We all laughed.

"Okay, we're coming up on the top of the hour and that concludes all the wisdom I have for you. I'll be around for a bit and then later on tonight if anyone has more questions or wants to chat."

There was a chorus of thank yous as we gathered up our stuff to head out to the next session. I told Nick I'd catch up and hung back, letting everyone else leave ahead of me. The line finally pared down to me.

"So, is everyone in Hollywood a fraud?" I asked.

"No. We all just think we are. And that no one else is. You'll never meet so many insecure people in your life as you will in the business."

"Great. So basically, I just paid two grand to find out no one knows what they're doing."

"Not at all. Most of these people are brilliant at what they do. The system is set up to make them think they're not—that they're failing."

"Why?"

"Because then they'll keep giving it everything they've got to the point of exhaustion."

"And not ask for more money."

"Exactly."

"So, are you going to work to the point of exhaustion? Wait til you crack? Because you look pretty close to it."

"Possibly."

I gave him a nudging look.

"I keep a little bit of myself for myself. I'm a writer. I have my own projects going, separate from the studio. Everyone does. Stand on a street corner in LA and ask random strangers how their screenplay is coming along. Nine out of ten will stop and tell you. No joke."

I nodded.

"Piece of advice?"

"Absolutely."

"Write a book. Write a series of books. Make them something that hits the tropes for whatever genre TV show or Hollywood movie is popular right now. And when you write your characters, think of a real actor who might play them."

"Really?"

"You have to make it easy for someone to visualize the project. That's why projects are described using other movies. Think *Death Takes a Holiday* meets *My Fair Lady*. Death goes on holiday, likes it so much that he decides to train his replacement. So, he grooms an uneducated street vendor, maybe a taco truck guy, in the fine art of helping people die."

"*Death Takes a Holiday* as a musical?"

"Hey, somebody gave the greenlight to *Sharknado*."

"Good point." I couldn't argue that.

"So, that's a silly example. But you get my drift—make the concept something simple and familiar, with all the expected tropes. You'll at least have a shot at getting optioned. That's whether the book is good or bad. Really, it's a way of getting seen. Most of the stuff that is optioned doesn't get made, but now people know your name. If your book fits a Hollywood story line, you're ahead of the game. All these people" he waved his arm at the now-empty chairs, "want to be stand-ups and eventually get sitcoms and HBO specials. Nothing wrong with that. But get your writing game going, too. It's multi-purpose. You'll write better stand-up material. You can help other comics and really, you've got a one in a million shot at stardom, but if you help ten or twenty other people, you've just upped your odds of riding their success. Still a long shot, but the odds are better. Write stuff that you can be in. You might not be the star, but put yourself in there. Write your own roles."

My brain was spinning. "You've just opened up a whole new track for me."

"You're welcome."

"I really appreciate your taking the time."

"Well, write something and send it to me." He pulled out a business card. "Don't share this. But if you write a book, a screenplay, whatever and want a critical set of eyes, I'm happy to help."

"Wow. Thank you." I surprised myself by giving him a quick hug. "You need to get some sleep."

"Yeah. They've got a room for us. I might get a nap in. Just have to make a few calls and check in with the show."

"Thanks again."

He nodded, pulled out his phone and looked at a text. "Shit."

I gathered up my stuff. I had a feeling he wasn't going to get that nap.

Chapter 14: Lost in the Sauce

THE POOL BAR WAS becoming our regular hangout. It was a bit hot today and most people had opted for the air-conditioned restaurant. By the time I got there, everyone had drinks in front of them.

"Did you order yet?" I asked, looking around for the server.

"Just drinks," Roger said.

"We thought about sending the cavalry after you," Luke chided. "You're not supposed to be walking around alone."

"I was talking with Rob. He walked with me back to the lobby and there were tons of people around."

The server arrived and we put in our orders.

I was finally junk-fooded out. Gabby and I both opted for the grilled chicken salad and I got a bottled water. Luke and Roger went all in on cheeseburgers and fries. Nick had blackened salmon on a bed of rice and a side salad.

Luke got down to business. "I take it you've heard nothing from Security about the guy who was in your room."

"No. But then, they didn't have a whole lot to go on. And nothing was missing. I don't think he had a lot of time to go through things."

"Or he may have figured out he had the wrong room," Gabby said.

"Girl stuff. We were the only ones who knew about that?" Roger looked to me for confirmation.

"We figured the fewer who knew, the better," I said. "And let's keep it that way."

"The guy who broke in knows," Luke said.

"If he had been waiting in the hall, he may have seen me come out the door. Gabby was already asleep and I didn't want to wake her up."

"Did you see anyone when you left?" Luke asked.

"No. But it's easy to step into a side corridor or the vending area or even the stairwell."

They nodded.

"And the security guard might have figured it out. He probably needed to put the room number on the report." Nick was thinking out loud.

"Which means the front desk will know, too," I said, sighing.

"But they haven't asked us to come down and change out credit cards or anything, so maybe they haven't picked up on it yet," Gabby said. She daintily dipped a piece of lettuce into her side of dressing.

"What do you think he was looking for?" Nick asked.

There was silence around the table.

"I don't know. If he thought it was my room, then maybe he thought I had information on the blackmailing? Or it's totally unrelated; someone is just breaking into rooms."

"Which would make more sense if they thought they were breaking into my room," Gabby said. They might have thought I had money or jewelry."

"Or it could be someone who is pissed about the private showcases and wanted to scare you off... or worse," Roger said.

"So, it's more likely that the person who broke in thought they were breaking into Gabby's room. That leaves us with two options. It might be an unrelated, run-of-the-mill robbery. Or it may be related to the private showcases."

"Would someone go that far just for a private showcase?" Roger asked.

"People have done worse for less," Luke said ruefully. "Seriously, after 25 comics last night, if you really wanted to be noticed by the agent, you'd want to be in the private showcase tonight. You're absolutely lost in the sauce doing the regular showcase."

"Thanks. That makes me feel better about paying $250 for six lousy minutes," I said.

"Still a deal on a per minute basis," Gabby pointed out. "You're paying about $42 a minute, I'm paying $100."

We all stopped eating. Gabby looked up from her salad. "What?"

"Did not have you down for a numbers girl," Roger said. "I like that."

"But it's not the dollars per minute. It's the increased visibility. And that is important to someone." Nick, as usual, cut right to the heart of it.

"Which means whoever broke into your room last night is probably not the blackmailer; just a disgruntled comic."

"That's a good persona," I said looking at Luke. "The Disgruntled Comic."

"Have to be an older person, a 'get off my lawn' type. We're too young to be disgruntled."

"Chad's disgruntled and he's not that much older than we are," I said. "What is he, mid-thirties?"

"Do you think it was Chad who knocked you over?" Nick asked. "Think back."

I closed my eyes and tried to picture the sequence of events last night. The problem was that the guy had lunged out of a dark room and barreled into me before I had a chance to get a good look. The hood was pulled tight which served to cover part of his face.

"Was he about Chad's height and weight?" Luke asked.

"I'm really not sure. I'm sorry. It all happened so fast. And he was kind of hunched over as he ran down the hallway. Could have been Chad. Could have been almost anyone."

There was a glum silence.

"But if we figure out who sent the notes, we'll probably figure out who was in my room."

"So, where do we go from here?"

"Eyes and ears open, I guess. The private showcases are this evening. Once they're done, it's game over on that."

"If that's what the threatening notes were all about. I'm still not convinced Chad has the skills to get people's phone numbers and send out a group text. That takes some work and Chad is more than a bit lazy. He'll bitch about the situation, but he really won't do anything to help himself out." Roger looked around the table. "I mean, think about it. He creates public stinks, complaining in front of everyone, but did he sign up for the wait list? Did he show up at the persona workshop to see if he could sharpen his game?"

"All talk, no action," Nick said.

"The list of names was cut off on one side," I said. "The room numbers could have been on there. I need to check with Juliet."

"So, Chad's back in play, then," Luke said.

"Roger's got a good point, though," Gabby put in. "What if the group text about the private showcases was the blackmailer, adding pressure to Juliet? She needs this workshop to go well and she's had to kind of scramble to make things work. It's keeping her off-balance."

"And Chad just kind of played into that," Luke said.

Nick's brown eyes were clouded over with concern. "That means you could have been the target last night, Kasey. Maybe the blackmailer wants to know what you know. They got lucky when they saw you leave the room."

"But it's not like I have notes written down. I mean, really, so far we have nothing."

"The blackmailer doesn't know that," Luke pointed out.

"So, eyes and ears?" Gabby said.

"Yes, and neither of you walks anywhere alone until this is settled," Nick's voice was firm. "Stay in groups, grab one of us, walk together. But nowhere alone."

"Except the bathroom. Gabby's a friend, but we are not that close yet."

It lightened the mood, which was exactly what I wanted. We signed for our bills and had a few minutes before the next sessions started.

"What's everybody doing next? I've got Danny's media darling thing," I said.

"Me, too," Gabby said. But I've got to run up to my room."

Before Roger could volunteer, Luke said, "I'm in that one, too. I'll walk you to your room then pick you back up when I come down again."

Nick was heading off to the gift shop. I took Roger's arm. "I'll have Roger walk me over to the next session."

People went their separate ways. I slow walked to let everyone get ahead of us.

"Roger, I need you to do something and you can't tell the others."

"Of course. Secret stuff, huh?"

"Super secret. You really can't tell anyone. Can you do some deeper Internet searches, more than just what turns up on Google?"

"Yeah. My company subscribes to all sorts of data bases."

I spoke quietly as we walked, explaining Juliet's situation, the accident and that she changed her name. "Can you see what you can dig up from that time, anything from the college she went to and anything under her old name, Joanne Preston."

"Joanne. Wait. That's the name Philipa calls her."

"Exactly. Philipa might be mixed up in this. Darlana and Danny knew Juliet back in the day. Whoever is blackmailing her is someone from her past. I think we need to look there."

We were at the door to my next session. "Danny is doing this session. Maybe he'll have more information from Juliet. I can ask him afterwards."

"I'm heading to Mo's Improv Games, but I can start the searches on the break."

"Great. And remember..."

"I know. Mum's the word."

He returned back down the hallway as I signed in for Danny's session.

Chapter 15: Don't Be a Bore, Darling

I wasn't too sure I wanted to "become a publicity darling" but I had written enough ad copy at the agency to recognize hyperbole when I saw it. Besides, I was very sure I didn't want to do Improv Games. While I really liked Mo, I was here for the business side of things. So, Danny's session on publicity was the logical choice. Besides, his first session on building a fanbase had been packed with valuable information. I figured this would be just as good.

I was right. I spent almost the entire 90 minutes taking notes. I knew the basics of a press release from working at the ad agency. But he added some good angles on how to approach feature and entertainment editors in the towns where you were performing. It wasn't something I had thought of doing—usually the clubs sent out notices of who was appearing each week and it seemed like only the big stars had articles written on them. Which made sense, Danny explained. If you worked for a newspaper or radio station and wanted to meet a big star, that would be your way to do it. He gave us timelines of how far in advance to contact people and how to put together a media kit, which I also knew about—I just hadn't thought to do it for myself.

The bottom line, Danny said, was that anything extra you could do to put more "butts in seats" for the club owner, was going to work in your favor. However, he cautioned, do check with the club owner to make sure you're not stepping on toes. And the club owner or manager might be able to give you their local contacts.

I should have thought of this myself. Sometimes you need someone else to point out the obvious for you. I made a note to myself to talk to the woman who did publicity at the agency to get her take on the best way to go about this.

I also knew that most press releases were ignored by media outlets—unless there was something that grabbed their attention. I raised my hand.

"Kasey?"

"I get all this, but what are the types of things that would get the attention of an entertainment editor or a segment producer? There are comics coming in every week and most of us aren't big stars. I guess this goes back to this morning's Honing Your Persona session."

"So, you're looking for a way to tie it all in. Figure out your persona, which gives you an angle to approach the media with."

"Yes. Exactly."

"Okay. Let's use you as an example."

Crap.

"What's special about you?"

"I'm a tall redhead. From a big family. Italian-Irish. I work fairly clean." I was out. "There's nothing super special about me."

Danny looked around the room. "How many of you here have nothing special about you?"

Most of the people raised their hands.

"Wow, you people are boring."

We laughed.

"Kasey, why are you boring?"

"I don't know about anyone else but I still work a day job. So, I go to work, I might have gigs for a couple of weeks each month, not every week. Sometimes they're only weekend gigs. So, I go to work, I hit the gigs, I go home to bed, and do it all over again."

"Is that the drill for most of you?"

People agreed.

"Who do you hang out with?"

"Mostly other comics," I said.

"Other comics. Other boring comics?"

"They're not boring."

"Look around you. You're with a bunch of comics who just admitted they were boring."

There was some nervous laughter.

"But you don't think they're boring."

I shook my head. "No."

"How many of you think Kasey is boring?"

"I know for a fact she's not in the least bit boring," Luke said.

Gabby tagged on, "Me, too."

"Luke, what's special about Kasey?"

"She's like a detective. She tracked down the person who tried to kill me. And she figured out who stole a Dax Arnota script from a local club."

Dax Arnota's name still had magic. People turned to look at me and I wanted to bury my head under the table.

"She's always thinking about stuff," Gabby said. "She anticipates what's going to happen."

"She's psychic?" Danny asked.

"No. Just smart."

"I paid Gabby to say that," I said, just to deflect some of the attention.

"What I'm hearing is that you probably study human nature. Yes?"

"Well, not formally."

"No, but don't all comics observe human nature? The weird, funny things we all do?"

People nodded in agreement.

"And you, Kasey, have some interesting stuff in your past—the stuff that Luke mentioned."

I nodded.

"There's your angle. 'Comic says observing human nature helps her solve crimes.'"

"I really don't want to be known for that. Honestly." Just hearing it put that way made me squeamish.

"Hell, I'll take it if you don't want it," someone on the other side of the room said. He got a big laugh.

"If you can pass yourself off as a tall redheaded babe, you might get away with it," Danny said. He suddenly got animated. "I have an idea. Everyone, get out a fresh sheet of paper. If you don't have one, ask for one. Let's take five minutes and everyone write down 25 things about you. Normal things. Weird things. Any awards you might have won, like being an Eagle Scout or winning the fifth-grade spelling bee, or, I don't know, you rescued a cat. So, normal factual things about you and then fun facts about you. Minimum of twenty-five things." He looked at his watch and pressed a button. "Starting... now."

The room went mostly quiet as we all started scribbling. A couple of minutes in, we were looking around. Danny was making a list on the white board: family, education, activities as a kid, musical instruments, dancing, acting, heroic feats, famous people you've met (non-comics), writings, health issues, superpowers. People would look up, out of ideas, start reading the list and you could see them remember something to add. Danny's watch started beeping.

"Okay. Looks like everyone has a list, yeah?"

"I got more than 25."

"Me, too," a few others said.

"Great. Now we're going to make headlines for press releases." He looked around the room. "Gabby, what's on your list?"

"Only child, studied acting, went to an all-girls' boarding school, snuck out of there to enter a local talent show, degree in Applied Mathematics from George Washington University..."

"Wait. Back up. You snuck out of your all-girls' boarding school to enter a talent contest?"

"Yes. I did a musical number. Song and dance."

"And you won the contest?"

"No. I came in second." She paused. "To a comic."

The room erupted in laughter.

Someone said, "Oh, she's got gold."

"And did that have any effect on your choice of careers?" Danny asked, a wide grin on his face.

Gabby started laughing. "Well, I guess it did."

"Singer Loses Talent Show, Gets Her Revenge as a Comic," Danny said. "Who else is boring?"

A shaggy-haired guy in the back of the room raised his hand. Danny pointed at him. "You."

"I really am boring. I work in accounting during the day. I live in the same town I grew up in—I only moved away for college and then moved back. I wasn't popular in high school, didn't do any sports." He thought for a second. "I played in the marching band."

"I'll bite," Danny said. "What instrument did you play?"

"Sousaphone. It's basically a tuba for marching bands."

"I don't know about a full persona, but man, you went from one non-chick magnet activity to another," I said.

He laughed. "I know. You can't exactly serenade a girl with a tuba. I've tried."

The class roared.

Someone asked, "Do you play rock n' roll tuba?"

"Yeah. Surprisingly enough, it's got a whole different sound."

"Hey!" Tim Norris spoke up. "Have you ever seen that bagpipe player that has flames shooting out of the pipes? Can you do that with your tuba?"

"Pretty sure I can't," the kid said. He got a good laugh.

"I don't know if you have a press release, but you do have something unique and different. I think you at least have a new bit," Danny said. Then he smiled. "Making the tuba sexy again. Comic will blow you away." He tilted his head. "Not great, but I think we have something there. If you don't mind carrying your tuba to gigs. Anyone have anything?"

"Sousaphone. Probably not. But, thank you. I do have a new bit." He gave a little wave and started scribbling some notes.

"Comic Finds Unusual Ways to Repel Women," Gabby said.

"Seriously, not helping," the kid said.

"That's the bit, though and maybe even your persona," Luke said. "If you don't mind that being your persona."

"You don't have to Sad Sack it," I said, to help move the idea along. "You can carry it off with a self-awareness that tells the audience you see the humor in it yourself. You're aware of how it looks to the outside world and you're okay with it. Which will make the audience okay with it."

I watched the idea catch in the kid's mind. He nodded slowly. "Yeah. I'm in on my own joke."

"Exactly! Great work you guys. So, you're getting the idea?" Danny's eyes swept the room. "Good. Now, if you're stuck, you guys help each other out, yeah? On one of the breaks or after the day's sessions. And if you're really stuck, flag me down. We'll find an angle for you. Here's the thing and it's really important. You must never, never tell anyone that you are boring again."

People laughed and there was a smattering of applause. He held up his hand.

"No, I mean it. The media doesn't cover boring people. You have to let them know that you are interesting and dynamic and fun and clever. That's who they want to cover. That's who their readers and listeners and viewers want to know about. People automatically think you're interesting when you're a comic or really, a performer of any sort. Don't let the cat out of the bag." He made a face and we laughed.

"Which brings us to sound bites. You all know what a sound bite is, yeah?"

And he was off again, showing us how to salt our interviews with sound bites, how to work things around and lead the interviewer into asking questions that would let you work in bits of your comedy. He closed out with a segment on keeping your cool, staying loose and light, and some basic good manners, like sending a thank you to the interviewer afterwards. He ended up getting a big round of applause from the group and he looked as pleased as a little kid. About a dozen people surrounded him at the end of class. Luke, Gabby, and I picked up our stuff and headed for the door.

"That was a really good session," Gabby said.

"Beat the hell out of Dolphin Auditions," Luke put in.

We laughed. "Darlana is…" I hesitated. "Just not really the right person for the job."

We were moving towards the main meeting room.

"What's next?" Luke asked.

"The event I have been waiting for. The ice cream social."

"I'm not even walking in there," Gabby said. "I can only be so good. Way too tempting."

"How long is the break?"

"Half an hour."

"I'm going to head up to my room and meditate."

"So healthy," I teased.

"Well, we got a lot of information from Danny. I think I need to grab another pad of paper, too."

"I'll walk you up to your room," Luke offered.

"No ice cream?" Gabby asked.

"Unlike Kasey, I can wait."

"Show off," I said.

I dropped them at the elevator bank and followed a group of people the short distance to the main room. I only looked over my shoulder once. Besides, ice cream was in the offing. Much better to look forward.

Chapter 16: Who Knew Hot Fudge Could Create a Slippery Slope?

I WAS SCOOPING HOT fudge onto my ice cream (one scoop chocolate, one vanilla) and eyeballing the bowl of whip cream. I was afraid it was getting a little low and that would not do. When I eat an ice cream sundae, I go all out. I was in luck. The staff brought out another bowl of real whipped cream (none of that canned stuff here!) and I shamelessly added half a dozen dollops. I accented my creation with a couple of spoonfuls of walnuts, skipped the maraschino cherries (too healthy), and went to find a seat. Part of me was already wondering if I could grab seconds.

Perhaps not my finest moment, but we're talking ice cream here. My dad is an ice cream freak and I inherited my passion for it from him. So, eating ice cream not only tastes good, it reminds me of all the times we went out for ice cream as a family or the times when Dad would meet me at the ice cream shop, picking me up from my guitar lesson. I thought he was treating me, but he finally admitted he was treating himself as much as me. I was good with that because either way, I got ice cream. I was a pragmatic child.

A minute or so later, Nick sat down next to me. I looked over at his bowl. One scoop of vanilla. With a few walnuts. No hot fudge sauce, no strawberry sauce, no whip cream or marshmallow.

"That's the saddest thing I've ever seen."

"I know what all that does to your body."

"It makes my body happy."

He looked down at his single scoop and sighed.

I took a big spoonful of whip cream and dropped it in his bowl. "It's dairy. Very good for you."

He ate some of it with his next spoonful. "Better."

"The hot fudge is pretty good, too." I offered my bowl to him, teasing: "You know you want it."

"I do." He met my eyes. "But I'm going to have to settle for the anticipation of it. I'm not allowed hot fudge at this point in my life."

I felt myself blush. "I understand. But seriously, it was only hot fudge."

"Hot fudge creates a slippery slope. Next thing you know, it's brownies and buttercream and biscuits with gravy."

I laughed. "All things I love. You've got me there."

"Things I love, too. But right now, I can't have them."

We both knew what he was talking about. "Yeah."

"But I'd love to get a hot fudge sundae with you at some time in the not-so-distant future."

"That would be fun." I looked down at the bowl. "It is a rather decadent, gloppy mess."

"I bet it's delicious."

I nodded and put another spoonful in my mouth.

"Your eyes are actually gleaming. You're probably addicted to sugar."

"Yeah. I'm good with that. It keeps me from craving other things."

"In that case, I'll give it a temporary seal of approval."

We sat quietly, letting the room buzz around us. Nick had a weird calming influence. Not just on me. I'd already seen him use it with Gabby and Luke. I figured it was a professional skill.

"What you're eating would seem decadent to Gabby," I said, kind of out of nowhere.

"Yeah. She's got some food issues. Not a professional opinion," he said quickly. "Just an observation."

"Don't need to be a professional to see that. I suspect her father has done a number on her."

He nodded. "Parents do the best they can but sometimes it is nowhere near close to what they should be doing."

"I would love to see her succeed. She puts a lot of pressure on herself."

"You do, too."

I looked at him.

"You aren't responsible for whatever is going on with Juliet, yet you've taken that on. You've assigned yourself the job of Gabby's protector. You're soaking up these sessions like your future depends on it."

"Well, my future does depend on it, pretty much." I took another bite. The ice cream had reached a perfect state of melt and it totally worked with the hot fudge and whip cream. "And really, I don't take these things on so much as they're thrust upon me. I mean, I somehow just find myself in the middle of these messes and if people need help, you help. If it makes you feel any better, I have no idea what I'm doing."

Nick laughed. "People seem to think you do."

"I know! Crazy, right?"

"Except you obviously do know what you're doing. You figured out who stabbed Luke at that competition."

"And nearly got killed in the process. Not all that smart."

"But you didn't. And Luke said you helped recover a stolen script or something?"

"Yeah. That one was self-serving."

"And there you go. Playing it off." He paused. "Look. I'm a damn good cardiac surgeon."

I nodded.

"Does that sound like I'm bragging?"

"No, you're just stating a fact."

"You're a damn good comedian. And you're damn good at figuring things out. Own it."

I shrugged. "I'm mostly fumbling around."

"Onstage?"

"No. I'm pretty good there."

"So, maybe you're pretty good at helping people out."

"I'm really not. I just get backed into a corner and have to do something."

"But you figure it out. And that doesn't come out of nowhere. You've got a good brain. Give it some credit."

"Sometimes it feels more like intuition. It really does come out of nowhere."

"No, it doesn't. It comes out of your brain recognizing patterns. Subconsciously, maybe."

I thought about that. "That makes sense."

"You're good at what you do, Kasey. Tonight, when you go up, I want you to remember that."

"You haven't even seen my act, yet."

"Well then, don't embarrass me. We've been hanging out for two days. I have a reputation to uphold."

I laughed. "So, no need to put pressure on myself. You've done it for me."

"You're welcome." He scraped the last bits of ice cream from the bowl. "The whip cream definitely improved it."

"Wait til you try the hot fudge."

"Really?" His face broke into a huge smile.

I blushed. "Oh my God. I didn't mean it like that."

"That's disappointing." He gave me a look that had me melting more than my ice cream. I wondered how long it took for a divorce to be finalized in New York State.

"Private party or can anyone join?" Luke walked up holding a dish of ice cream with hot fudge and caramel. Not in mass quantities. Lightweight.

"Have a seat," Nick said. "Kasey was just schooling me on the joys of hot fudge."

"One of the many beauties of Kasey," Luke leaned in conspiratorially, "is that she is always up to go for a drink or a meal or a coffee. She is not one of those women who pretends she has no appetite."

"New York women," Nick nodded. "You wouldn't believe how many of them eat tissues to stay thin."

"Tissues? For real?"

"For real. They're all going to have osteoporosis by the time they're fifty."

"I really just eat ice cream for the calcium. I'm preventing osteoporosis."

"How do you explain the hot fudge?" Luke teased.

"Chocolate is good for my soul."

Nick laughed and stood up. "I've got to check in with my office before the next session."

We watched him walk away.

"You and Nick... getting a little friendly there." Luke sounded casual.

"Nick? He's out of my league."

"Why would you even say that, Kasey?"

"The guy's a world-renowned cardiologist."

"And you're about to become a world-renowned comedian."

I looked at him as if he were an idiot. "Really? You really think those two professions are on the same level?"

He laughed. "Well, you know…" He shrugged. "Not everyone can do what you do, Kasey. You have that spark that will get you to the top. I have that spark. Gabby has it. That's not bragging or ego; it's just talent and hard work. Nick has that spark for cardiology, not so much for comedy and that's okay. Everyone has their talents. You need to recognize that in yourself and own it."

I nodded.

He went on. "But he is married."

"Divorcing." It was an automatic response and I probably snapped it out a little too quickly.

"Are they still living together?"

"Yes." I squirmed. "And that's one reason why nothing is going to happen. On either side."

Luke nodded. "I just don't want to see you get hurt."

"Well, that makes two of us." I smiled at him. "Really, it's not happening. We're both adults and we're both aware of the situation. When he is free…" I hesitated. "Maybe. That's all."

"If and when," Luke said.

"It's in process. And really, none of our business."

"You mean none of my business."

"Not mine either, really. It's Nick's marriage. Maybe it's just a rough patch."

"And you get to wait around while he's deciding that."

"I just met the guy. I'm hardly going to be putting my life on hold for a possibility." I looked hard at Luke. "Do I like the guy? Yes. Do

I hope something will happen? Yes. He's a great guy. Smart, funny, good-looking. What's not to like?"

"Married."

"Yeah, I get that part."

"I just don't want you to waste a whole lot of time waiting around for something that may not happen. Waiting for someone to come around is not fun." He looked away. "Not fun at all."

I nodded.

"There are other smart, funny, good-looking guys around. Single."

"Point taken, but they're not exactly lining up at my door."

"Well, maybe you should open it. Sometimes they're standing right in front of you."

Shit.

"Luke, look..." I started.

"I get it and don't panic. I'm just in here pitching." He smiled at me. "It's good for my ego to get shot down every so often. Keeps Luscious Luke in check."

"In that case, I've done the women of the world a great service."

He stood up and gave me a little salute. He started to walk away and then turned back to me. "Kasey, Nick is safe. He's in New York; you're in Florida and if it doesn't work out, you probably won't see each other again."

That stopped me short. "I like Nick. I'm not looking to bail out before it starts."

"Maybe. But I've known you for a couple of years now. You've made an art form out of dodging me. And from what I've seen, you've dodged every guy who has even thought about asking you out."

I started to protest but he waved his hand. "That's okay. I can take being friend-zoned. But Kasey, you don't date anyone. Not comics, not insurance agents."

"Insurance agents?"

"Well, I figure that's a pretty boring job."

I nodded.

"Do you know what the guys call you?"

I flinched. "Not sure I want to know."

"Fire and Ice. You look hot but you're ice cold."

I felt my face start turning red. I went into defense mode: snark. "Is there a pool going? Cuz I'd like to get in on the action."

"You're not getting any action."

I had to laugh. "Tell me about it."

He sat back down. "I'm telling you this—as a friend since that's where you want me. You're attracted to Nick because there's no risk involved for you. He's unavailable. He's far enough away that he's geographically undesirable."

I looked away and then back at him. "Well, nothing is going to happen there anyway."

"Exactly. That's what I'm saying. You're playing it safe. Love is about risk. Life is about risk. Shit, even with your act, you're not taking any risks. You're funny, you're solid. But you're not batting anywhere near where you should be."

"So, you hate my act, too."

"I'm not saying that."

"What, then?"

"We both sat through all those comics last night. Who do you remember?"

"Roger and Nick, of course. Tim, the number 23 guy." I thought back over the sets from last night and came up empty. I shrugged.

"Exactly. We've worked on material together and I know you have stuff that could be brilliant. But it's not in your act."

"That's because it's not brilliant. Yet. Or it's just too offbeat. People like stupid stuff."

"Yes, but people don't remember the stupid stuff. They remember the people who said the smart stuff. You just have to make the smart stuff understandable to drunks."

"Yeah, well…"

"Listen. When we first started out, you had a bit about souls and Disney World."

"You remember that?"

"I only heard you do it about five times in the space of two weeks. But you don't do it now. It's a great bit."

"Phil liked that bit, too."

"Why don't you use it then?"

"It's kind of offbeat."

"Yes." He looked at me. "And memorable."

"And memorable."

"Put it in tonight. You might have stronger stuff, but that bit is strong enough and it will make you memorable. It will make you stand out from the twenty-four other comics up there."

I nodded at him. "You're very smart."

"I keep telling you, not just a pretty face."

"I like your face, too."

"Throw me a bone. Gee, thanks." He rolled his eyes but he was smiling.

People were shifting out of the room. "Where to next?" he asked.

"I've got *Write Faster, Write Funnier* with Rob," I said.

"*Playing to the Camera*. Darlana. Not sure why I'm bothering."

"Maybe she'll do a better job today. The presentation she did this morning with Juliet was pretty good."

Luke seemed undecided. "Well, if it sucks, I'll go get some pool time."

We left the main room together. Passing through the lobby, I saw that Stavon was, once again, behind the desk.

In front of the counter was a spindly man with a rolling suitcase. Behind him, in a little Hawaiian shirt, khaki shorts, and a bucket hat, with aviator sunglasses hung around his neck by a neon pink Croakie, was a monkey, with his own little rolling suitcase. He looked like his stylist was Bill Murray.

I stopped short. Luke was half a dozen paces ahead of me before he realized I had stopped.

"What?"

He followed my gaze, then shook his head. "Coincidence."

"No such thing," I muttered. I looked at the monkey. He looked down at the floor, then looked up at the ceiling.

I approached the man. "Excuse me, cute monkey. Does he have a name?"

The man's face broke into a wide smile. "This is The Incredible Jax." He had the voice of a circus announcer. He added in a more normal voice, "but you can call him Jax."

"Well, aren't you a handsome guy, Jax."

Can a monkey look sheepish? Apparently, they can.

I turned to the man. "It's so cool that you take your monkey on vacation with you."

"Oh, we're here on business. He's got a couple days work over at Disney."

I threw a triumphant look at Luke. He rolled his eyes.

"Does he ever work at Disney Orlando?"

Jax suddenly became engrossed with checking his fingernails.

His owner got excited. "Yes! Have you seen him? He has also worked some of the shows at Busch Gardens in Tampa. We live in Florida."

"What a coincidence. So do I." I stared hard at the monkey. "He certainly gets around."

Jax dipped his head but I could see his lips drawing back. I didn't know if that was a smile or if he was about to attack me.

"Well, maybe I'll run into Jax again then. So very nice to meet you. Both."

The owner nodded and turned back to get his credit card from Stavon. Jax looked right up at me and winked.

I leaned down and whispered, "Cheeky monkey."

He made a little chattering noise as he hung his head.

Chapter 17: Why Didn't the Cougar Cross the Line?

ROB GAVE ME A smile and wave as I came through the door. I found a seat near the front of the room and got out my pad of paper and pen. Rob was getting repeat business. I saw Philipa and Tim sitting towards the back and recognized a few other faces.

"Okay, let's get started." His energy level seemed higher today. He must have finally gotten some sleep. He was more like the onstage Rob Tolland that I had seen in a few YouTube videos.

"Write Faster, Write Funnier. Well, I can help you for sure with the first part. First drafts are all about getting the words on the page. That's all, just words. The funnier part—well, I'm going to show you some of the writing formulas that we use. Sound like fun?"

He got a chorus of affirmatives and started in. "For those of you who were in my sitcom class, remember how I said you had to be able to take criticism? Well, the worst critic you will ever have is yourself.

That voice inside your head that tells you everything you've just written is crap."

"Sometimes it is crap," one of the women said.

Rob brightened. "Oh yeah, for sure. It's all crap. That's why it's called a *first* draft. Hemingway said the first draft of anything is shit and really, some of his finals weren't all that great, no matter what your high school English teachers told you. The important thing here is learning to make your inner critic shut up long enough for you to get words on paper."

He talked about imposter syndrome and then he showed us his process for shutting up his inner critic. It was really learning to allow yourself to write badly. He talked about all the rewrites that shows go through and how they could always look at a show when it was finished and come up with at least half a dozen better punchlines. "It's the nature of the beast. It's like when you have an argument with someone and an hour or a day later you think, *Man, I should've said this.*"

We all nodded in recognition. He gave us a ten-minute writing exercise and the goal was to write as badly and as "hack" as possible. There was a lot of giggling going on in the room and more than a few groans. I heard someone whisper, "This is truly awful!"

Rob heard it. "That means you're doing it right."

When we finished he said, "How horrible is your story?"

People responded with everything from "the worst" to "pure shit."

"Okay, now I want you to tear it up."

"What?"

"Rip it up."

No one did.

"If it's crap, why aren't you tearing it up?"

Tim said, "I think I have the start of something here. I mean it's not good, but it's a start."

Rob threw his arms in the air, triumphant. "EXACTLY!"

We all laughed.

"Even though it was bad, you didn't want to just toss out your work, did you?"

Nos all around.

"Now you have something to work with. It might become something, it might not, it might morph into something completely different. But until you have something on the page, you can't make it better. And that's why we work in writing sprints, just getting as much down as possible in whatever time you want to set. Sprints are exercise. You need to do them every day. Keep track of how many words you write in your set time period. If you're writing fewer words, you're listening to your inner critic." He wagged a finger. "Stop that. Now, let's work on making you funnier."

He gave us some writing formulas, a couple I already knew from some of the joke writing I had done. About halfway through the session, I got a text from Roger. *Look at this* followed by a grainy image. I enlarged it as much as I could on my phone. It was a picture of a group of students: Joanne Preston, Darla Beaver, Danny Shillingford, Betsy Recker, Tom Krintz, and Robert Tolland. It was captioned "Picnic in the Quad at Franklin College" and named off the students, right to left.

I tapped a quick response to Roger: *Will ask Rob about this after the session.*

Juliet hadn't mentioned that she had known Rob in college, but it made sense. Friends from college, all going into some aspect of show business. And Juliet was not the only one to change her name. I looked at Darlana, nee Darla: She already had a theatrical sparkle going about her whereas Juliet looked like the girl next door. Rob had said it was all about creating a network. This was a pretty close network.

Rob gave us another writing exercise: Write a scene in ten minutes. Make it funny.

We all groaned.

"What?"

"Well, what kind of scene? Like, anything?" someone asked.

"I'll help you out. You all know the show I work on, *Luck Be a Lady*, yes? Let's do a scene where Jackie's character comes in to find her mom has let herself into her apartment and discovered a man in Jackie's bed." He paused for a minute. "This is like a bad improv setup," he muttered.

"Do we have to keep things in character for Jackie? Because I've seen the show a few times, but I don't really know the characters well."

"Sacrilege!" Rob thundered and we all laughed.

"No, you can take that situation any which way you want to, character-wise. I just want a scene that has some sort of action and hopefully, a few jokes. The key is that I am timing you, so it's how fast you can come up with an idea, put it on paper, and then make it funny. And if you were paying close attention, I just gave you the order of things." He glanced at his watch. "Get started."

My mind went blank. I was hoping everybody else's did, too. I started by writing down the situation. Jackie's mom lets herself in and finds a guy. Why did she let herself in? Did Jackie know she had a key? Where's Jackie right now?

I wrote, *Enter Mom. She is carrying groceries and drops them in the kitchen. She goes into Jackie's bedroom, opens the curtains to bright sunlight, slaps the rump of the body under the covers, who she assumes is Jackie.*

Mom: Come on, Sunshine. Mommy's here to make your day!

The covers move, the pillow shifts, and a good-looking, naked (at least from the waist up and we'll assume down) sits up, shaking himself awake and starts standing. The sheet dips lower.

Mom: If that sheet drops any farther, you're going to make my day.

He jumps, covering himself up.

Guy: Who are you? Where's Jackie?

Mom: I could ask you the same things.

Then I got stuck. What could happen next? Maybe Jackie's mom is a cougar. Of course she is; this is network TV. Too easy. Maybe she's down-to-earth, matter-of-fact.

Mom: You first.

Guy: I'm Chip. Jackie's date. From last night.

Mom: Hope for Jackie's sake you're packing more than a chip.

I looked at what I had written. I needed a more suggestive name than Chip. I underlined it and put "find better name."

Chip: And you are?

Mom: Jackie's mom. I hope you used a condom, Chip.

Chip (embarrassed): Umm, pretty sure we did.

Mom: Pretty sure? Don't make me check the bathroom wastebasket. I told her to stop using wicker years ago.

That was kind of weak. Maybe too obscure. Well, it wasn't like I knew what I was doing.

Chip: Uh, no. We definitely used condoms.

Mom (Sits on bed, pats the space next to her, crosses legs and is clearly enjoying herself. Chip sits next to her.): Condoms. How many exactly, Chip?

Chip (uncertain what number he should say but clearly lying): Three?

Mom (disparaging): Three?

Chip: Maybe four?

Mom (confiding): If you tell me, you'll feel better.

Chip: Four.

Mom waits a beat: I'll make breakfast for you.

Chip (a little proud): Six. What's for breakfast?

Mom: I'm thinking about muffins. (Under her breath) *Stud muffins.*

Rob called time and there was a collective groan.

"Who's got more than five lines of dialogue?"

Everyone raised their hands. I started counting the lines on my paper. Twenty-one

"Keep your hands up if you have more than ten"

A few hands went down.

"Fifteen?" Rob looked around the room. "I'm impressed. Twenty?"

Three of us still had our hands up.

"Twenty-five?" My hand and another guy's went down.

Rob looked at the woman who had more than twenty-five lines written. "Well, let's start with you. How many lines do you have?"

"Twenty-eight. They're not particularly funny though."

"That's okay because you've got something on paper to work with and that's the important thing. Bestselling author Jodi Picoult nailed it when she said 'you can't edit a blank page.' So, getting something—anything—down on paper is your first step."

I wrote down the name Jodi Picoult. I should see what kind of stuff she wrote.

He leaned against the front table. "For those of you with fewer than ten lines, your inner critic is killing you. First drafts are just author vomit on the page. And, just like when you drink too much, you will feel better after you puke."

People groaned and laughed at the same time.

"How many of you made Jackie's mom a cougar?"

It looked like every hand went up. "Easier, who didn't make Jackie's mom a cougar?"

I raised my hand.

"We'll get back to you, Kasey."

I looked around. Just me. Of course. Talk about screwing up publicly. I ducked my head down.

"And who let Mom slide under the covers with the guy?"

Half a dozen hands went up.

Rob shook his head. "Naughty, naughty."

"Ladies, why is that bad?"

"Crosses the line," Philipa said. "Big time."

"Yes, it does. This is Jackie's mom, a recurring character in the show. Now, I know I said you didn't have to stick to the characters' personalities in the real show, but if Jackie comes home and finds her mom in bed with her new boyfriend, that's going to do some real relationship damage. This is a sitcom. Finding a naked man in your daughter's bed can be funny. Finding your mom in bed with your boyfriend is devastating."

"But Mom can be a cougar, right?" a woman asked.

"Yes, and that's direction that most sitcoms would take the scene. What's the other direction? Kasey."

My head snapped up. "Well, I don't know if it's the other direction..." I hesitated.

"Where did you take it?"

"I made the mom kind of, well, she messes with him, gets him flustered, but she has no intention of sleeping with him. So, she's kind of wise-cracking, but down-to-earth."

"Why didn't you make her a cougar?"

"I thought about it but it just seemed too easy and overdone."

"Good instinct." He gave me a quick smile. "There's nothing wrong with making her a cougar. That works, so those of you who did, you understand American sitcoms pretty well. But if you want to keep a show fresh, you need to change it up, go in a different direction sometimes. Either way works... as long as the jokes are funny."

I felt relieved. And, I'll admit, a little chuffed.

"Who has jokes in there?"

All of us raised our hands.

"A room full of comics, go figure. And who got as far as having the scene lead to the next scene?"

"I think most of us didn't get that far," someone laughed.

"Could you explain what you're looking for?" Philipa asked.

"Is there mention of what's going to happen next?"

I half raised my hand, "She said she would make him breakfast. Do you mean like that?"

"Sure, that works. Because the next scene is Jackie walking in on Mom and her new boyfriend chatting over breakfast like old friends or whatever, right?"

"Oh yeah, I had that whole scene already worked out," I said as insincerely as possible. I got a nice laugh.

We were closing in on the end of class. Rob fielded some questions and then we ran out of time.

A few people waited to talk to Rob when class was over. I was one of them. I looked at Nick. "I just need to ask Rob a quick question. You don't have to wait for me."

"I'll hang." He indicated that he'd be outside the door.

A couple of people asked Rob to look over what they had written and give some pointers. That went pretty quickly because there wasn't that much for him to read. The woman with the 28 lines was in front of me. He took a little more time with her. He gave a snort at one of the lines. We call it the headliner laugh. Headliners don't really laugh at jokes; they do more of a "Ha!" or they'll snort when they think something is funny. Rob laughing at a line told me it was pretty good.

"Thanks, Rob. Appreciate all your help," she said. She gave me a friendly smile as she turned around to leave.

"Want me to take a look at what you've written?" Rob asked.

"That would be great, but it's not why I stayed. I need to ask you about something else."

He gave me a curious look. "What?"

I pulled out my phone and showed him the picture Roger had sent me.

"You knew Juliet when she was Joanne," I stated.

"You know Juliet's real name?"

"Yes, I've been working with her on something."

"I'm sure she'd prefer that people don't know her real name."

"Understood and we're keeping it under wraps. But you went to college with her. You, Danny, Darlana."

"Yeah. They were all in the theatre department together. I was a journalism major but I hung out with the theatre kids. Just more fun. Then Juliet had that horrible accident and she left school. She felt so guilty."

"Were you in the car that night?"

Rob shook his head no. "Darla and Danny were. They were tighter with her than I was. I was always kind of on the edges. But you should know that Juliet hadn't been drinking. The cops breathalyzed her. The kid ran a red light. There was a traffic camera; she was never even charged. Just a stupid accident."

"Did you know Juliet is being blackmailed?"

His head snapped up. "What? No! Who would do that?"

"That's what we're trying to find out."

"No wonder she's been so tense. I knew something was off with her. I can't believe this is coming back to bite her."

"Do you know of anyone who is here that knew all of you back in the day?"

Rob thought. "Not really."

"How about Philipa?"

"Which one is she?"

"Heavyset, long dark curls, glasses?"

He shook his head. "She spoke up in the session. I didn't recognize her, though. She's doing the private showcase, right?"

"Yeah."

"I'll pay closer attention and see if I recognize her. I mean, people change after college. We gain weight, go grey, or lose our hair."

"Change our names..." I prompted.

"Yeah. Darla became Darlana. DeLuz, of all things. Joanne became Juliet."

"You were fine with the name your parents gave you," I said, smiling at him.

"Named after my dad and no way was I going to change it. That would hurt him beyond belief. And Danny quickly shifted to behind the scenes work once we were out of college. He did not want to go the whole starving artist route. He found a niche doing voiceovers and then IT and faded into the background. It keeps him in touch with the supposed excitement of show biz without having to step on a stage."

"I saw his price sheet. He must do pretty well."

"I think so. Nice car, nice address. He's built a good business."

"What about the other two people in the picture?"

Rob shook his head. "Tom Krintz went on to legit theatre. He's in New York and is doing pretty well. I don't know about Betsy; haven't seen her since college. Juliet might know."

"I'll ask her." It was kind of a dead end but you have to check out everything, if only to make sure it's going nowhere. There was a bit of an awkward silence.

"So, you're going up tonight?" Rob asked.

"Well, just the regular set; the private showcase was too rich for my blood. Not that I was asked."

"Yeah. That's kind of a weird thing. Got tagged on to the agenda a couple of days before the event began. Very last-minute."

"Stirred up some feelings, too."

"Like that jerk who made such a fuss. Chad something? Do you think he's behind the blackmail?"

"Juliet was being blackmailed before the event started. So, probably not. It's got to be someone who knew her from college."

"Well, let's hope they show themselves because there were over 15,000 students at that school. The car accident was a big deal when it happened, but I'm sure it's faded in most people's minds."

"I wonder if the guy who got killed had a girlfriend at the time..." I was thinking out loud.

"No idea. But it's a long gap between college and now. How long has this been going on?"

"A little over a year."

"Maybe Juliet did something a year ago that triggered all this."

"Great thought," I said. I was excited. "I'll check with her. Thanks. And now I have to get ready to attend the private showcase, prep my set, and hopefully swallow some food to tide me over."

"And I'm going to go get a beer because my work is done for the day."

"You're a brat."

"Thank you. Hope you do well tonight."

"Well, I'm counting on you to laugh even if I'm not funny."

"You'll be fine."

I nodded. "Six minutes. Piece of cake."

We headed out of the room and there were still people hanging out, talking in the hall. Rob got buttonholed by a woman who was trying to hand him a large envelope. I heard him say "Happy to take a look," as they walked away. I suspected he was not happy to take a look.

Nick was still in the hall, talking to one of the guys. He ended his conversation when he saw me.

"Taking this bodyguard stuff pretty seriously."

"Absolutely. Don't want my handiwork messed up."

We were close to the elevators when my cell phone rang.

"Kasey, can you come to my room? Right away?"

It sounded like Juliet was in full panic mode.

"Sure, what's the room number?"

"1010."

"See you in a few."

Chapter 18: Everybody Wants to Get into the Act

We got into the elevator. Nick pressed the button for the fourth floor and I pressed for ten.

Nick looked at me questioningly.

"Juliet. And she's—"

"Yeah, I could hear her. Do you want me to ride up with you?"

"No. I don't know how long this will take."

The elevator dinged for the fourth floor, and Nick hesitated a bit, then re-pressed the button for ten.

"It'll be fine."

We continued on up to the tenth, and as it turned out, top floor. Nick watched me as I knocked on the door and waited for the door to open before he punched the button to go back down.

So, this is how the other half lives. I tried not to gawk as I walked into a large sitting room. It had gorgeous views of the Santa Ana

Mountains. Quite an upgrade over my room. I bet the mini-bar snacks were better, too. Well, it gave me something to aspire to.

Danny came through a doorway that must have led to the bedroom. I wondered if Danny was staying with her or if he had his own room.

Juliet shut the door behind me and started in. "I can't believe the bitch is actually doing this to me!"

"Which bitch is doing what?" I asked. I looked at Danny to see if he could fill me.

"Darlana," he started.

"That bitch is trying to blackmail me!"

The gears in my brain clicked. *Of course she was.* Once she found out Juliet was paying someone to keep quiet about her past, Darlana figured she could get in on the action. So much for the friendship being mended.

I restrained myself from telling Juliet to calm down. But now I understood why guys said it. "When did this happen? It looked like you two were getting along fine this morning."

"I thought it was all smoothed over, too. Then at our daily meeting, she waited until everyone else was gone and told me I had to pay her an extra $2,000 to keep her quiet. She's already overpaid for this event as it is!"

"That's pretty ballsy. But it probably means we can rule out Darlana as your original blackmailer."

"One down, 99 to go," Danny deadpanned.

"She should really watch her step. She's not exactly Miss Squeaky Clean." Juliet's eyes narrowed.

"Really? Tell me about that."

"It's nothing big. She didn't kill anyone. Like me." Juliet deflated, her anger momentarily checked by guilt.

"It was an accident, Jules." I wondered how long Danny had been telling her that.

She waved the sentence away. I waited.

"She has screwed someone for every role she's ever gotten. Directors, producers, stars... well, supporting actors."

"So the Dolphin Technique is...?"

"Please." Juliet rolled her eyes. "She couldn't audition her way out of a wet paper bag. The Dolphin Technique is pure bullshit."

I called that one right at least. "So, there's a little leverage there. Something we can use against Darlana."

"Well, the casting couch is more of a hard reality than something to blackmail her over. A lot of actors, male and female, have done it," Juliet observed.

"Yes, but that's changing. And," I paused for effect, "If she's staking her claim on how her Dolphin Technique can get people cast, then telling people it is BS is going to kill that for her. She's getting older. Roles will be getting scarcer." I was thinking out loud. "And she's really not made it at this point. So, is teaching auditioning techniques her main paycheck these days?"

Danny nodded. "I do her website. We've been running ads to her workshops and she's working on an online course using videos."

"How's that going for her?"

"About as well as you'd expect. She wants a minimum of ten people per class and she's trying to charge $500 for the day. But beginning actors—and that's what she is getting for these sessions—can't really afford even that. So, if she gets five people, she's doing well. Especially since she's not a celebrity. No name recognition."

I nodded.

He went on. "But there are expenses: the advertising, renting the room for the day. She gives them lunch and snacks. All organic, of course. So, the costs aren't huge, but it's not all profit."

"And LA is an expensive town to live in."

"You're looking at a couple of grand for a studio apartment anywhere decent. So yeah, she needs the money. But most people in our profession do. Unless you hit into steady work, you're living paycheck to paycheck."

"Same as most people," I commented.

"It still doesn't give her the right to blackmail me." Juliet was winding up again.

"Nobody said it did. I'm just trying to get a picture here. Figure out the playing field." I thought for a minute. "I can't say it's the brightest move in the world."

Juliet looked at me.

"Well, you don't know who your blackmailer is, right? So, you can't go after him or her. But you know Darlana. All you have to do is turn her in to the cops."

"But then the story will get out about the accident and my career will go right into the toilet."

"That's what she wants you to think. But really, it was twenty years ago. Not to be disrespectful to the young man who died, but it will cause a ripple for about a week and a half and then become a trivia question. At most."

"So, what should I do? Confront her?"

"You can. Let her know that you're not paying and that you will go to the police and report her if she says anything. Look up the sentencing for blackmailers, talk about suing for damages, let her understand that trying to blackmail you is going to cost her big money." I looked at Danny and shrugged. "What do you think?"

"That's the upfront way to do it," he agreed.

"I should just tell everyone how she lands what few roles she has," Juliet fumed.

"Threatening Darlana makes you no better than her," I said. "But it's a nice thing to have in your pocket should you need to use it. I wouldn't pull it out yet, though. You and Danny talk to her and see if you can make her see reason. But you have to sell her on the idea that you will definitely go to the police if she doesn't back down. She has to believe you on that."

Juliet nodded, but she was not at all happy.

"If you talk with her, this will probably all go away. Look, Juliet. You're the big dog in this fight. She needs you more than you need her. Point out that she's going to look like the bad guy attacking you for something that happened when you were a kid. Tell her flat out that you will survive the story coming out. And you will." I looked Juliet in the eyes to make sure she was getting it. "Okay?"

"Yes."

"Darlana is just a bump in the road. And not particularly bright. Get her handled and we can concentrate on the main problem: your unknown blackmailer." I switched gears. "Something else has come up."

Both Juliet and Danny straightened up. I showed them the picture that Roger had sent me.

"I'd forgotten this!" Juliet said. "God, we were babies."

"Back when Darlana was still Darla," Danny sniffed.

"You didn't mention that you knew Rob back then."

"I didn't?"

"No. You mentioned Danny and Darlana," I hesitated for a second. The alliteration of their names threw me a bit. "But Rob was a friend back then."

"Rob hung around with the group, but he was a journalism major. He was there, but on the edges."

"He was more observer than participant," Danny said.

"We met back up again in New York, when we were both on the circuit."

I pivoted. "The other two people in the picture... do you know what they're doing or where they are?"

Juliet gave me about the same information on Tom as Rob had. I asked about Betsy. She shrugged.

Danny spoke up. "Married for over fifteen years. Three kids. A dog. Lives in suburban Connecticut. She left before you had the accident."

We both looked at Danny. "Old girlfriend?" I asked.

"For the record, I dumped her. As nicely as I could. I actually introduced her to her future husband."

"Jeez, you never fixed me up with anyone like that," Juliet teased him.

"You didn't need fixing up. And I wouldn't have dumped you."

"Maybe you should run a matchmaking website," I said.

"Cut my teeth on those. I learned a lot about copywriting, too."

"I bet." I turned to go and then turned back. "Does Philipa look familiar to either of you?"

"Philipa? No." Juliet was firm. Danny shook his head.

"Okay." I figured I'd keep the fact that Philipa had gone to the same college to myself. It might just be coincidence.

I shifted back. "So, Rob knew about the accident and about you changing your name."

"Rob wouldn't do this," Juliet said.

Danny agreed. "Rob's a sweetheart. He might be the only guy in LA without a mean bone in him."

Truth was, I didn't think Rob would do something like this, either. But I wasn't going to count him out just because I thought he was a nice guy. I got up to leave and Danny followed me to open the door.

I took the opportunity to enlist his help. "Right now, Juliet's defensive and hurt and angry. When you meet with Darlana, Juliet's got to be confident and cool. Can you get her into the right headspace?"

"Yeah. She goes through this. Spirals a bit then pulls out. It's just a lot of stuff is happening to her at once."

"And at the worst possible time. I know you care for her. I'm sure she appreciates it."

"In her way." Danny looked away. "It's all good. Or it will be."

"We'll find the real blackmailer and get her back to good." I smiled at him reassuringly.

"Do you think you can find the guy?"

"I'll do my best."

"Thanks. We really do appreciate your help."

I headed back to my room. I wasn't going to have much time to shower and change before the private showcases. And I still needed to put the Disney World bit into my set and run through it at least once. I was thankful it was only a six-minute set. I thought about Tim's set from last night. Loose, not appearing as if he cared. I needed to capture that energy. With that idea settled, I prepped for the night.

Chapter 19: Are You Ready to Rumble?

Gabby was nervous. She had knocked on my door early and of course, I wasn't ready. She sat on the bed waiting for me, and I rushed as I put on a pair of dangly earrings that I knew would catch the light. I did one last check in the mirror: black DKNY pants suit with a long jacket. Cobalt blue blouse. Chunky necklace. Nine West heels again. I had a nice, wide gold cuff bracelet that made it look like I was doing okay. I checked my pockets. Key cards, credit card, a bit of cash, and my set list.

"Ready!"

"You're not wearing lipstick?"

"Shit." I dashed back into the bathroom, found the right color and put it on. The lipstick went into my pocket. Should I bring a brush? God, I hated carrying a bag, especially when I was going up. I looked out at Gabby sitting on the bed.

"Can I put a brush and comb in your bag?"

"Sure. Better give me the lipstick, too. It's creating a bulge in your pocket."

"Crap. Thanks."

She put my stuff in her Gucci bag. We looked at each other in the mirror. Gabby was, of course, gorgeous and just the right mix of girl-next-door and Barbie-doll sexy. She was wearing a medium pink sleeveless dress with a sweetheart neckline that had a full skirt dropping almost to her knees. She had topped it with a matching bolero jacket. Both the dress and jacket were decorated with a few scattered sequins—just enough to catch the light. She was wearing a short pearl necklace, diamond and pearl drop earrings and Louboutin stiletto heels in a matching pink. The outfit had a girl next door wholesomeness to it, if you lived in Beverly Hills. I looked like I was doing okay; she looked like a million bucks.

We switched rooms, closed the door between them and locked it, and we came out of our doors at the same time. We pretended to be surprised.

"Great timing!"

"We're going to need it tonight."

Each person doing the showcase had been allowed to bring two guests so there would be a bit of an audience. Gabby had invited Nick and me as her guests; Luke invited Roger and Amber.

We walked in to the main room. Pamela was handling the door and as we came in, she told us everyone was sitting at the front tables so the video shots would pick up a bit of audience. Normally I sit in the back, but tonight I was happy to sit down front and help my friends.

I took a minute to look around the room. The service bars were stationed in the room but they weren't set up yet. But there two big buckets filled with ice and bottled water and sodas for us. There'd be about a fifteen-minute break between the private and regular show-cases.

In all, there were about thirty people in the room; not enough to get big laughs, but enough to fill. That's a lot more than people got at any audition. I had auditioned for a few local shows and I hated the process. Usually, you were onstage, with three people sitting somewhere in the darkened audience, not reacting to anything you said or did, and passing judgment. At least the showcase I was doing was more like a regular comedy night. For the first time, I was glad I wasn't asked to participate in the private showcases.

The guys were already there, of course. Roger jumped up and got waters for us while we checked in. Gabby was going up third, Luke was number seven.

Philipa was at the next table over with Tim Norris and someone I didn't know. She leaned over to say hello.

"What number are you?" I asked.

"Eight."

"Right after Luke."

"Hope they won't be too tired by then," she said.

"Ha! I'm doing the showcase tonight. They're ten in before we even get started. I think I'm just going to have a good time and hope the video comes out okay."

She nodded. "Yeah. I'm not sure I'm happy I paid $1,000 for this."

"Don't worry. You'll kill it. And you'll stand out. I'm just going to be a redheaded blur to them."

"Sounds like a superhero name. The Redheaded Blur. Like the Flash."

"Maybe not."

She laughed.

The lights dimmed, and the sound man's deep voice came over the speakers: "Ladies and Gentlemen, America's Comedy Sweetheart, Ms. Juliet Hartwell."

We applauded loudly to make up for the lack of people in the room but it felt a bit weak. Luke twisted open a bottled water and looked around the room. "Oh, joy."

Juliet welcomed everyone and explained how the showcases worked. She reintroduced Ross and Solly, as if we didn't all know who they were. But there was no real warm up. On the other hand, these were more auditions than anything and you wouldn't have a warm up at an audition. Unless you counted the people who auditioned before you. I noticed the intros were a bit more involved: Juliet gave credentials that included any acting work as well as comedy credits.

The first two comics were good, but they were starting from zero: cold crowd and no alcohol. I guess the point is if you need the audience to be drunk to be funny, you're probably not that funny. Gabby was standing near the stairs and I saw Juliet leaning over and whispering with her. The second comic finished up, we gave a good round of applause because he had earned it. It also brought some energy up for Gabby.

"Gabby Leigh is a quadruple threat: singer, dancer, actor, and stand-up comic. She danced the role of Clara for two seasons in the National Theatre's annual presentation of The Nutcracker, spent three seasons playing various roles at Williamstown, including Laura in *Glass Menagerie*. And as a singer, she once lost a talent competition to a comic." Juliet landed a nice laugh on that. I am sure Danny had mentioned it to her. It was nice move; it softened the audience towards her. "Ladies and Gentlemen, please welcome Ms. Gabby Leigh."

I looked around the table. "Sheesh. She tell any of you guys that?" I whispered.

Everyone shook their heads no.

She must have been a hell of a dancer. That horseback riding accident was more than a broken leg; it must have been a huge blow to her. She had made it sound like a small incident.

Gabby got up to a polite round of applause and launched in with more confidence than I have ever seen her display. Gone was the uncertainty and the need for reassurance. She was totally at home on a stage and she looked it. She took the mic out of the stand, a vision of pink femininity, swung the stand back, and looked out over the audience as if there were a thousand of us.

"Are you ready to rumble?" She roared.

The unexpected worked. She got that first laugh immediately. She shrugged prettily, then she was off and running. Her material wasn't strong, but she had good timing and she was good at acting out the bits.

"I went to an all-girls boarding school. So, my high school experience was absolutely normal. Let's just say that an all-girls school works out better for some than others. It was a unique experience. People often assume that being surrounded by teenage girls all the time means endless gossip and drama." She did a take to the audience. "No shit, Sherlock." She got the laugh and continued on. "Our school had its own rumor mill that could rival any high school; the bathroom stalls doubled as confessionals."

"My second year there, the school instituted a new policy: They would only hire male teachers who were gay. So, I guess we know what our parents were really paying for. Though I'm pretty sure a chastity belt costs less than four years of private school tuition. Hashtag: Parent math." She threw up her hands in disgust.

"So, all of our male teachers were gay. It was FABULOUS for us because who better to teach hormonal teenage girls how to get boys? Someone didn't think that one through." She rolled her eyes and shrugged.

"It was a well-rounded education. We learned Shakespeare's sonnets *and* the importance of smokey eye." She paused for the laugh.

"Chemistry was great. We created an entire makeup line. Which led into Trigonometry which was basically learning how to contour our cheekbones to create the best photographic angles. These guys might not have known quadratic equations, but they sure knew how to 'Yaaas queen' at our talent shows. They were like our personal cheerleaders, complete with pom-poms and glitter. School dances were entire Busby Berkeley musical numbers." Pause. "A ***lot*** of jazz hands."

She relaxed down a bit, took a breath, pretended she was remembering back to high school.

"They really went over and above. The history teacher liked to dress up as whatever historical person we were learning about. We learned a lot about women in history that year. Every week was like a new episode of *RuPaul's Drag Race*. We had to wear these ugly uniforms. The teachers took one look and were like, 'Girl, that plaid is so last season. MAKEOVERS!' Within a week, we went from looking like Anne Hathaway at the beginning of *Princess Diaries* to walking around like Reese Witherspoon in *Cruel Intentions*."

She moved on to a bit about college and being in the STEM program. None of the material was super strong, but it was pretty good for an opener and she knew how to deliver a line. It was petty of me to think it, but with her looks, all she had to do was not trip over her words. She got a nice round of applause at the end and I saw the agent making furious notes. The club owner didn't seem to react one way or the other. She was more actor than comic and she had the right person paying attention. I hoped something would come out of it for her.

We had three comics to go through before Luke's set. Half an hour. They went quickly and I was impressed by the quality of the sets. People were definitely bringing their "A" game to this. I couldn't see the club owner booking everyone or even anyone, though. There was enough talent in LA without having to look outside. It wasn't even about being good-looking—LA was filled with gorgeous people. I admit that I tuned out a bit to the showcases. I was working on the question "How do you stand out when everyone is good-looking and is about equally funny?" Maybe for Luke and Gabby, it would be the combination of extraordinary looks along with talent. They were built for Hollywood. I was not. Which meant I was going to have to be super-talented. No pressure.

Luke had gotten up from the table ten minutes earlier and was waiting on the side near the stage stairs for the comic in front of him to finish. Philipa was reapplying her lipstick using a small mirror.

"So unfair—half the guys don't even shave and we have to spend forty-five minutes to an hour just to look natural," I whispered.

"Hell," Philipa said. "I shaved my legs and I'm wearing pants!"

I wished Philipa luck as she left the table and went to stand near Luke.

Juliet brought Luke up on stage and I noticed the agent was once again making notes. The club owner, not so much. The perfect crystallization of Luke's looks working for him and against him at the same time.

He had jettisoned much of the material that went with his "Luscious Luke" persona and, while his act wasn't exactly wholesome, it was more in keeping with his actual good guy character.

He opened with his ugliest one in the family bit. When he got to the part about having to take his ugly cousin to prom ("she's only a Victoria's Secret Model"), he threw in, "Wish I had known Roger's grandma back then!" which got a laugh from our table and some recognition from the rest. He segued into a bit I hadn't heard.

"I have not had good luck dating. My last girlfriend stabbed me. Pro tip: If you're breaking up with someone, don't order the steak." There were some uncomfortable laughs. "What? Too dark? She didn't stab you, what's your problem?" This got a better response.

He launched into his next bit.

"I'm a late-night breakfast restaurant connoisseur. IHOP, Waffle House, Denny's, Huddle House... Huddle House is like Waffle House but not as elegant. Forget eating healthier when you are on the road. Literally, the healthiest fast-food menu is at Taco Bell. I shit you not. Well, actually, if you go to Taco Bell..." He trailed off letting the audience fill in the obvious and got the laugh. He moved through some material about being on the road and went into a bit that we had worked on together.

"I make extra money as a male model, and let me tell you, it's not nearly as glamorous as *Zoolander* makes it out to be. People often assume I live this fabulous life, but the reality is I stand around looking sulky for hours. I mean, why do I even get my teeth cleaned? I now excel at blank expressions, which is perfect for inter-departmental meetings."

He put a blank expression on his face and stared out over the audience. He got a ripple of a laugh. Then he slowly raised his arm and pointed into the distance. Bigger laugh. "Ah, you've seen my work!" He thrust his hands on his hips and stared out: "Underwear man!" Big laugh.

"People think modeling is easy. 'Just stand there and look good.' But the truth is, modeling is a workout. I've mastered the art of holding a flex for hours. My biceps are basically permanent cramps in disguise."

He shook his head to indicate how silly he thought the whole business was. "The hardest part of being a male model is trying to hold onto your dignity when you're sent down a runway wearing something billed as the latest in office attire and it would be banned on the beach at Club Med. I'm walking down a runway in front of 500 people" he paused, "many of whom are taking PICTURES..." people were laughing now, "in the equivalent of a paper onesy held together by some designer's hopes and dreams."

"You know how people say, 'you couldn't pay me to do that'?" He waited for a response. "Apparently you can pay me to do that." Big laugh. "I'm so proud."

Luke came off to a nice round of applause, but when he sat back down at the table, I could tell he wasn't overly happy with the set. He nodded to acknowledge the "nice job" comments but he turned a bit in his seat to look like he was focusing on Philipa. There was not a damn thing wrong with his set for the level that we were at, but I know

Luke well enough to know he was already critiquing his performance. It was the nature of the beast.

Philipa knew how to work a showcase. Her ten-minute set involved a lot of acting out bits, creating several characters using different voices and accents. She reminded me of a young Lily Tomlin in that regard. I noticed that she was hitting the sitcom supporting role tropes—the wacky neighbor, best friend, crazy sister. This truly was a showcase set: It demonstrated her versatility as an actress, allowing the agent to visualize her in various roles. *Smart, smart, smart*, I thought. She did a funny bit about her time as a teacher, dealing with teenagers.

"Everything is life or death at that age. They get dumped by a boyfriend and it's the end of the world. They don't know that by the time they're thirty, they can fix that shit with a couple of pints of Häagen-Daz and a box of wine."

She segued from there to talking about her family.

"My sister is this emaciated little thing, five feet tall and barely one hundred pounds. I know people look at the two of us together and think, "Damn. That big one ate all the little one's food." She took a beat, then adopted a proud stance. "Maybe I did."

"My sister sabotaged every diet I ever went on. As if I couldn't do that on my own..." She paused for the laugh.

"My sister would say, 'Let's go for ice cream sundaes!' And of course, I'd say yes. I'm chubby, not stupid. We'd go to the ice cream shop, order our sundaes. She'd take one bite—I swear, ONE BITE, then hold her stomach and say, 'Ooh. I'm stuffed.'" Philipa used a squeaky, childish voice for her sister. She mimed scooping spoonfuls of her sundae into her mouth and looked over to the side, as if eyeballing her sister's sundae. "Not a problem." She said it as if she had a mouthful of food and gleeful enthusiasm. She mimed grabbing her sister's sundae. She got about as big a laugh as you can get from a small audience.

Then she threw in, "Yes, I am the fat best friend in case you're looking for a type" and she snapped her head around to stare hard at the agent. He cracked up, as did the rest of us.

"Too subtle?"

She packed as much into ten minutes as you could possibly pack. I leaned over and whispered to Gabby. "We just got a master class in how to do a showcase."

Gabby nodded. "I feel like an idiot even getting on the stage after seeing that."

"She's got seven years' experience on you. But now we both know what to work towards."

Philipa closed her set to an enthusiastic round of applause. She gave a very graceful, grand diva curtsy. She had nailed it and she knew it. We all excitedly whispered congratulations to her when she rejoined the table. I felt bad for the final two people who had to follow her, though they turned in good sets.

Juliet closed out the showcases with a short set of thank yous to the judges, audience, and comics. "And, I have it on good authority that the bars are open for business, if any of you are interested." There was an immediate pushing back of chairs and people heading for the bars. She laughed. "I guess you're interested. Okay. We're taking a fifteen-minute break and then we'll get started with the next set of showcases. Thank you all."

There was a smattering of applause as the houselights came up. Luke, Gabby, and Philipa headed over to the bar nearest our table.

The doors to the room opened up and more people started filtering in for tonight's show. It was too early to start counting heads, but the audience felt lighter than last night. Sitting through another twenty-five comics if you didn't have to was probably not high on anyone's list.

Roger, Nick and I were still at the table. Roger was slouched down in his seat, watching Gabby as she walked away. "I can't believe I ever thought I had a chance with her."

"Roger, she really likes you. And you delivered a great set last night. You can hold your own with her."

"She's got it all: acting, singing, dancing, money." He groaned out the word money.

"Dude, just invent a stupid app, become a multi-millionaire, and you're all even again."

"Thanks," he said flatly. "I'm out."

"Kind of sexist of you," I said.

"What do you mean?"

"Taking the decision out of Gabby's hands. You've known her for two days and you already think you know what's best for her."

"I don't think that!"

"Then why don't you let her decide if she wants to date you or not?"

He looked at me. "I'm a geek."

"Yeah, and she has her issues, too. No one's perfect, not even Gabby. And she could probably use someone like you in her life that appreciates her and not her money."

"She's pretty intimidating."

"And you're being a wuss. If you want her, you better man up and do it fast, because Tim looks like he is trying to move in on your girl."

I inclined my head over to the corner bar where Gabby was in the center of half a dozen men. She was smiling, but by now I knew her well enough to see the discomfort. "Go rescue her from the riff-raff."

"I'm just more riff-raff."

"Yeah, well. You're riff-raff she knows and trusts. And likes! Go."

He bounced up from his seat and made his way over to Gabby, slowing his walk a bit as he approached. She looked up as he got there and smiled with relief. I don't know what he said, but she disengaged herself from the group with a smile and she and Roger walked off together.

"Young love," Nick said, raising his bottle of water.

"Nice to see." I returned the salute.

We had about ten minutes before the showcases started. I had over an hour before I would go up. I would hit the ladies' room about the time number nine went up, pee, check my makeup, and get back to the showroom with time to spare. Luke came back to the table and set down a beer. Amber was right behind him. He seemed to welcome her company. I had mixed feelings about that, but I also knew that I had no right to feel anything on that score. I focused on my water bottle.

Chapter 20: It's Showtime!

Juliet kicked off the show, by reintroducing Solly Vincenzo and Ross Zieff. They got a solid round of applause because no one sucks up like a comic in need of a gig. Tonight's showcases were pretty much a repeat of last night's, with the exception that I had a huge knot in my stomach. I had checked in and really, it was just a matter of pretending to enjoy the other comics while I waited my turn. I felt like one of the contestants at a beauty contest who hadn't made the cut but still had to smile during the big number. Which was ridiculous, because I hadn't even gone up yet and it was a showcase, not a competition. *Yeah, keep telling yourself that and don't think about the agent and club owner who are going to be judging you.* At least there wasn't a swimsuit competition.

Three women had gone up in the first group of ten. Amber was number six. She had a solid set and I was grateful that she didn't talk too much about her "lady parts" as the other two had. One had actually been a little too graphic. And yes, I get it, club comedy, but I am surprisingly repressed for a comic. I'm good with that.

Amber had a sweet bit about taking up golf to get closer to her dad.

"Saturday and Sunday afternoons my dad watched golf. I decided to watch with him, you know, to bond. Three minutes in, I'm lost—it's like learning a whole new language. They've got words like 'birdie,' 'eagle,' 'camel' –that's hitting it into a sand trap—" she said this last bit with pure pride. "'ferret,' 'ostrich.' I'm like, am I watching golf or Mutual of Omaha's Wild Kingdom? Then a ball goes the wrong way and they yell 'fore' instead of shouting the obvious..." she looked out at us. "Duck" someone supplied. "Thank you! Like, you've got a whole animal motif working here and now we're doing numbers?" She sounded exasperated. She got a nice laugh.

"The whole game is backwards. The guy with the lowest score wins. I'm thinking some loser made this game up." She nodded knowingly. "And jeez, who dresses these guys? Do their wives hate them that much?"

"I took some lessons so I could go golfing with him. Come to find out, 'golf' is code for going drinking with the guys. Hell, I didn't need to take lessons for that."

"We definitely bonded. When my mom is getting a little high strung, I look at my dad and say, 'You wanna go hit a bucket of balls?' He waits until we pull out of the driveway and then, every time he turns to me and says, 'Make that a bucket of highballs!' That's his joke. I laugh every time cuz he's buying."

Not a lot of women comics talk about golf. That bit would help her stand out. Although we would all take a back seat to Philipa. I was glad Amber had a good set. If someone has a crap act, I have a hard time finding something supportive to say when they come offstage. I looked over at Luke as he watched Amber. He had shaken off his earlier gloom and seemed to be watching Amber with admiration. Not that I noticed. Much.

The guy after Amber was a trainwreck. I watched the next guy try to dig his way out of the hole and decided now was a good time to hit the ladies' and get my head together. I got my brush and lipstick from Gabby and quietly got up from the table. Luke followed me through the door into the brightly lit lobby area.

"Are you going to follow me into the ladies' room?"

"No, I'll wait outside." He walked me around the corner and leaned casually against the opposite wall.

"I was going to get my energy up in there. You might be waiting a bit longer than you expect."

"Are you doing the souls bit?"

"Yeah, I need to run through the set in my head."

"I'll be here. Go do what you need to do, killer."

I went in and took care of business, freshened my makeup, and quickly went through the set, mouthing the words, but not acting anything out or stopping for the pauses. I wasn't too worried about the order—most of my bits led from one to the next. I had put the souls bit toward the end, right before my Charmin toilet paper/fart closer. If it didn't go over, the last bit would make up for it. My set wasn't as solid or as packed as Philipa's, but I could show some versatility and be a bit different from everyone else in the lineup. I looked in the mirror. Luke was right about putting that bit in tonight. I wasn't doing my act for a club full of drunks; this was for Solly and Ross. I was ready to sell the entire act hard. I did a couple of jumping jacks (yes, in heels! I am just that good) and smiled at my reflection. Time to turn on the energy.

I walked out and Luke pushed himself off the wall. He took one look at me and grinned.

"You're out for blood, aren't you?"

"You make it sound so vicious. I just want to own the stage and every other comic going up tonight. That's all."

He gave me a side hug as we walked the short distance back. "I have no doubt in my mind that you will do just that."

"You looked like you weren't super-pleased with your set. It was solid, Luke."

"Yeah. It was okay. But not Philipa level, for sure."

"It was solid." I repeated. "And the stabbing stuff was pretty edgy."

"Yeah. I was trying it out to see how it would go over. Not huge, but…"

"If you're going to get stabbed, you might as well get some mileage out of it. We'll work on it a bit to add some more and then tighten it. No one else is going to have a bit like that."

He laughed. "Let's hope not for their sakes."

"Can you do me a favor? Would you watch the judges and see if they write anything down while I'm up?"

"Sure. Did they write anything down about me?"

"As a matter of fact, they both did. But the agent did more writing."

"Works for me."

We got back to the table and I handed Gabby my things. "What number are we on?" I whispered.

"Ten. He's almost done."

I nodded. Three more then me. I looked around the table. Everyone else was done for the night. They were sitting through this waiting for me. I felt guilty and grateful at the same time.

I wondered about the way the comics were listed. At first, I thought there was no real pattern behind the order. But I realized that the final comics last night had all been headliners or features working to headliner. Amber had said she was a feature, but she had gone up pretty early in the night, when most of the openers were going up. Which explained why the guy after her had bombed—he was a new opener. There was nothing wrong with that; openers bomb all the time. We're just not that good. Our material is not as strong, we don't have as much experience. Putting Amber in a group of openers made her stand out from the others. Either she wasn't really a feature or maybe Juliet was giving little pushes here and there to help people.

Maybe she was giving little pushes for the women. *Leveling the playing field?* I smiled at the thought.

Number eleven, Steve somebody, did a nice job. Even set, good rhythm, strong punchlines. I could see the club owner make a few notes by his name. The agent wasn't paying much attention. I got up from the table and received a whispered round of "good luck" and "break a lip," the comedy equivalent of break a leg. I moved to the wall where everyone going up waited. Juliet thanked Steve and brought up the guy with the dark curls that I saw in one of Rob's sessions. I looked around for the guy who was supposed to go up before me. He should have been standing here by now. Maybe he was taking a last-minute pee. Three minutes in, he still was missing.

Juliet came by. "Where's Topher?"

"Beats me."

"Okay. He's got one more minute to get here or he's out. Looks like you're going to be next."

"Not a problem."

I glanced back at the table. Everyone was watching the comic on-stage except Amber, who was watching me. I gave her a smile and a wave. She ducked her head and turned her attention to the stage. *Weird.*

The curly-haired guy was pretty good. He talked about a lot of the stuff that most comics talk about—girlfriend, his car, sports. There were a few good punchlines but nothing really new. He had a very nice delivery though, almost a little shy and that created a likeability factor as well as a bit of a persona. He just needed stronger material. Didn't we all?

Juliet thanked him and repeated his name as he left the stage. She looked over to where I was standing, checking one last time to see if Topher had shown up.

"A little change-up in the order. Topher seems to be among the missing, so we're moving onto showcase number 14." She paused and looked over at the judges to make sure they had the right name in front of them, then she launched into my short intro. "...runner up in last year's Florida's Funniest New Comedians, please welcome Kasey McCormick."

I launched myself up the two stairs to the stage, shook Juliet's hand, and took the mic.

A six-minute set when you're used to doing twenty or twenty-five minutes goes really fast. I focused on being animated without looking like I was trying too hard.

I opened with my nearsighted bit because it has a tiny bit of physical humor—I mime walking into a wall. It's a nice opener because it is easy to understand, no complex setups, and I actually ask for applause less than thirty seconds in—it preconditions the audience to clap. (Ha! And people think I don't know what I'm doing!) It also leads directly into my dating bit which was great for this showcase. It allows me to do a couple of voices: one is a bimbo-esque squeak and the other is a TV character. Both are short pops, just enough to let the agent know I can do that. It also has a little bit at the end that is just a tad on the naughty side. It gives me a bit of an edge.

"...Shortly after that we split up. He took up with a bimbo. Excuse me, that's not politically correct. He took up with an intellectually challenged woman." I did a take to the audience and gave it a beat.

"Physically victorious." I tilted my head, as if it had just occurred to me.

"Virginally impaired." Boom. Big laugh.

"Repeatedly." I got the tag laugh.

"I'd hate to malign the tramp." I gave a big grin to the audience to let them know that I took great pleasure in maligning her. "Oh please, she had the names and phone numbers of hundreds of men written on her vaginal wall. Kind of like the Viet Nam Memorial, but bigger."

I heard a woman say, "Oh my God" somewhere among the laughs. I plunged on.

"I'm gonna flat out say it: She was stupid. She was what I call one of those Etch-A-Sketch girls. They shake their heads and everything's erased." I shook my head from side to side, bopped my own nose, and made a squeaky "huh" sound and got a good laugh. It's a set up line. "Which is okay because there's always some guy around ready to twist her knobs and set her back up again." I mimed twisting a breast. Women and men laugh at that joke, but the men don't know the women are laughing for a different reason than they are. I gave a knowing smirk.

I took a pause and let the audience settle down a bit. I didn't have a segue into the Souls bit so I pretended a thought had just occurred to me.

"Hey hey! Did you hear about this? I saw a headline in the newspaper the other day, Britain Considers Recycling Graves." I paused for a fraction of a second. "Initial Reaction Negative." I moved my hand across to indicate the imaginary sub headline.

I did a take to the audience. "You don't say."

"Apparently in Europe, they've run out of space, so they dig up the old bodies to make room for the new. Kind of freshening up the place. It will probably be the next reality TV show: Extreme Grave Makeover." That got a fair laugh.

"Of course, they've got to get the family's permission to dig up the old body. It's only polite."

I hit the mic three times to make a knocking sound. I launched into my not-very-good British accent. It's good enough for Americans apparently. This part was almost a throwback to Bob Newhart's phone conversation bits. I like to think it's an homage.

"You want to what? Dig up me mum? Took me 35 years to get her out of the 'ouse." Pause for a beat as if listening to someone. "Well, you can't bring her here. Not enough room. Not to mention the smell. That's why we buried her in the first place." I switched back to my normal voice. "The English, so sentimental."

"I got to thinking, if the cemeteries are overcrowded, then heaven must be absolutely jammed. At that point, there's only one thing to do." I looked out at the audience expectantly. "Call in the Disney people."

I shielded the mic with my hand and pitched my voice lower. "This is God. Get me Bob Iger. No. *I'm* God. He just thinks he is." It's a little inside, but this was California. Both the agent and the club owner laughed. I checked.

"Next thing you know, the velvet ropes and stanchions are being set up. You start doing the Disney shuffle." I put my hands stiffly by my sides and mimed walking in a queue, making the turns. I stopped and looked up at an imaginary sign.

"Only 400 years from this point. That's faster than Space Mountain." Knowing laughs. Nothing like shared experiences.

"Finally, you reach that big tram in the sky. You get a three-minute ride through heaven, end up in the gift shop. And an angel's voice floats over you:"

This is where the delivery is everything, because really, it's not that funny. But there's a certain "resort park inflection" that all the announcers and tour guides use and I had it down pat.

"The sidewalk is moving at the same speed as your tram. Please look about the car for any emotional baggage you may have brought with you, take small souls by the hand, and exit to the right. Have a heavenly day."

Again, people recognized the experience and laughed. I shrugged like it was nothing and pivoted to my close, which is, I am not proud to say this, a bit about Charmin toilet paper. Okay, it's really a fart joke. I get to act a little bit exasperated and outraged. And it always works. Which is what you want your closer to do. And it did. Like a charm. I thanked the audience and Juliet came back on the stage and gave me a hug. And if you think people don't notice when you get a hug from the host as opposed to a handshake, you are sadly mistaken. I knew it was because I had been helping her with the blackmail situation. Solly and Ross did not. It was a mini-endorsement and I appreciated it. Everything helps at this stage.

I was number fourteen. I assumed Topher never came back, because I was sure Juliet would have fit him in at the end of the lineup. We did get six minutes of Chad. He was—disappointingly—pretty good, if foul-mouthed. He had not upgraded his look. He took the stage in black jeans and the ubiquitous untucked shirt, and running shoes. A couple of minutes in, he started a set up with "I'm sure some of you people here are hating on me," and as he took his beat, Gabby said "At least ten of us" which was the exact number of special showcase participants. Apparently, our girl had some pent-up anger in her because it was louder than she probably meant it to be. There was a ripple of laughter through the audience as people did the math. Chad's face turned red and he forced a laugh. "I had that coming." He got a real laugh on that one and he continued on with his set. It won him a bit of likeability but I could see the defensive stiffness in his movements for the next minute or so. He seemed to relax back down but he didn't wait for Juliet to come back onstage at the close of his set. He brushed past her as she came up. Poor etiquette.

Juliet pretended not to notice. "Chad Warder, from Atlanta, ladies and gentlemen" garnering him a second and undeserved round of applause.

Gabby leaned in and whispered, "Do you think he knows it was me?"

"He can't be sure." I could tell she was already feeling bad about needling him. "That was so perfectly timed, Gabby. I am in awe."

She smiled and leaned back. Her right hand was in her lap but I would have bet money she was clenching and unclenching it.

We dutifully sat through the rest of the comics. The audience was noticeably smaller tonight and it had thinned further as we got to the last few sets. I was starving, but a sense of fairness kept me in my seat. They sat through me; I'd support them.

When the houselights finally came up, we were all ready for a meal.

"I cannot eat at the pool bar one more time. At least not today," Gabby said.

"I need breakfast foods. Do you think the restaurant might have a late-night omelet?" I asked.

"Only one way to find out," Philipa said. "Let's move. My ass fell asleep four comics ago."

We settled into a booth at the back of the restaurant. There were still people eating even though it was late. We put in our orders, which included another round of drinks. Almost everyone was several drinks ahead of me. I was fine with that—I'm a bit of a lightweight and I hadn't eaten since my snackie-snack at 5:30.

The server put the drinks in front of us and Roger raised up his glass. "To us. We are damn funny people."

There was a chorus of "Here, here" and a lot of clinking.

We probably sounded like the mutual admiration society, talking about everyone's sets. Chad was a brief topic of conversation, but really, we were in too good a mood to give him much of our time.

Luke looked over at me. "The souls bit went over."

I nodded. "Yeah. Did they take any notes?"

"Solly scribbled something."

"I'll take it."

"Hey, what happened to the guy ahead of you?" Philipa asked. "All of a sudden, you were getting called up."

"I know, right? He bailed, I guess." I shrugged.

Gabby spoke up. "That would have thrown me. I mean, I'm new and all, but if I'm going up and the guy in front of me disappears..." she trailed off.

Nick nodded. "Yeah, you're not quite in the right headspace when you think you've got another five or ten minutes."

Amber was watching us all. "Well, Kasey is a pro. It takes more than getting your time slot moved up to throw her." Her words were kind, but the tone was just a bit off.

"Well, I'd already peed, so at that point..." I grinned at her.

"We're eating here," Roger said, but he laughed along with everyone else.

A warning bell chimed in my head. I tested my theory. "Still, it was weird that he just disappeared." I was watching Amber's reaction. "Do you think something bad might have happened to him?"

People grunted or shrugged.

"He probably just chickened out. I mean, performing in front of other comics is always hard, especially when you're an opener," Amber said.

"He's an opener?" I nodded as if that explained things. "How do you know him?"

"Oh, we just got talking after one of the sessions. His name is unusual which is why I knew who he was." She looked away uncomfortably.

"Was that the guy you were having drinks with earlier?" Philipa asked. "He looked like he was getting trashed."

"Yeah. He skipped the second afternoon session and started drinking early. Maybe he passed out in his room." Amber started peeling the label off her bottle of beer.

"If I paid two hundred and fifty dollars for something, I'd show up," Roger commented.

"Me, too. Now I'm curious. I'll check with Juliet tomorrow to see if she knows what happened to him." I swished a piece of pancake around in a pool of syrup and popped it in my mouth. There's nothing better than breakfast food late at night.

The talk turned to other subjects but I kept half an eye on Amber. Something was up with her. We were discussing who was taking which sessions the next day when all of a sudden, I was exhausted. The adrenaline had worn off and my head started to pound again. I caught the server's eye and signaled for my check.

The server asked if anyone else needed anything, and came back in a few minutes with all our checks. We walked out as a group, but Philipa, Amber, and Luke split off, heading for a nightcap in the lounge. Roger and Nick escorted us to our rooms.

"Let me take a look at your cut, as long as I'm here." Nick's voice was a little louder than normal.

We went into Gabby's room, leaving Roger and Gabby in the hall. The door was unlocked between the two rooms and we walked through. Nick flipped on the bathroom light.

"This has the best lighting."

"I thought you were just giving Roger and Gabby some alone time."

"I am. But I want to check you out. Headache is back?"

"Yeah. It's funny. No matter how bad I feel before I go up, I never hurt onstage."

He nodded. "Adrenaline, partially. And you're focusing on something other than what hurts. Once you drop that focus…"

"Yeah. It's like all my energy disappeared in an instant."

"Take two Acetaminophen."

"And call you in the morning? Really?"

"Old jokes still work." He laughed softly. "Get some sleep. Your shiner is really going to come out tomorrow. It's starting to go purple and yellow under the makeup."

"Lovely. Thanks for taking such good care of me."

"Anytime." He went back through the door to leave from Gabby's room. "I'll tell Gabby to hurry it up so you can get to bed."

"Roger won't appreciate that."

"Roger will do just fine. Patience works for those who are in it for the long run."

I gave him a little smile. Message received.

Gabby came through the door a minute later, looking happier than I had ever seen her. I did the mature thing and started singing the kissing song at her. She just grinned.

"I told you he liked you."

"Yes, he does."

"Good. Now get out of my room. I'm so tired I am ready to fall asleep standing up."

We hugged good night and I closed the door between the rooms. Five minutes later, face washed, teeth brushed, jammies on, I was in bed and on my way to dreamland.

Normally, I sleep like the proverbial rock. I went down like a tranquilized gazelle, only to wake up two hours later with my head pounding. I wondered if I could take more Acetaminophen or if I had to wait. Coffee was good for a headache. I knew just where to get some.

Chapter 21: You Always Hurt the One You Love

"Geez, Stavon. You do work all the time."

Not gonna lie: I walked into the lobby hoping he'd be there. He was easy to talk to and had a way of looking at things that gave the situation clarity. Plus, his coffee rocked.

"Buying a resort costs money. I've got to save up."

"I don't want to harsh your buzz, but it's gonna take a lot more hours to have enough to buy a resort."

"Of course. I will ladder up. Buy a motel. Fix it up. Make it profitable. Sell it for a down payment on a better hotel. Fix it up. Make it profitable. Like shampoo. Rinse repeat, but every time I start with better hair." He smiled. "Eventually, I will have enough cash flow and a history of success to get the financing for the kind of property I really want."

"You've got a plan."

"Yes. Now, I do. Life throws you a ball with a curve."

"When you least expect it."

"Where you least expect it."

I looked at him. "Sounds like a story."

"Oh, it's a sad story. You don't need a sad story."

"You have listened to mine. I owe you."

"There is no owing between friends. Real friends." He smiled but his eyes were sad.

"So, your tale of woe..." I led in.

"First, coffee." He went into the back and returned with two fresh cups of coffee. I added cream from the little stainless-steel creamer and stirred in some sugar. I looked at him expectantly.

"I come from a very wealthy family." He paused. "I am the oldest son, so much is expected of me. But, if I meet these expectations, much will be given to me."

"And those expectations?"

"Very simple. Do well at university, go into the family business, help my father until it is my time to take over."

"Very normal."

"Yes, with one little catch: Marry the woman you are supposed to marry."

"Arranged marriage?" I tried to keep the surprise out of my voice. He nodded.

"I take it you're not in love with the girl." It was the obvious issue.

"And she's not in love with me. But love has little to do with it. In our circles, marriage is a business alliance. With luck, you like and respect the other person. You treat each other well because you don't want to cause a... break? It's not quite the right word."

"A rift? Or a break, sure. Nice girl?"

"Very nice girl."

"But you love another." I was feeling clever, treating this like just a story. "And this is where the problem comes in. Who is she, the one you love?"

"She," he paused, "is the brother of the woman I was betrothed to." He pursed his lips.

"Oops. Did not see that coming."

"And he feels the same way about me."

"That's good!"

"Yes and no. It's good, but it's impossible." Stavon was becoming agitated. "He is also betrothed to a woman. I tell him I cannot marry his sister when I am in love with him. I tried to talk him into coming away with me. I want to break off the betrothal to his sister. I want him to break off his betrothal."

"But he doesn't."

"No. But I cannot live a lie. I don't want to live a lie. So, I break my betrothal. She is crying every day because now she is ruined—a broken engagement. Obviously, people think there is something horribly wrong with her. No other man will want her. Her family is berating her—she obviously did something wrong. But Raj cannot stand seeing his sister cry. He blurts out that I am a homosexual."

"Whoa! He outed you?"

"I don't think it was malicious. Raj is tenderhearted. His father was beating his sister. What could he do? He just wanted to protect her."

I nodded. "Don't suppose he thought to mention that he was gay?"

Stavon gave a short laugh. "That would be the no. Then, of course, their father calls a meeting with my father. My father asks if it is true, if I am homosexual. I am done with living a lie. I tell him the truth. Yes. I am homosexual." He drank some more of his coffee. "And so, I am no longer part of the family. I do not exist. My brother steps into my place, marries Prarthana. And I..." he faltered. "I make my own way."

"They just threw you out?" I was horrified.

"It is not uncommon. It is not uncommon here in these United States."

"So, you had to start from nothing."

"Oh, no. I have a university degree. I had my own money that I had gophered away."

I smiled but didn't correct him. He caught me.

"What?"

"Squirreled. You squirrel away money, like a squirrel hides acorns for the coming winter."

"Ah, squirrel. I squirrel the money. I had more than enough to get to Paris and live while I attended culinary school. With a degree from there, I know I can go anywhere in the world, any restaurant, any hotel, and get a job. I have jewelry I can sell if I ever need to. My mother sends me money behind my father's back. She is a squirrel, too." His face twisted. "My only regret is that it is hard for my mother."

"It's hard for you, too."

"Yes. But I am young. Everything is in front of me."

"Do you ever hear from Raj?"

"No." His face hardened. "I know why he did it. I understand. I forgive him but…"

"That was a betrayal you don't forget."

He nodded. "I forgive. I don't forget. No one can hurt you as much as those you are closest to."

I drank the last of my coffee as he said that and I almost choked.

"Kasey, are you okay?"

"Yes. But you're right. Betrayal comes from those closest to you."

"Sadly, yes."

"Stavon, if I hit it big, I'm investing in your resorts."

"From your lips to God's ears."

I gave him a quick peck on the cheek. "And you will find love again. You are too good to sit on the shelf."

"Business first. With enough money, no one can ever tell me who I can or cannot love."

Stavon had spoken truth. You have to be who you are. If you're going to move forward with your life, you have to step into yourself, you have to be yourself. I walked back to the elevator bank, thinking about people wanting to be seen in a different way. Or maybe just wanting to be seen. Wasn't that why we were all here? I pressed the button for four and thought about what Stavon said, how people who have known you a long time don't want you to change. You're a known quantity and they don't want to have to relearn you. Known quantity. I thought back to what Rob had said about certain actors being hired because the producer or director was confident in their abilities to do the job. There was something there, but I couldn't connect the dots. I really didn't even know if it was important or not.

I lay in bed thinking about stage personas and people hiding the parts of themselves they didn't like or in Juliet's case, felt guilty about. We hold ourselves back by being afraid to be ourselves. But the people we are drawn to are the ones who are comfortable with who they are. It's not that they don't try to become better versions of themselves, but they know who they are and they are good with it. Nick was there. Luke was getting there. I was not even close and Gabby, poor Gabby! She had a lot to chew through.

I fell back to sleep only to have a strange dream involving Juliet and Amber drinking while a faceless drunk guy was passed out at their table, his head in his arms. Danny came by and yelled at Juliet because she was late for class and was going to flunk the mid-term. Juliet looked at Amber and said, "You shouldn't have gotten me drunk!" and Amber laughed and said, "But it's two-for-one!" Then they all ordered another round and made toasts to the drunk guy who they kept calling Two-fer. A glass fell off the table and smashed to the floor and I woke up. The sound in my dream had come from Gabby's room. I heard her say "Damn!" The bedside clock read 5:10 am. What the hell was she doing up at this hour?

Chapter 22: You Never Know When You Might Need an Emergency Bagel

I knocked on the door between our rooms. "Gabby? Are you okay?"

"Shit." Then, "Sorry."

The door knob turned and I made way for Gabby to come in.

I took in the cute workout ensemble (really, it was an ensemble). "Going to work out? This early?"

"No, I just threw this on. I couldn't sleep."

I sighed inwardly. That meant I wasn't going back to sleep, either.

"Tell you what, let me put something on and we can go grab coffee in the lobby."

I threw on some leggings and a big shirt (NOT an ensemble) grabbed some money and my keycard. We switched rooms and went out the respective doors. The elevator dinged softly as the doors opened at the lobby level. It was, for the most part, deserted. Stavon was gone and a light-haired man was behind the lobby desk, laughing at something on his computer screen. He stood politely as we came through.

"May I help you?"

"We were hoping to grab a cup of coffee. Too early for the restaurant?"

"Yes, but you're in luck. The night crew just brought out a fresh carafe." He raised up a cup from behind the desk. "It's on the table across from the restaurant."

We gave him an enthusiastic thanks and went around the corner to the restaurant. The coffee was set up as promised, but the restaurant area was dark.

"Kind of creepy," Gabby said.

"Yeah, let's drink this out by the pool. Sun should be coming up and we can enjoy that along with the coffee."

We continued down the hallway to the pool. The area was deserted, as expected. Some light bled out from the hotel hallway and we could see the walkways leading to and from the pool area outlined with low level landscaping lights. Most of the pool and deck area was in shadow. We stretched out on lounge chairs, with our coffee on a table between us.

"Now this is the life," I said, taking a sip.

We could hear the water lapping at the pool sides. There was the quiet sound of the pump humming. Light was just starting to tinge the edges of the sky.

"I think the last time I saw a sunrise was at summer camp," Gabby said. "I used to go for eight weeks every summer. Performing arts camp."

I didn't even know they had those. "I never went to camp. I think one of my brothers went to Boy Scout camp one year." With six kids, there wasn't a lot of money for extra stuff like camp in my family.

We weren't poor, but eight weeks of some expensive camp for six kids would add up fast. "Eight weeks?"

"Yeah, it was a whole summer curriculum. Music, dance, performing. Gymnastics if you did that. I mean, we did the fun camp stuff, too. Swimming, canoeing, cookouts." She trailed off.

"Making s'mores around the campfire." There was no response. "Gabby?"

"Now that I think about it, the cookouts probably weren't ordinary camp cookouts. How embarrassing."

"What?"

"I am just now realizing that... this is horrible." She took a long drink of coffee. "I'm just now realizing that it was probably all catered. We had steak and grilled lobster and French fries and an entire dessert bar every time."

I started laughing. "Oh. My. God. For real?" I was so glad I hadn't had a mouthful of coffee; it would have come out my nose.

"We thought we were camping!"

"Oh, my God. You have GOT to put that in your act!"

"I was today years old..."

We dissolved into laughter.

"It feels good to laugh," she said quietly. Almost an afterthought.

We talked for a while about the showcases and the whole mess that Chad had created.

The darkness was fading and the tables and chairs of the pool table were just starting to separate from the night. I looked at the pool and saw a shadow.

"What's that in the pool?"

Gabby looked over. "Where?"

"Down the other end. Something's floating down there."

"Maybe one of those lounge floats."

We sat up in our chairs for a better view. A dark figure was floating in the pool. We started walking the short distance to that end of the pool.

It was still too dark to see clearly. I took my phone out of my pocket, flipped on the flashlight app and shone it on the dark mass. It was a body, face down in the water. There was something beside the body, but I couldn't quite make out what.

"Not just a pool float," I said flatly.

Gabby gasped in horror. "We have to do something."

"I'm pretty sure we're past that," I said. "We've been sitting out here for over twenty minutes and never heard a splash."

Gabby was frozen, staring at the body. I had to get her out of there. Hell, I'd like to get me out of there.

"Gabby, we need to get someone from the hotel to call the police."

She didn't react.

"Gabby? Go to the front desk, tell them there's a body in the pool and you need the police." I took her by the shoulders and forcibly turned her towards the doors leading back to the lobby. "Go get help. Now."

She nodded and headed back into the hotel. I checked the time. Almost 6:00 am. There would be more people up now. Hotel personnel would be coming in for the day shift, guests would be heading for the workout room. I hoped no one wanted to take an early morning swim.

I played the light over the body. I realized with a sinking feeling that it was Darlana DeLuz. She was still dressed in the black gauzy outfit she had been wearing last night at the showcase. Her blonde ringlets dark from the water, flowed around her. Floating next to her was a big inflatable dolphin pool toy. It looked like Darlana was riding it and it had tipped over sideways.

I blinked and tilted my head, then I tilted the flashlight to different angles. It was a strange and surreal sight. I wondered if I was still in bed, dreaming. No such luck.

Gabby arrived back with a security guard. He flipped a switch and the pool lights came on along with seemingly every other light in the vicinity. It was even more surreal in the light.

"Shit." The security guard got out his two-way radio and connected with the front desk. "We've got a floater. Call the cops and send whoever's around to help me secure the area."

He walked over to the pool pump shed and came back with a pool hook.

"Are you supposed to do that?" I asked.

"Can't leave her floating in the middle of the pool. And I don't want anyone looking down from their room and seeing this."

"Not your first time?"

"No. Doesn't happen that often and I wish it never happened. People get drinking, think it would be fun to go for a swim..." He shook his head and extended the hook to its full length. I snapped off a couple of quick pictures with my phone. Cops might want them.

Gabby had sat herself down sideways on one of the lounge chairs. She was watching the security guy, but not really seeing him. Her hand was clenching and unclenching rhythmically. I sat down next to her and took her hand.

There was a weird lapping sound as the security guard pulled the body closer to the edge and over to the pool steps. He looked down at the body and then over to us. "Do you have any idea who this is?"

"Yeah. She's one of the instructors at our seminar. Darlana DeLuz." I thought for a minute. "Someone needs to contact Juliet Hartwell. It's her seminar. She needs to know."

The security guard spoke into his radio again. He angled the pool hook so it secured Darlana's body in the stair area. I looked away and then back again. The dolphin pool float had come with her. I wondered if perhaps rigor mortis had clamped her legs around the float. But that didn't make sense. It takes a couple of hours for rigor mortis to set in—I'd watched enough episodes of *CSI* to know that. Why was the dolphin still attached to her?

I walked over to the edge of the pool and forced myself to look at her body. Her ankles were tied under the float. I nudged the security guard to look.

"Yeah. I saw that. Pool is definitely closed today."

Darlana's death summed up as an inconvenience to the guests. I felt sorry for her. I went back to where Gabby was sitting and took up my seat next to her again. Gabby had been crying.

"This is how she's going to be remembered. Drowning on a plastic dolphin."

"Slightly better than being remembered for the STD commercial she did." Did I mention I'm a blurter?

"Oh my God!" But then she let out a little giggle. "She did a sexually transmitted disease commercial?"

"It was in her presentation. I hear they get paid extra for that."

"Well, she was that much ahead of me."

"You might want to skip that stage of your career."

We waited because we really didn't know what else to do. We could see hotel staff setting up "Pool Closed" signs. A couple of maintenance men set up a portable screen so Darlana's body was hidden from view. At least ground floor view. Someone who must have been the night manager came out to talk to the security guard. Then he walked over to us.

"The police are on their way. They're going to want to talk with you."

"I figured." I didn't feel the need to mention that this was not my first rodeo.

"What were you doing out here?" he asked.

"Just sitting and talking. Having coffee."

"And you didn't see or hear anything?"

"It was dark and the pool lights were off. But as the sun started coming up…" I didn't finish. Someone who works nights knows how darkness turns to shapes and then the shapes become recognizable objects.

His radio crackled with the news that the police had arrived. He walked toward the doors closest to the lobby and two cops came through at almost the same time. I watched him shake hands and the three walked together to the pool stairs. They seemed to know the security guard. I wondered how many people had drowned in that pool. Then I realized that the night shift cops and night shift security chief would probably know each other better from handling unruly drunks and whatever thefts took place. There was always something happening at a hotel; most guests are oblivious. The hotels liked to keep it that way.

One of the cops radioed for the Medical Examiner and I heard him say the words possible homicide. I didn't see how she could have tied her own feet around the dolphin, but maybe it was a weird sex accident. I try to keep my knowledge of kinky sex limited. I might not be a practicing Catholic anymore, but some things stay with you for life. And she had seemed kind of turned on by the whole dolphin thing. Southern California. Anything was possible.

The other cop made his way over to us.

"You two found the body."

"Yes, sir," Gabby squeaked out.

He took down our names and asked how long we would be staying at the hotel. Got our cell phone numbers, too. Then he got down to the real business.

"What were you doing here in the dark?"

I took over. "We woke up early. We're still on East Coast time. We came down for coffee and decided to sit out by the pool instead of sitting in a dark corridor." I indicated our cups sitting on the table where we'd been.

"When did you arrive?"

I thought back. "Maybe around 5:30? The desk clerk saw us."

"And you didn't hear or see anything?"

"No. It was dark. The pool lights weren't on. Then, as it got lighter, we saw a shape in the pool."

"Pool lights were off?"

"Definitely."

He jotted that down in his notebook. "And you recognize the victim."

Gabby nodded and her eyes welled up again.

"Darlana DeLuz. She's one of the instructors for the seminar. I was in one of her sessions the first day and we've seen her in the group sessions."

The cop looked at Gabby's face. "Did you know her well?"

"No. Not at all. It's just... so horrible."

He nodded. Just then Juliet came through the door and ran up to us.

"What happened?"

"And you are?"

"Juliet Hartwell. I'm in charge of the seminar." She was looking around wildly. A second later she realized the black clump in the pool was Darlana.

"Oh my God!" She made a move to go to the body but the cop stopped her.

"We need you to stay back for now. We've got a forensics team coming. I'm going to need your information." He looked at Juliet a little more closely. "You're that lady comedian."

Juliet nodded. As she spoke with the cop, I could see a small number of people looking out the windows at the pool. I saw Danny's blond hair and a few seconds later, the door open and he joined us.

"Danny!" she hugged him and started crying. "It's Darlana. She's dead. This is a disaster."

I wasn't sure if she was talking about Darlana's death or if she was just worried about bad publicity for the seminar. I am not particularly charitable on one cup of coffee.

Danny put a comforting arm around her. "We'll get through this, Jules. It will be all right."

The officers asked Juliet and Danny a few questions. I broke in. "Are you done with us? You've got our contact information."

"The detectives will most likely want to speak to you, but that could take a while."

"We're not going anywhere. Just call and we'll make ourselves available."

The cop looked around but the detectives hadn't arrived on the scene yet and neither had the medical examiner. I could tell he didn't want to let us go, but there was no reason to keep us standing on the pool deck. Or sitting. We'd been cooperative. We were booked in for another night at the hotel.

"I really need more coffee," I said.

"Don't we all," he mumbled. "Yeah. Keep her identity under wraps. Not a word to anyone. We'll need to notify next of kin."

He turned back to questioning Juliet and Danny. "Have you noticed anything strange or suspicious about the victim's behavior in the past few days? Maybe boyfriend trouble?"

I heard Juliet answer in the negative and I was glad the cop couldn't see my face because my eyebrows shot up so far they probably disappeared into my hairline.

Gabby looked at me and I could tell she was about to say something.

"Just keep walking. Nothing to see here. We'll talk when we get back to the room."

We both entered through my door. No pretenses right now. I called down to room service to get coffee and bagels sent up. There was no way we could hit the breakfast buffet without being bombarded with questions from people.

"Did you hear Juliet say everything was normal?" Gabby was incredulous.

"Yes, I did and we're going to pretend to Juliet and Danny *and* the cops that we did NOT hear that. I don't know why Juliet lied to the cops, but it's not a good sign."

"Do you think the cops think we did it?"

"Well, they're going to look at us, that's for sure. But we don't have any motive and the desk clerk can put us in the lobby around 5:30 am. So, we're not going to be their leading suspects."

"My father will kill me if he finds out about this!"

"Your father will call an incredibly over-priced lawyer who will intimidate the police commissioner or whoever is in charge out here and the detectives will treat you with kid gloves," I observed.

"Spooky. It's like you've met my father."

"I just know that people with money have connections and a few phone calls solve a lot of problems. Let's hope we don't need to tell your dad."

She nodded. "What if the detectives ask us about Darlana?"

"We tell the truth."

"All of it?"

"Yeah. Not our circus, not our monkeys. If Juliet wants to lie, that's her thing. We don't have a vested interest here. I'm not lying to the cops for someone I met three days ago."

Gabby nodded, unsure.

"Juliet is supposed to do the first session today. It will be interesting to see if she shows up."

"I can't imagine having to do a presentation after waking up to that," Gabby said.

"Let's get showered and dressed. Coffee is coming and time is tight."

There was a knock on the door.

"Right on cue," I smiled.

We poured ourselves coffee and I managed to grab a couple of bites of bagel before jumping in the shower. Gabby, of course, just had coffee, black. We kept the door open between the rooms while we showered and changed. I wolfed down the rest of my bagel waiting for Gabby to finish and wrapped up the other bagel for later. You never knew when you might need an emergency bagel.

The first session was starting late. No surprise there. Juliet was supposed to be leading the Book Yourself Solid training and all the attendees were gathered in the main meeting room. It was ten past the hour and people were restless.

Of course, the rumor mill was going full tilt boogie. It was hard to miss the police presence at the pool. The hot rumor was that someone had drowned in the pool and I felt no need to name that someone. Our little group, Gabby, Nick, Luke, and Roger were the only ones who knew Darlana was dead. Danny and Juliet knew, of course, but they had yet to make an appearance. From the way Robbie and Mo were whispering together and looking around, I suspected they didn't know yet, either.

I saw Robbie check his phone. He shook his head, said something to Mo, and disappeared into the back for a couple of minutes. He came back with a sheaf of notes and grabbed Mo by the hand, leading her onstage with him. They turned each other's mic battery packs on.

"Good morning," Rob's voice came over the speakers and we all quieted down.

"Sorry for the delay in getting started. Juliet had an emergency come up and Mo and I are going to pinch hit for her. As it so happens, I am incredibly brilliant at getting and staying booked. And Mo is going to open up your eyes to the joy of high-paying corporate gigs and how to get them."

Mo took a seat in a director's chair and Rob moved to center stage. "How did I get so good at filling my calendar?" He rubbed his head, looked down at the floor, and sighed. "It's a very sad story but as with many things we learn the hard way, some good came out of it. Short version: I came home from two weeks on the road one Monday and found my wife had cleaned out our bank accounts, taken most of our worldly possessions, and, well, left me."

We groaned in sympathy.

"Her loss, Rob!" a woman called out.

He grinned. "Thank you! I like to think so. It gets a bit better. She didn't just leave me—she had maxed out our joint credit cards, including taking cash advances, and the only thing I had to my name besides my devilishly handsome looks, was my nine-year-old car with a couple hundred thousand miles on it—"

"Road car!" a guy shouted.

"Oh yeah. It was beaten pretty badly. So, my gorgeous face, my beat-up car, and the checks from the two clubs I had just worked." He took a beat. "And I was a feature."

We all groaned again. Feature pay was barely subsistence level.

"Fortunately, it was enough to cover the next month's rent, but I also like to eat. And have electricity. So, I needed to bring in cash like yesterday. That's when I learned how to book myself solid. Now, Mo is going to come at it from a different angle later in the session, and that's how to leverage your experience into better paying private gigs."

Mo gave a little wave, and returned to furiously scribbling notes for herself while Rob spoke.

Rob pulled one of the director's chairs towards the front of the stage. "I'm going to sit back in my chair and drink my coffee while I do this because I am NOT a morning person." Then he launched into what he did to get booked and make sure his calendar was only empty when he wanted it to be.

Considering they were thrown into it at the last minute, Rob and Mo did a great job covering the topic. It was possibly not as well organized as Juliet's presentation would have been, but we got some good real-world tips on getting booked as well as picking up last-minute, fill-in gigs. I knew the clubs in my area had their back up comics lined up; every so often I got a call seeing if I was available to fill in on short notice. I made a note to myself of a couple of "pop-up" clubs to contact, those clubs that used local hotel bars or meeting rooms to run a comedy night. Rob advised contacting meeting and event planners and the venues themselves to get listed as a fill-in emcee, something I hadn't thought of yet. He also told us to go to benefits and charity events to get a feel for how clean the comedy acts were and to watch how the emcees moved things along.

"If you work clean, you can pick up a lot of gigs. These are the gigs that you will hear comics make fun of, but they pay well. Believe me, if they could land those gigs, they wouldn't be making fun of them. Private gigs pay way better than clubs and you can make obscene amounts of money with corporate gigs."

Mo stepped up at that point. "Speaking of obscene amounts of money, I hold improv workshops for trial attorneys as well as work with some of those clients one-on-one. Trial attorneys have to be able to think on their feet and improv is great training for that. Courtrooms are sort of weird little theatres—an attorney has to be able to convincingly act as if his client is not guilty, even when he knows the guy is a three-time loser. Law firms are very good about hiring coaches to help their team members level up, whether it's in courtroom theatrics, learning how to bring in business, or even getting over shyness to deal with clients effectively. I do improv for the love of it, but honestly, there's not a lot of money in it. It's really not a living wage until you get up to my level. Attorneys keep me in premium tequila."

Mo showed us how she constructed various trainings: ninety minutes, half day, and full day events. I was very sure I wasn't ready for that, but maybe one day this information would come in handy. I wasn't the only one taking a lot of notes—I could hear people around me scribbling or tapping on their tablets.

They did ten minutes of question and answer and then we broke for coffee and pastries. The body in the pool was momentarily forgotten. I wondered how long it would be before the news of Darlana's death hit.

As we were walking out to the next session, I saw Juliet come through the side door. She looked around and quickly signaled to Rob and Mo to follow her to the back area. I had a feeling they were about to get the bad news about Darlana. Rob had the Handling Hecklers session next. I wondered if Juliet would actually make it to the Cruise Ship Bookings session I had been looking forward to. The sense of gloom, that had been hanging over me all morning deepened.

Chapter 23: Crime Scene Tape is a Conversation Starter

Juliet did make the Cruise Ship session, but she was distracted and a bit flat. Not that I expected her to be Little Mary Sunshine, but I could tell other people in the session felt a bit confused.

I was disappointed, though, because this was a subject I particularly wanted to hone in on. Cruise ship work paid well and Florida had a lot of cruise ships coming in and out. You used to have to be squeaky clean, but audiences have grown more sophisticated (which is code for they aren't shocked by the F-bomb) and most cruise lines had a late-night comedy show that included "adult" material. There are ranks as to how dirty comics can be. You never want the opening act to be dirty because it brings down the "level" of the room. If you've got a somewhat clean headliner, the opener is probably going to offend the headliner's audience. And it's the headliner who puts butts in the seats.

I took notes but found myself almost as distracted as Juliet seemed. Gabby was in the session with me and a few times, when Juliet got lost in her notes or backtracked, she shot me a questioning look. I shrugged.

The session actually let out about five minutes early and people seemed eager to grab some lunch.

"Kasey, could I have a minute?" Juliet asked.

"Sure."

Gabby stayed with me and Juliet gave a questioning look.

"Gabby's been helping me out trying to figure out who is black-mailing you."

Juliet nodded. "First, I just want to thank you both for keeping Darlana's drowning quiet."

"Of course," I said. "But we all know she didn't drown."

Juliet's eyes flashed and then she looked down at the floor. "No. The police said it was a homicide. I spent over an hour with them this morning and I probably have to go back tomorrow."

"Did you tell them you were being blackmailed?"

"No. Danny said it was unrelated and it would just complicate things."

"That's not going to play out well if they find out about the black-mail, Juliet." I was concerned. I'm not a total goody-two-shoes, but the idea of lying to the police in a murder investigation did not sit well with me. Then again, I hadn't mentioned it, either.

"Well, the blackmailer is complicating things all on his own" She pulled out her phone and flipped through to her email messages. "He knows I made $10,000 on the private showcases. He wants that money, too!"

She handed me the phone and I looked at the message. It was nasty:

There's a reason why the cops are looking at you for Darlana's death and we both know it's because you're no innocent. You killed Ted all those years ago and you had a fight with Darlana the day before she died. I can make sure the cops sew this case up fast. You've already killed one person. It won't be hard to make them believe you've done it again.

Unless you pay me the $10,000 you collected for the private showcases, the person they'll be arresting for Darlana's murder is YOU. I'll be in touch.

"Does the blackmailer always contact you by email?"

Juliet nodded miserably.

"Can't Danny trace it back? He's an Internet guy," Gabby asked.

"He's been trying ever since this began. No luck. Says the guy goes through multiple servers and uses a VPN or something." She looked up at the ceiling, trying not to cry. "What am I going to do? Most of that money was going to pay Danny back. I'm barely going to clear enough on this event to cover my own bills."

"I'm sure Danny will understand," I began.

"He needs the money, too. He loaned it to me but said he needed it back by the end of this month. It would have been tight, but we had enough people signed up that he knew I could pay him back." She sighed. "He didn't ask for any interest or anything. Just a loan from one friend to another."

"Ten thousand dollars is a good friend." I said flatly.

"If I pay the blackmailer, I can possibly pay Danny back half..." Juliet was thinking out loud.

"But then you're still stuck owing money and having someone bleed you dry," I said. "We need to stop this guy once and for all."

Juliet nodded. She was back to looking down at her phone. "What am I going to do?" she asked in a whisper.

Gabby moved over beside Juliet and took her hand. "We're going to find whoever is doing this to you and get you free. Look at me."

Juliet looked up and met Gabby's eyes. "This is going to be settled this weekend. Kasey and the rest of us are working on it and we're making progress. It's going to be okay." She nodded at Juliet who automatically nodded back.

"How do you normally get the money to the blackmailer?" I asked.

"It's a little different every time. I leave the money in an envelope addressed to a different name each time at a place that has a lot of walk-up traffic. Sometimes it's a ticket booth. Or a hotel front desk or concierge. One time it was a coffee shop. He instructed me to leave it with the cashier and say I was supposed to meet a friend, but I had an emergency and wanted to leave a note. The girl was so nice."

"You said you'd paid out thousands of dollars. Does he always ask for $10,000?"

"The first few times it was $1,000."

"A month? A week?"

"About a month. He called it accident insurance. Like it was his little joke. Then it went up to $2,500. But three months ago, it jumped to $10,000."

"Good God! How much have you paid this person in total?"

"Almost $50,000 now. I had some savings but the last few months just wiped me out. I make good money, but most of it goes right back out again."

I nodded. I knew how that worked all too well.

"I hate to victim blame here, but why didn't you just circle back and see who picked up the envelope?" Gabby asked.

"The first time I was too scared. The second time, I did go back. I changed clothes, put on a hat. Stupid, of course. I got an email from him saying I had one minute to leave or the price would double." She shrugged. "I left."

"And he upped the price anyway."

"Danny said he would go and watch for the guy, but I was afraid the same thing would happen again."

I thought a bit. "Well, this blackmailer doesn't know that we're helping you. We can probably position ourselves wherever the drop-off point is and keep watch for who collects the envelope."

"I don't know…"

"Juliet, you're at the point where it's unsustainable. He's got to know that you're close to broke. If you don't do something now, you're not going to be able to pay the next time or the time after and the story of your accident is going to come out anyway."

She nodded. "It's all my fault. If I had been paying more attention, I could have stopped the car on time." Tears were spilling over onto her cheeks. "I deserve this."

"No. You don't." Gabby's voice was harsh. "No one deserves this. It was an accident. Even if you had been paying attention, he was on a motorcycle. Even at low speeds, people die. There's no protection. He ran the light. He ran into you. Look at me." Juliet looked up.

"Not. Your. Fault."

Where the hell did that come from? I watched this in amazement. Normally, Gabby was pretty unsure of herself. Here she was, almost yelling at Juliet.

They looked at me.

"Um… What she said?"

It broke the tension and we laughed nervously.

"Okay. Here's the plan. The blackmailer is going to contact you. Odds are good he's going to make the drop location somewhere here in the resort. Let us know and we can arrange ourselves casually in whatever location."

Juliet nodded.

"Do you think the drop will be tonight?" I asked.

"Probably. He likes to make me race around, keep me off-balance."

Sadistic twist, I thought. *Controlling. That's personal.* I said, "It's a Sunday. Can you get that much in cash?"

"Yes. I have most of it. I had cash set aside to pay the instructors. I can use that and then just pay them out tomorrow after the bank opens. I also have a couple of thousand in case any problems come up. I can get to an ATM and pull the rest of it, if I use my credit cards. Danny could probably pull from his accounts if I need him to, but I already owe him ten thousand. I don't want to ask him for more."

"You may have to. See what you can scrape together and we'll figure it out if there's a shortfall. I mean, the guy has to know that it's hard to raise that kind of money on a weekend. It's almost like he wants you to fail."

She nodded, but she looked beat.

I hated to ask, but ever since Rob pointed it out, it had been bothering me. "Nothing happened for almost twenty years and all of a sudden you start getting blackmailed over this. Something must have changed in your life a year ago."

"Or the blackmailer's," Gabby pointed out.

"True, if they had known all along. But we don't have the luxury of asking the blackmailer. Did you change anything around that time? Meet someone new? Start working with someone?"

Juliet thought for a minute, then shook her head no. "Same apartment, same job. I do this event every year about this time—I've been doing them for the past five years, so that wasn't new."

"Same instructors?"

"I usually have a couple more, but this year money was obviously tighter and I couldn't afford to bring them in."

I nodded. "New friend? Did you randomly run into someone from college? Move?"

She shrugged. "No. My therapist retired. Pretty sure she's not the blackmailer."

"It's hard when you have to change therapists," Gabby said.

"Yeah. My new one is good, but Danny doesn't like him."

"Does Danny go to your sessions with you?" I asked.

"Oh, no. He thinks all therapists are quacks. He didn't like the one before that, either."

"How long had you been seeing that therapist?"

"Oh, years. Really miss her."

"Have you told your new therapist you're being blackmailed?"

"Oh, dear God, No!"

"I thought you were supposed to be completely open and honest in those sessions."

Both Gabby and Juliet laughed.

"What?"

"Getting down to the actual truth is really what the process is about. There's the stuff we tell others, the stuff we tell ourselves, and the stuff we don't even tell ourselves. That's the hardest stuff," Gabby explained.

"But you told both your therapists about the accident?" I asked Juliet.

"That's why I'm there. Do you think my therapist is blackmailing me?" She was horrified.

"That would be a tremendous breach of ethics," Gabby said. "They'd lose their license if they were found out. Frankly, an extra $50,000 might be nice, but most therapists are doing well over six figures. The risk-reward isn't there. Especially paid out over a year."

She really was a numbers girl. "That makes sense. But let's not take the possibility out of the mix. Text me both therapists' names. We can check their backgrounds, see if there are any professional complaints against them. And, if either one of them is here, that will be a rather huge tip off."

"It would be nice if it were that easy," Juliet said.

"I doubt it's either one, but we'll check just to eliminate the possibility. It's lunch break. Go back to your room and get yourself together. You've had a rough morning, to say the least."

She gave us hugs which I think were more for her sake than ours. We all left the meeting room together and we dropped her at the elevators.

I checked my phone and found the expected text from Roger. *Where are you guys? We're at the main restaurant.*

On our way.

I looked at Gabby. "Well, at least we'll have a change from the pool restaurant."

She shrugged. "Last night I realized that everywhere I go, I get the grilled chicken salad. Doesn't really matter where I eat it."

"We're going to have a chat about your eating habits. You need to have more fun in your diet."

"Oh, get in line. That was three therapists ago."

I laughed. "Ah, so that's why you knew what to say to Juliet. You certainly did some amazing therapy in there. Did you go to school for that, too?"

"Hell, no. I'm a STEM girl all the way. What I pulled out for Juliet is the result of a solid 12 years of once-a-week counseling. We all know the words. The problem is believing them. For Juliet, it's guilt. For me, it's feeling like I'm never going to be good enough." She looked at me. "So, yes, I know the words that are supposed to make me feel better. I'm kind of looking for solid proof, though."

"For the record, you were more than good enough just now. You really helped her."

Gabby smiled and I was reminded once again of just how extraordinarily gorgeous she was. What had Luke said? She had electricity, star power. All she really needed was a confidence boost. Who didn't?

"Let's get the guys up to speed on this."

The restaurant was crowded, most likely because the pool restaurant was closed down, and there were people constantly around us. I didn't want to be overheard, so we kept the conversation casual, talking about the sessions. Most of the people were talking about the body in the pool. Face it, crime scene tape is a conversation starter. It didn't seem that anyone had missed Darlana at all. I checked the schedule. She hadn't been scheduled for any of the sessions today. Well, except the final panel.

People finished their lunches and the restaurant started clearing out. In a low voice, I updated the guys on the latest threat.

"How the hell is she going to get $10,000 in cash on a Sunday?" Roger asked.

"She has most of it. She had cash for the instructors plus money for any contingencies. She says she can pull the rest from an ATM."

"My bank limits withdrawals to $400 a day," Luke said.

"She's probably using her credit cards, too."

"She's scraping the bottom," Nick said. "This guy needs to be stopped."

We all nodded. Juliet had texted the names of the therapists and Roger looked them up through the state licensing board. He added their photos on the group chat with a BOLO—Be On The Lookout—headline.

"Too bad this all ends tomorrow. Not enough time to order us all secret decoder rings," Luke said.

"We'll have to settle for wearing our sunglasses indoors," Gabby replied.

"Like Chad," Roger rolled his eyes.

"Are we sure he's not behind it? I'd really like it to be him," Gabby said.

"He's a real long shot. As are the therapists. Once we find out where the drop is, we can position ourselves casually nearby. The operative word here is casually."

They all nodded.

Roger checked his phone. "Next session is starting up. Kasey, if you hear from Juliet, just text us."

"You got it." I looked at the schedule. "It's really just this next session, then the cookie break and the panel. Juliet's probably going to let people know about Darlana then."

"That should put a damper on the farewell party tonight," Luke said.

"It's actually good timing. There's about a three-hour break between the end of the session and the party. It will give people time to absorb the news. People are amazingly callous about these things," Nick said.

"How so?"

Nick laid out his thinking. "Well, most if not all of the attendees didn't really know her. They may have attended one or two of her sessions and then she was in the larger sessions, but her interaction with people was limited. They didn't have a relationship. So, it's going to be 'Oh, that's a shame' and then they'll move on."

"Yikes. I hope people will be a little more upset when I pass away," I said.

"Jeez, don't even say stuff like that," Luke gave a weird shake, as if warding off evil spirits.

"Superstitious?"

"I know enough not to tempt fate."

"Well, this is cheery and all, but we have to go. Or do we?" Roger was looking at his schedule. "Comedy Trends or Screenwriting."

"I'm going to Screenwriting," I said.

Nick started getting his things together. "Me, too."

Roger looked at Gabby and Luke. "I'm thinking nap time."

"I was definitely up way too early today. Napping sounds fantastic," Gabby said.

"I had been planning on sitting poolside, but that's off the table."

"Comedy trends?" I asked.

"Hell no! Nap time!" The three of them giggled like kids playing hooky.

I could use a nap just as much if not more than all of them, but I didn't want to miss the screenwriting session. I'd load up on coffee at the break and hope it would power me through whatever happened in the next few hours. I should have known it would take a lot more than coffee.

Chapter 24: There's No Slippery Slope to a Cookie

ROB'S SCREENWRITING CLASS WAS pretty full. He had gained a lot of fans with his morning session. We were all hungry for real-world information and Rob had it in spades. That, or no one wanted to be politically correct. Two nights of showcases illustrated just how much some of these comics should have been sitting in the front row of Mo's PC session. There are certain lines you don't cross in comedy and some of these folks never got the memo.

Rob began, "This is going to be more about how to tell a good story, how to structure it so people get sucked in. What I'm teaching you today can apply to comedy or drama, so you're getting a bonus. You're welcome." He paused, took a sip of water, then went on. "For those of you who were in the sitcom session, some of this will be familiar to you."

Rob went over the hero's journey and the three-act structure which seemed to me like it should be four acts, but what do I know? An hour in, he started talking about the specific types of comedy films: buddy films, road trips, romantic comedy, slapstick, action, zero to hero. He gave us a few examples of each type and then he talked about combining the types and how the combinations can make a movie seem unique. He brought us through the plot of *Hunger Games*, matching up the scenes to the points of the hero's journey. Then he discussed tropes—those elements of a genre that the audience has come to expect. A romance has to have a happily-ever-after. The detective has to tell the suspect "Don't leave town."

"Aren't those things overdone?" Tim asked.

"Yes." Rob shrugged. "But you still need to put them in because if they're not in there, the audience will at the very least sense that something is missing and feel slightly disappointed."

And then he was off again, giving us still more information. It was like drinking from a firehose. I was grateful that Juliet had the AV team videoing each session. I would need to watch this more than once to get everything that Rob was saying. When he finished up, people broke into applause. He took a slightly embarrassed bow but he looked more than a little pleased.

For once, I wasn't in the knot of people waiting to talk to Rob after the session. Nick and I headed back to the main conference room for the cookie break.

The cookie break seemed to be losing its appeal for people, which was both appalling to me and joyous because... more cookies for me! I grabbed yet another coffee and two chocolate chip cookies as well as a ginger cookie. I wrapped up the ginger cookie for later. I didn't think it would pair well with the chocolate chip cookies.

Nick grabbed a bottled water and a chocolate chip cookie. I was glad to see he wasn't completely without weaknesses. We found a couple of seats in the back row and watched people filter into the room. We had about ten minutes before the final panel started.

I spoke in a low voice. "I imagine Juliet will make the announcement about Darlana at the start of the panel."

"Too many people in the room to see who reacts or doesn't react."

I liked Nick's logical approach to things. We hadn't really talked among ourselves about who we thought could be behind the blackmailing, so I asked him.

He thought for a minute, taking his time chewing on his cookie. I tried not to focus on his white, even teeth or on his full lips.

"It is most likely someone who went to the same college as Juliet, so Rob, Danny, or Philipa. Darlana is in the clear."

"Not a great way to clear your name."

"No. The most likely is Rob, but I just don't get that vibe from him." He shrugged and popped the rest of the cookie in his mouth. "I hate to say it, but it is most likely someone we have no knowledge of. I mean, we didn't know Philipa went to the same college. There could easily be someone else here who went there at the same time as Juliet."

"Well, that would narrow it down to someone about the same age, then."

"And a man."

I picked up my second cookie and was about to take a bite, then stopped. Nick looked at me expectantly.

"Do you want half my cookie?"

"I thought you were about to tell me you figured out who the blackmailer was!"

"I wish. I've got nuthin' in that regard. But I do have a cookie." I held it up.

"You would give up half a cookie for me? I'm in shock."

"Yes, I would."

"How much are you hoping I'll say no?"

"Percentage wise?"

"Never mind. No thank you. I want you to enjoy that cookie completely."

I happily complied.

"There's no slippery slope to a cookie," he observed.

"I think we learned our lesson with the hot fudge yesterday."

He smiled, remembering. I felt my face flush just a bit. My own fault.

I was debating another cookie when Juliet and the rest of the staff came through the side door. There was no voice over introduction of Juliet this time. Everyone took their seats onstage and people in the audience quieted down.

Juliet hesitated slightly before starting. She looked back at the row of instructors behind her. No one had thought to remove the extra chair for Darlana and it sat empty.

"Um, well, thank you all for coming. This is our last official session and then we have the farewell party tonight. This is the "Ask Us Anything" session, so get your burning questions ready."

She paused and looked back again. There was an audible intake of breath.

"But before we start, I have some very sad news to report. Most of you know that someone drowned in the pool last night."

There was an immediate buzz of whispered voices.

"We lost Darlana DeLuz, who has been our colleague and friend for years. Darlana and I went to college together for several years, as did Danny and Rob. We all started out together and have come up through the business over the years. This has been a great loss to us. I'd appreciate it if you could join us in just a few moments of silence to remember Darlana with us."

There was an awkward pause of about twenty seconds. She was smart not to let it go on too long. As it was, it seemed like forever. I could feel the people around me trying not to burst with questions.

"Thank you. We cannot answer any questions about Darlana's death due to the police investigation, but anything you want to know about the business, anything at all, we will do our level best to field your questions. Do we have our mic runners ready?"

The two runners waved the cordless mics over their heads.

"Great. Who has the first question?"

I recognized Patti Minette from that first morning breakfast. She asked a question about comedy condos, especially in the context of safety for female comics. A bit of a touchy subject, which worked to distract people from whispered speculations about Darlana's death.

The session was supposed to be ninety minutes long, but people seemed to run out of steam after an hour. Juliet closed out the session, thanked the instructors individually, making sure they got big rounds of applause.

"Okay. We've got a little bit of extra time. The farewell party starts at 9:00 pm in this room. We will see you all back here then!"

People applauded briefly, but they didn't stick around. They were eager to talk about Darlana's death and polite enough not to do it in front of her friends. I was more than ready to go back to my room and drop my stuff. It had been a long day. I didn't know when the blackmailer would set up the drop and I figured I should grab the chance for some quiet time to organize my thoughts.

I got all of twenty minutes.

Chapter 25: Now You See It, Now You Don't

JULIET TEXTED THE DROP information to me. The money was to be sealed in an envelope and placed behind the magazine display stand at the back of the gift shop before 5:30. The blackmailer really did keep her on a tight schedule.

I went into the gift shop to see exactly where the drop location was. I had been in and out of the gift shop getting snacky-snacks all weekend. No one would pay attention to me picking up another package of Twizzlers or Hostess cupcakes. The blackmailer had chosen a spot in the back that couldn't be seen from outside the store and was fairly hidden from the cashier. Of course. But that meant he would have to walk the entire length of the store. If nothing else, the security cameras would pick up everyone who was in the shop around that time. I sat in a chair outside the gift shop with my notes in my lap, chewing on Twizzlers. Gabby and Roger were a little ways down the corridor to the left in a sitting area. They were partially obscured by greenery. Luke and Nick were down the corridor to the right, near the front of the lounge where they had a good view of the gift shop entrance. They had beers in front of them and looked suitably casual.

Juliet went in and I saw her head disappear as she walked to the back of the store. Less than a minute later, she walked out of the gift shop and studiously did not look my way as she hustled towards the elevators. There was nothing we could do but wait and watch. I figured the money would be picked up fairly quickly—who wants to leave that kind of cash sitting around for some passerby to find? People went into the gift shop and came back out with purchases but no one looked suspicious. Five minutes passed. Then ten. Another meeting must have gotten out because half a dozen people entered the gift shop at one time. I couldn't stand it anymore. I went in to keep an eye on where the money was dropped but everyone seemed more intent on getting food and drinks. They cleared out and I followed, buying a package of Lorna Doone cookies for cover. I went back to my seat and texted the group.

Nobody went near the drop.

Is the money still there?

I don't know. I couldn't tell and I didn't want to tip off the black-mailer if he hasn't been there yet.

What do we do?

Wait, I guess.

Danny came walking down the corridor from the pool area. He was trying to be nonchalant but as he passed me, he gave me a questioning look. I shrugged. He kept walking. I figured he would let Juliet know, not that there was anything to know. We waited some more. Finally, at 45 minutes in, I texted Luke.

Luke, walk in and see if the money is still there.

Luke came out from his position in the lounge. He gave me a wave and said, "Be out in a minute. Are you hanging for a few?" Very casual, very cool.

"Yeah, sure."

He was back out a couple of minutes later carrying a bottled water. He sat down in a chair next to mine.

"Money's gone," he said softly.

"What the ----?"

"You know that bit you did last night, the one about Disney," he said just a bit loudly.

"Yeah."

"I've got some ideas for it. You want to go up to my room and we can work on it?"

"Sure. That would be great."

We rose and I was hoping that if anyone was watching, they'd just assume we were going to have sex. Yes. That's how awkward the conversation sounded to me.

I hit the group text: *Money gone. Meet in Luke's room.*

Luke pressed the button for five, I pressed for ten. He looked at me.

"I've got to talk to Juliet, then I'll be back down. See you in a few."

I knocked on the door of 1010 and Danny opened it. I just looked at him. "I am so sorry."

"Come on in."

Juliet was crying. I couldn't blame her. She turned on me.

"You mean to tell me you didn't see anyone collect the money?"

"No. We were positioned as best we could be, but the blackmailer is smart. He knew exactly where to place the drop so we'd have to be standing in the gift shop the whole time in order to catch him. And he knew you wouldn't do that."

"Well, that's ten grand you just cost me."

Danny jumped in. "Juliet, you would have paid it with or without Kasey watching."

"Whatever." She rubbed her forehead.

Danny looked at me. "What next?"

"You can ask security to pull the video and see if there's anything on it. There's video of everyone who walked through the door of the gift shop. It's got to be one of those people."

"Great," Juliet said flatly. Then more to herself, "I am so screwed."

Danny put his arm around her. "We'll figure this out, Jules."

Juliet looked at me. "Well, I guess you tried."

"I'm sorry. But we might get lucky with the security video."

"Could have done that ourselves."

I nodded. There was nothing else to say. I left Danny consoling Juliet and I went back down to Luke's room. Everyone was there waiting.

"Well?"

"What you would expect. She's crying and mad at me. Danny's trying to calm her down. The best we can do is pull the security footage. That's up to her—she's the one holding the event."

"Well, we must have seen whoever it is, even if we didn't recognize them," Gabby said.

"How did someone get in, take the money, and out again without being seen? It's got to be someone we'd know."

"Magician's trick. If Darlana wasn't dead, I'd say she did it. She was a magician's assistant," Luke said.

"Trick. That's it." I looked around. "Magic is just a trick; it's not real."

"Stage magic at least," Roger said with a surprisingly sweet innocence.

"Well, yeah, of course. My point is that the money didn't magically disappear."

Nick stated, "So, another way into the gift shop."

"Exactly."

"We're idiots," Roger said.

"If there is another way in, we're idiots. If there's not, the blackmailer did it a different way."

"Only one way to find out. Let's go check."

We all trooped back down to the lobby and went down the hall towards the gift shop. I looked around. "Maybe not all of us at once."

"Kasey and I will go in," Gabby said. She turned to me. "Follow my lead."

She dragged me in a rush up to the young woman at the counter.

"Oh my God, can you help us? This horrible alpha male," she rolled her eyes as she said the words, "totally toxic, keeps following me and all I want to do is have a quiet drink with my friend and some girl talk. He keeps butting in. Does this place have a back door we can sneak out of?"

The girl came to life. "Oh, my God! That is like, so icky." She looked around checking to see if anyone else was in the store. She lowered her voice. "You can go through the store room."

She led us to a flush-mounted door that was partially hidden behind a display. If you didn't know it was there, it looked like any other section of wall. And it was almost exactly where Juliet had dropped the payoff. Crap.

The clerk led us through a store room filled with shelves of boxes to a back door. "That's weird. I could have sworn I locked this."

Gabby and I looked at each other.

The clerk shrugged. "Whatever." She opened it. "Go left and when you get to the door, take another left. At the end of that hallway, there's a door to the outside. It will put you out kind of near the pool area."

"You are a total girlfriend. Thank you!" Gabby said.

"Girls have to stick together."

We went through the door and heard the lock click behind us. We followed her directions and sure enough ended up outside, around the corner from the pool area. I texted the guys. "Meet us at the pool bar."

We grabbed a table and a minute later the guys showed up.

"Ta-da!" I said, laying on the sarcasm.

"That confirms it. We're idiots," Luke said.

"There's a store room with a back door for deliveries. There's a door around the corner there" I waved my hand indicating the direction, "away from the guests. They bring in deliveries through a couple of back corridors."

"Makes sense," Nick said.

"We totally got played," Roger groaned.

Disappointment settled around the table.

"Okay. Let's rethink this," I started.

"I think better with beer," Roger said.

"Amen, brother," Luke agreed.

We looked around for the server.

"Maybe *he* took the ten grand and split," Roger commented.

"Won't get him very far," Nick said.

The bartender saw us looking and came over. "Sorry, your server is on a break. Apparently. What can I get you?"

We all ordered our usuals.

"We're starting from zero again," Nick said.

"Juliet is starting from less than zero. Ten Gs less," Luke said.

I was thinking. "Whoever did this knows the back hallways of the resort. To some extent, at least."

"So, everyone who works here."

"No, just the people on Juliet's staff and maybe one or two nosy attendees," I said.

"Like us."

"Who went snooping down the back halls..."

"Who would go snooping?" Gabby asked.

"Whoever was blackmailing Juliet, of course."

"Or someone who's naturally nosy," Luke said, looking at me.

I ignored him. "Most likely it's a member of the event staff... we haven't checked out Pamela and Trystan."

"Or it could be someone who has attended the event before," Nick pointed out.

Just then our drinks arrived. We all stopped talking which seemed obvious so then we all started talking too much. We waited until the bartender walked away to start again.

"I forgot about them. Roger, can you run a background check on them? As for someone who attended last year..." I was thinking out loud, "Maybe it's someone who attended last year and felt like Juliet didn't give them enough attention or maybe slighted them in some way."

I texted Juliet. *Can you send me a list of people who have attended this event before?*

Give me a few.J

"Let's think. Who had a past attendee ribbon on their badge?"

"Those are the purple ones, right?"

"Yeah."

"Well, not Chad."

"Something tells me he's not ever coming back to one of Juliet's events."

"No purple ribbon for Chad."

"Sad Chad." We raised our glasses in a mock toast. My phone pinged. There was a list of about a dozen names and I read them out. "Anyone recognize anyone? A name?"

We looked at each other, disappointed.

"Well, we might not know their names but we might know their faces. Let's check the Internet and see if we can match some of them up."

"Some of these names are pretty common," I said.

"I'll add the word comic after the name and see if that helps," Roger was working his phone keyboard like a pro.

"Give me a name," Luke said, pulling out his phone.

In no time we had ten faces to go with the names. We couldn't find two people.

"What kind of person isn't on social media at this point?" Roger asked, shaking his head.

"The kind who blackmails people," Nick replied.

"Fair enough."

"Or it could just be someone who isn't Internet savvy. They're going to need Danny to build a website for them to get them up and running."

"Won't matter," Roger said offhandedly. We looked at him. "If they're not Internet savvy at this point, they're not going to be able to maintain their own website. Even a simple blog site. I mean, it's not complicated, but you have to make some effort. You wouldn't believe the people I work with who can barely turn on their computers to do basic work. Still."

"Okay. So, new plan. We look for these people at the farewell mixer tonight. Chat them up, ask how they liked the conference, was it different last year..." I trailed off. "See if anything sets off your Spidey-sense." I looked around the table. "I know. Not much of a plan."

"We should chat up the staff, too. Mo, Rob, the two assistants—Pamela and the guy," Nick said.

"Trystan or whatever"

"Yeah, that's it. And Danny."

"Danny loaned Juliet the money for the payment before this one. I think that rules him out," I said.

"That makes sense. So, just the others."

"I don't think it's Rob. We've had some pretty good talks," I said.

"Yeah, but he was at school with Juliet," Roger said.

I shook my head at Roger.

"Shit. Sorry," He said.

"Shit what?" Luke asked. "You holding out on us, Kasey?" His tone was easy but there was no missing the underlying current at the table.

"Yeah, I was." Might as well come clean at this point. "You all know Juliet was being blackmailed but you don't know that she changed her name."

"And?" Nick prodded.

"Roger did some Internet digging and found a picture of her from college."

"Before the accident, I'm assuming," Nick said.

"Yeah." I pulled the picture up on my phone and they passed it around.

"So, Juliet is Joanne," Nick said.

"Joanne! Isn't that the name Philipa mentioned?" Gabby asked.

"Yes."

"We need to add Philipa to the suspect list, too," Luke said.

"Yeah, but I didn't want you guys acting all weird around her."

"You know Kasey, we can't help you if we don't have all the information." Nick's voice was calm but it was like hearing your dad say he was disappointed in you.

"Yeah, I know. But I'm trying to protect Juliet here. It didn't seem that important to the whole thing."

"Either we're in or we're out, Kasey. You trust us or you don't. You can't have it both ways."

"Kind of important info," Luke was definitely not happy with me.

"Look, I'm sorry." It came out more defensive than I wanted it to be.

"Anything else we don't know about Kasey?" Nick asked.

"I think we're good," I mumbled.

There was silence for a minute.

Roger checked his phone. "Well, it's almost 7:00. Party starts in two hours. I have to catch up on a little work or I'll be buried when I get back."

"I'm going to start getting ready," Gabby said. We all looked at her.

"Hey. This all takes work. The natural look is NOT natural."

She broke the tension and I was grateful. But there was still some residual hard feelings. We stood up to go our separate ways.

"Coming, Kasey?" Gabby asked.

"No, I think I need to take a walk and think this over."

No one objected but no one offered to come with me, either. Roger gave me a sympathetic glance as he held the door for Gabby. Luke and Nick headed over to sit at the tiki bar. *Well, at least they're bonding*, I thought.

I knew I had mis-stepped, but what the hell. I'm not a private investigator. I was asked to help and I tried. I had enough stuff to figure out in my life without people putting crazy expectations on me. And yet, here I was, still trying to figure out the puzzle. Maybe I should see a therapist.

Chapter 26: Tricks and Schtick

I DIDN'T FEEL LIKE going back to my room and decided to hit the resort lounge. I could use the dark and the air conditioning as well as the time to think without everyone looking at me.

I sat at the bar and eyeballed their top shelf scotches. I ordered a Glenfiddich 15 with a water back, knowing fully well it would be over-priced as hell. The bartender nodded his approval and gave a generous pour. At least someone didn't think I was a loser.

I added barely a splash of water to the scotch and let it sit for a minute. I took a sip and let it slide down my throat. Then another slightly bigger sip. I was going to make this thing last and enjoy every bit of it. I pulled out a pen and began scribbling the various points we actually knew on a napkin.

1. Juliet had been blackmailed for over a year. $50k.

2. Juliet, Darlana, Danny, and Rob had all gone to school to-gether.

3. Darlana knew about the blackmail and she was dead. Danny also knew. Rob had not.

I crossed out the last sentence. Rob said he hadn't known. Maybe he did. I kept going.

1. The blackmailer knew the back corridors of the resort.

2. Someone had broken into my room. Maybe thinking it was mine; maybe Gabby's.

3. The only real change in Juliet's life had been her therapist.

I took another sip. Someone set a drink down next to me. I looked up to see Philipa.

"Mind if I join you?"

I flipped over the napkin. "Be my guest."

"Working on material?"

"Trying to sort out some stuff in my head."

She nodded. "Helps to write it down."

"Yeah." I wondered how to change the subject. Fortunately, she did it for me.

"You're usually surrounded by your posse," she noted.

"Yeah. Everyone is doing their thing. Packing, napping, whatever. And I needed a little alone time."

"Oh, I'm sorry." She started to stand up.

"No, no. Sit. You're fine. Probably best that I'm not drinking alone."

"Happy to be your enabler."

"Thank you."

"Rough day."

"All around."

"More so for you. Rumor has it you found the body."

"Not a good start to the day. How did you hear that?"

"Someone saw you and Gabby at the pool with the police. Danny and Juliet, too."

"Yeah, Gabby and I woke up early and decided just to sit and talk by the pool. It was dark. And then, as it got more light..." I stopped remembering the black blob that had slowly become visible. I shivered.

"What are you drinking?" Philipa asked, giving the bartender a wave.

"Oh, I'm good."

"That wasn't the question. We'll have another round. Put it on my tab."

"You're going to regret that. I'm drinking top shelf scotch."

"You have had a very bad, terrible, awful day."

"Not as bad as Juliet," I said, thinking about Darlana's death and losing another ten thousand dollars. I was wondering how I was going to bring up the subject of going to the same college as Juliet. Subtlety is not my strong suit.

The bartender came back with our drinks. Philipa raised up her glass. "To Darlana."

"Darlana."

"But the Cold Auditions class was truly awful."

I half-choked on my scotch. "She really thought she had something there."

"I went to the same college she went to."

"Really? Did you know her?"

"No, she was a year or two ahead of me. I didn't recognize her at first. Danny looked familiar but I couldn't place him. Then in Cold Auditions it hit me. Danny and Darla."

"They were a couple?"

"Oh, no. He had a magic act and she was the assistant. I had forgotten all about them. They used to play in the talent shows on campus. I mean, it was almost twenty years ago. But when she showed that slide where she was in the little magician's assistant outfit, I put it together."

"Did you know Juliet back then?"

She shook her head. I decided to take a risk. "She was known as Joanne. Juliet's a stage name."

Philipa looked puzzled. "Joanne. That's scary. Maybe she was in some of the shows, too? I was just kind of breaking out of my shell back then."

"It's hard to imagine you were ever in a shell."

She laughed loudly. "Oh yeah. What you're seeing now is ten years of being in front of a room teaching junior high school kids followed by seven years of playing crappy clubs. But back then, I was pretty mousy."

I tried to sound conversational. "Was Darlana as bad at magic as she was at teaching auditioning?"

Philipa took a minute to think. "Well, really, all she had to do was prance around and then fold herself into tight spaces." She thought for a minute. "Bring up volunteers. Danny was pretty good, though. He did a stage hypnosis act that college kids loved. You know, make the guys act like girls, have people quack like ducks, all the schtick."

"I hate hypnotist acts. I never go to the bathroom during their act because I don't know if I'm going to the actual ladies' room or if I just think I am and I'm up on stage and about to pee in public."

She laughed and actually slapped her thigh. "Oh, my God, that's funny. Is that in your act?"

"No, I'm serious!"

"Put it in, girlfriend. You've got a bit there somewhere." She finished up her drink.

"Let me get the next round," I said, though I was only half through my drink.

"You can buy me one at the mixer tonight."

"Deal."

"See you there."

I waited a few seconds and flipped over the napkin. I added, "Also Philipa" to point number two.

1. Danny and Darla had a magic act together. Hypnosis.

2. Danny had loaned Juliet $10,000 to pay the blackmailer.

Had Danny mentioned his magic act in his talks? I didn't think so. And Darlana's slide didn't include Danny. Odd that neither one had mentioned working together, even if it was back in college. Come to think of it, none of them mentioned having gone to college together. Mo was the only one who hadn't been part of that clique.

I replayed the drop in my mind. The blackmailer went in the back way. Slipped in unseen, slipped out unseen. Really, he could have just reached his arm through the gap to retrieve the envelope. And he must have come out by the pool bar. He had probably picked up the money within minutes of Juliet placing it and walked right past me sitting outside the gift shop. I tried to think back to the people who walked past. Some of the people from the seminar. Hotel guests. Danny did a walk by check in.

Danny.

I looked back at my list of facts. Danny could definitely be the blackmailer. He knew about the accident. He knew the back corridors. He was stealthy and excelled at sleight of hand. *Why had he loaned Juliet the money?* I asked myself. *To be a good guy. To have Juliet be grateful to him.* Danny certainly had a thing for Juliet.

"Duh."

The bartender looked over at me.

"Nothing. Sorry. Could I get my check please?"

Of course, Danny loaned her the money. He had it back in his pocket again within hours. He looked like a good guy for helping her out and she now literally owed him.

I signed for my drink and only blinked once at the price. I would have to buy Philipa several drinks tonight.

I walked outside to be alone and called Juliet. "Is Danny with you?"

"No. Do you need him?"

"No. In fact, I need you to not tell him what I'm about to tell you."

"Why?"

"Because I think Danny is your blackmailer."

"That's ridiculous. Danny loaned me money."

"Yeah, that's why I originally ruled him out. But think about it. He got his money back immediately. And you still owe him the money."

"But I've known him forever. He's my friend!"

"And only your closest friends knew about your past. Let me ask you, does your new therapist do any hypnotherapy?"

"Yeah, he does. I think that's why Danny doesn't like him. Danny used to do hypnosis."

"And Danny has done hypnosis on you."

"Yeah, to help me with anxiety."

"Even back in college?"

"Oh yeah. He said he needed the practice. And it really helped my anxiety about exams."

"How about Darlana? Did he practice on her, too?"

"Sure. He hypnotized anyone who would let him."

"And when you started working with this new therapist, did the therapist hypnotize you to take you back to the night of the accident?"

"Yes. But it didn't do any good. I couldn't picture myself in the driver's seat. The therapist said that I was subconsciously in denial and I wouldn't get past the accident until I truly owned it. But I have truly owned it. I killed Ted. It was my fault."

A horrible thought occurred to me. I didn't tell her what I was thinking. If I was wrong, it would just bring more pain.

"Why would Danny do this to me?"

"To manipulate you. Rob talked about how comics that make it help out their friends, right? You're one of those comics who made it.

Danny wants to keep you close because being in your circle gives him stature and paying clients."

"So, he's just using me. I feel sick."

"Well, there's another part to it. He's in love with you."

"Oh, he was, but that was ages ago. We're just good friends."

"You may think that, but he is not happy in the friend zone. Who do you turn to when you need help?"

"Danny."

"And you appreciate him."

"Of course."

I let it sit.

"Oh, God." She paused "I knew it. I just didn't want to see it. I brought this on myself."

"No, you didn't. It's what happened but this is on him. He knew he was friend-zoned and didn't accept it. And, let's not forget that he purposely manipulated you to his benefit, never mind whatever ethics boundaries he may have crossed when he hypnotized you."

"I'm going to confront him on this!"

"No, no, no, no. Don't do that. We have no proof at this point. He's just going to pretend to be hurt. Then he'll call you crazy for even thinking it, go out in a huff, and disappear with your money."

"What do we do?"

"I have an idea. But you're going to need to pull out all your acting chops." I went over my new plan with her.

Half an hour later, I knocked on the door of Juliet's suite. Danny opened the door within seconds. I wasn't even through the door when he blurted, "So, you know who the blackmailer is?"

He was wound pretty tight and that was exactly what I wanted.

I sat on the sofa next to Juliet. Danny sat in one of the side chairs.

Juliet pretended to be anxious. "Do you know who it is? Tell me!"

I waited a beat. Out of the corner of my eye I watched Danny involuntarily lean forward a bit in the chair.

"No. I'm sorry." I saw Danny relax and the corners of his mouth twitched.

"Then why are you even here? This has been a disaster." Juliet sat back with a huff.

"I think I have a solution to your problem."

"What?"

"Juliet, the only way out of this mess is for you to come clean. Admit what happened all those years ago."

"That's career suicide!" Danny said.

"Not if you control the narrative. Juliet, this guy will bleed you dry and when you're out of money, he's going to expose you anyway."

"So, your solution is to rip off the Band-Aid quickly?" Juliet was not impressed.

"Bad idea. Very bad idea," Danny piled on.

I could tell he was frustrated that he wasn't sitting next to her. I took Juliet's hand.

"Juliet, think about it. It's the only way to get you out from under."

She pretended to waiver.

"If you announce it at the farewell party tonight, you'll be in a safe spot with a sympathetic crowd."

"I don't know how sympathetic they are. Some of them are still pretty pissed off about the private showcases." Danny was trying to cast doubt.

"You can explain that the private showcases were added because the blackmailer wanted more money. Once you tell them that, they'll understand."

"I don't know, Kasey. It could all backfire on me."

"You bet your ass it could." Danny was standing now and started to pace. "The blowback will be devastating. Career ending."

He over-enunciated the last two words to make his point.

"Lots of celebrities have overcome huge issues. I mean, Hugh Grant picked up a transvestite hooker."

"He was pretty funny about it, too," Juliet said, as if remembering back.

"Exactly. It was a big deal for about a month. It was embarrassing. But he hit the talk shows, did damage control, put out some sound bites, and it faded away when the next big celebrity blow-up happened. And face it, they're happening a lot faster these days."

"He lost his girlfriend," Danny huffed.

"Yes, but not his career. Are you seeing anyone, Juliet?"

"Uh, no."

"Well, you won't have to worry about that then. And, if a boyfriend dropped you because of that, he's not the one anyway."

"Perhaps you're right," Juliet agreed. "But I killed someone. What I did was a whole lot worse than picking up a transvestite hooker."

"Absolutely," Danny jumped in. "Can't tell a funny story about that."

"Of course not. But Juliet, you're America's Comedy Sweetheart. You've carried this weight on your heart for years. You are honestly still torn up about this. I think keeping this secret, not owning it, holds you back."

"That's what my therapist says."

I picked up her hand again. "I think it's time."

Her eyes had welled up with tears. She wasn't acting now. I realized that I had pushed her into something she wasn't ready for. No going back now.

"Do you want me to stand next to you when you announce it?"

"Would you? I don't think I could do it any other way."

She had returned to the script.

"I'll be there for you."

She gave me a side hug. Danny huffed but didn't say anything.

"Okay. Think about what you're going to say, but think in bullet points; don't write it all out. You want this to come from your heart. Clear and honest."

She nodded.

I stood up to go. Danny's face was bright red. I realized that he wasn't a natural blond. He was a ginger, same as me. Coloring gives us away.

"This is a very bad idea," he started.

"Do you see another way out for her?"

He was silent. I dug in.

"She's going to need your support, Danny. I know you'll be there for her."

I opened the door and looked back. "Juliet, in just a couple of hours, you'll be free."

I didn't get the door closed before Danny started trying to talk her out of it. I smiled. All Juliet had to do was waiver a bit, mention that she couldn't do it without me. And all Danny had to do was take the bait. Which was me...

Chapter 27: You Call This a Plan?

"Damn it, Kasey, No!" Luke's blue eyes blazed at me.

I had called an emergency meeting in my room and laid out the plan.

"Luke's right," Nick's voice was calm but tight. "You can't hang yourself out there."

"It might be Danny's way out. Juliet confesses her secret and Danny gets off clean as the blackmailer," I said.

"He's also Darlana's killer. He's not going to stop there. He's in too deep." Luke wasn't going to budge on this.

"That's why I am putting you guys in charge of seeing nothing happens to me." I smiled at them.

Roger said, "We screw up and you're dead. No pressure."

"The guys are right," Gabby said. "This is too dangerous."

"Does anyone have a better plan?"

"How about we go to the police," Nick stated the obvious. "Like normal people."

"Because we're a bunch of comics with a theory and no proof. They're going to make a note of it and get around to checking it out sometime in the next few days. In the meantime, the seminar is over, everyone goes their separate ways, and Danny gets off scot-free. For the blackmail and the murder."

They all looked at me, not budging.

"We've got nothing. The only thing I can do is try to push him into confessing. And, he'll confess to me if he thinks I'm not going to live to tell about it."

"You call this a plan?" Nick said.

"It's worked before, right Luke?"

"Yeah, but that time the stakes were a lot lower and the person we were dealing with was not a murderer. If we're right, Danny murdered Darlana and he won't hesitate to kill you." Luke took a breath. "It's a very bad plan, Kasey."

"It's all we've got."

"And what are we going to do once he confesses and we corner him? Tie him up and sit on him?" Roger asked.

"We call hotel security. They can call the cops."

"I'd feel better if they were close by," Gabby said.

"Security got here pretty fast the other night," I said. "Stavon at the front desk is good."

"Let's see if he's working tonight," Nick suggested. A quick call to the front desk confirmed that he was.

"Is there a problem, Kasey?" Stavon asked.

"We hope not, but there might be. Could you maybe tip off Security to be on their toes this evening? Maybe be prepped to come to the event room if we need them?"

"I can. But Kasey, this seminar has been bad business. You be careful."

"I will. Thanks, Stavon." I hung up the room phone. "Stavon's on top of it. As usual."

"Now what?" Nick asked.

"We wait, I guess. Either Danny is going to try to stop Juliet from making the announcement or not."

"You mean Danny is going to try to stop you," Luke pointed out.

"Yes. But really, he's not going to have the time or the opportunity to do anything. He confesses, you guys show up, nobody gets hurt." I looked at my phone to check the time. "We have about half an hour before the mixer starts. It's going to take him a bit of time to figure out what to do, so let's get ready for the mixer and meet there. We can be a bit late. Can we all be ready in forty minutes?"

Everybody looked at Gabby.

"Why are you looking at me? Of course, I can be ready. My hair's already done. Just need to finish my makeup and put on my dress."

"You look fine just the way you are," Roger said.

"Thank you," came the simple reply.

I watched them make eye contact and suppressed a smile. *Go, Roger.*

"Why don't you all leave from Gabby's room—that's the one Danny thinks is mine. It will look like our meeting broke up and I'm on my own. If he's watching the room, he may just decide to knock on the door."

"Oh, that's brilliant," Luke said. "Let's all leave Kasey on her own in case the murderer wants to stop by."

"Except, Gabby calls through the door. We just won't let him in. She'll tell him I'm just out of the shower and to give me a few minutes. And if that happens—a very big if, by the way—I'll text you guys. You wait by the elevator. Once Danny comes in, Gabby can unlock her door for you. Come through Gabby's room and boom! We've got him."

"Or he decides to hurt both of you, makes it look like a robbery gone wrong, and boom! You're both dead. No." Nick said. "How about you don't let him in at all. Tell him you'll see him at the party."

"Well, he's probably not going to show up here. We've got to get ready. So, go and we'll meet up at the party."

"We'll come down and escort you two," Roger said.

"Nothing will happen if Danny can't get me alone," I said. "If he shows up, I'll do what Nick said."

"And if he insists?"

"I'll meet him in the lobby in a few minutes."

The guys didn't look happy.

"Then I call you guys and we go into action as planned, just in the lobby. Let's get moving."

We said loud good-byes to the guys and shut the door. Gabby looked at me.

"So, what are you wearing?" she sing-songed. I cracked up.

"Well, I was going to wear a hot little number and my three-inch heels, but now I'm thinking I should wear something I can run in."

"Maybe I should wear something more practical." Her eyes went over to her closet door. There was a royal blue dress with bugle beads and a plunging neckline on a plush, non-hotel hanger.

"Oh, no! That will be a perfect distraction if we need one. Besides, I think Roger likes blue."

"Do you think he likes me?"

"I'm sorry. Were you not kissing at the door last night?"

"Yeah, but no, I mean..."

"I know what you mean. Besides the looks and the money."

She nodded.

"He thinks you're smart, funny, and is totally intimidated by you. And he's worried about the money. He feels like he can't measure up. You're gonna have to help him a bit."

"When this is all over."

"When this is all over. But you know, if you see the chance for him to be heroic or something..."

"Oh yeah. I'll go total damsel in distress."

We grinned at each other.

"Okay. Throw the latch lock on your room door just to be safe and let's leave the door between the rooms open. And if your room phone rings—"

"I know. Don't answer it."

I went back to my room and had the fastest shower I could get away with. I could hear Gabby getting ready in her room. I sighed as I pulled on my black jeans and a starched white shirt. At least it had some sage green embroidered detailing on it. I buttoned the cuffs. No flowy sleeves allowed. Unfortunately, my running shoes would not work for a party. Most of the men, of course, would be wearing running shoes. I looked over my limited shoe selection cursing my childish need to emphasize my height. My best bet was my black and snakeskin Tony Lama boots. They had a two-inch heel, but it was square and substantial. I pulled them on. At least my feet wouldn't hurt tonight.

Gabby was talking herself through her makeup application. I heard an "Oops" and a "That's better." I wondered how long it took her to put on makeup. I needed about five minutes, eight if I was going super-fancy which would turn into ten because at some point, I would mess something up and have to scrub off all or part of my efforts and start again. I took my time, went a little heavy on the concealer around my eye, and still did it in eight, knowing Gabby was at least another ten minutes from being ready. Makeup done, I turned on the TV in the room and found a cable channel rerunning episodes of *NCIS*. I settled on the bed with my booted feet hanging off it. My mother raised me right, even if it didn't show most of the time.

Gabby surprised me five minutes later when she walked into my room, looking absolutely stunning.

"All ready. Shall we call our dates?"

I texted the group. Luke responded first.

I'll come down to your room. Wait for me.

I sent an okay and Gabby went into the other room to get her purse.

She called through the door, "Luke sure likes to keep an eye on you. What's the deal?"

"No deal. Just old friends."

"Um-hmm. He definitely doesn't like Nick buzzing around."

"No. But that's because Nick is married and Luke doesn't want me to get hurt."

"Yeah, I bet that's the only reason."

"It doesn't matter anyway because Nick *is* married and I do not go there. And neither does he."

"That's good to hear." She paused and then, "Why not Luke?"

"Too good-looking," I said it without thinking.

"So good-looking people are what? Self-centered? Shallow?"

"No, that's not what I meant. Just that he's... too much, you know. He's gorgeous, a truly good guy, smart, funny, not stuck on himself..."

"Yeah, he sounds horrible. The downside?"

I shrugged.

"I'm asking because I don't want to run into the same problem with Roger. So, what is it?"

"I don't know." I did know but I wasn't ready for that yet.

"Do you think you're not good enough for him?"

There was a knock on the door. I was saved. I looked at her and smiled. "Nah. I'm a catch."

She threw a pillow at me as I crossed to look out the peephole. Luke was outside with Roger. I opened the door.

"Double our pleasure," I said.

We made sure both rooms were locked securely and headed down to the party.

Chapter 28: Never Break the Mic

NOTHING LIKE FREE DRINKS to get comics to show up to a party. The room was already crowded when we got there. We had our drink coupons in hand, but the service bars were backed up. I wouldn't be drinking just yet anyway.

I had kind of gotten used to Luke's looks and I expected Gabby to turn heads, but I hadn't considered the effect of the two of them entering a room at the same time. Their entrance created a strange rolling full three seconds of silence. Like a lack-of-sound wave spreading through the room and then, the murmuring started back up until it returned to the full throttle noise of a hundred people interacting.

"That was weird," Roger said.

"What was?" Gabby asked.

Roger looked confused. "Like, the whole world just stopped when you walked through the door!"

"Oh, that. Happens all the time. Don't pay any attention to it."

"Sure. Nothing to see here..." Roger looked at me and rolled his eyes.

"We are rubbing shoulders with greatness. But let's not forget why we're here," I said. "Does anyone see Danny?"

"No, but there's Nick and Philipa," Gabby said. We walked over to the table they had staked out. Nick had his ever-present bottle of water. Philipa had somehow managed to get a drink from the bar and she was about halfway through it.

"Any sign of Danny and Juliet?" I asked.

"No sign of any of the event people except Pam and Trystan at the door. And, the AV. guys, of course."

"Guess we can't get too wild with cameras rolling," Roger said.

"And yet, comics and free booze." Luke paused for effect. "Let's just wait and see."

"As long as we're here and Danny isn't, I'm going to go get miked up," I said.

Philipa looked at me, curious.

"Juliet is making an announcement tonight and she wanted me to kind of hold her hand. I don't expect to talk, but just in case she needs a little help..." I trailed off and shrugged, as if it were just a bit of weirdness.

"I'll walk you over," Nick volunteered.

We went over to the sound and light board. Juliet had already arranged for my mic and the guys clipped the battery pack to the belt at the small of my back. I untucked the front of my blouse and ran the mic and wire up the inside, clipping it near the collar. We did the fastest of sound checks, then they turned off my mic at the board. We kept the battery pack live. Danny would also be miked up, as would all the instructors. It was up to the sound guy to flip our mics on at the right time. Roger was in charge of making sure he didn't miss his cue. I could feel another knot forming in my stomach and I forced myself to breathe more deeply. I would have a live mic and three guys ready to charge in if anything went wrong.

I spied Juliet and Danny entering from a side door. Another AV guy was hovering around them, making final adjustments to their microphones. He had been instructed to turn Danny's battery pack on. Danny didn't know it, but he was our back up.

Juliet was scanning the room and she stopped when she found me. I looked at our group.

"I need to talk to Juliet for a minute," I excused myself. As I walked over to Juliet, I turned on my phone and called Roger. He picked up and made sure we were connected. I put the phone in my front pocket, upside down so the mic would pick up what was being said. I just had to hope we wouldn't lose signal or that I wouldn't accidently bump it off.

Juliet hugged me and said, "I am so nervous. I'm glad you're here."

"Hey, we'll get through this together," I replied. "People will support you." I grinned at her. "You seem to forget that we have plants in the crowd."

"What?"

"I prepped my friends. When you make the announcement, they'll shout out something supportive and positive."

"How many friends do you have?" Danny asked. "Because we've got a hundred people in this room and a couple of people aren't going to be very loud when everyone freaks out."

"I've got enough and they know to scatter around the room. Danny, this is the best course of action. Juliet can't go on like this anymore."

"Danny, I really need your support in this. You want what's best for me, don't you?" Juliet had some acting chops.

"Of course. Which is why I don't want you to do this."

"With you and Kasey beside me, I can weather this storm. That and my lucky charm."

I took my cue. "Your lucky charm?"

"Oh, it's silly. It's a stuffed animal, a plush St. Bernard puppy. He's supposed to be pre-set..." she looked around at the stage area, pretending to be confused. "Oh, he must be back in the staff room."

"Hey Juliet, can I get a selfie with you?" Luke pulled up to us right on time.

She smiled at him. "Sure. Um, Kasey, I hate to ask but could you run back to the staff room and grab Bernie for me?"

"You got it. I'll be right back."

I went through the side door and down the hall to the staff room. I waited at the door for a few seconds and sure enough, I heard the door to the party open and close and footsteps coming down the hall. I scooted inside.

"Okay, Roger. Hope you're listening. He's about ten seconds behind me."

I had no way of getting confirmation. I just had to trust that everyone else was doing their part. I looked around the room and saw the plush toy on the table. Well, that part was easy enough. I was just reaching for it when the door opened and Danny walked in.

"Kasey, we need to talk. Confessing to the accident will tank Juliet's career. You don't know what you're doing."

"Danny, I might not know about big time careers, but anyone can see carrying this guilt is breaking Juliet. If you were truly her friend, you would help her with this."

"I've known her for twenty years and you've known her for three days. I know what's best for Juliet. You need to butt out."

"If I don't?"

"You don't want to know."

"Sounds threatening. Could you be more specific?"

He glowered at me. "Just back off. This is not your business."

"Did you tell Darlana to butt out?" I tried to steer him into admitting something. Anything, really.

"Darlana was about to tank Juliet's career. And you're about to do the same thing. You need to tell Juliet not to go ahead with this."

"Or what? I'll end up like Darlana?"

"Maybe you will."

He moved closer to me and I forced myself not to step backward.

"Seems like you just didn't like Darlana muscling in on your cash cow."

His face was beet red. "It was never about the money."

*Gotch*a. Step one complete. "Funny, because Juliet is almost broke thanks to you."

"She would have gotten it all back when we got married."

"Oh, you two are engaged? I didn't see a ring on her finger."

He backpedaled. "Well, no. But it's just a matter of time. She depends on me and I come through for her. I'm the one she calls on when she needs help."

"You caused the problem in the first place!" I felt no need to keep the exasperation out of my voice. "But I believe you. It wasn't about the money. I know you love Juliet."

I saw him relax a bit. He saw a glimmer of hope in the situation. I was about to smother it. I silently prayed that the sound guy had our mics on and we were going out over the speakers. He still hadn't confessed to Darlana's murder. I also had a theory I wanted to prove. I decided to go for it.

"I think you killed Darlana because she knew you were the one driving that night, didn't she? And she was happy to keep quiet about it, leveraging her friendship with Juliet all these years—until she found out you were making a profit off of it. Maybe Darlana decided to blackmail you when Juliet sent her packing."

"That's ridiculous."

"You were both riding Juliet's coattails."

"You're wrong. I wasn't riding Juliet's coattails. I'm the one who helped her get to where she is today. I. Love. Her."

It was the angriest declaration of love I had ever heard. But he didn't admit to driving the car that night. Could I have been wrong? Maybe Juliet was driving that night. Time to poke the bear.

"Funny way to show your love, Danny. Blackmailing her into bankruptcy. Maybe that's just payback for her friend-zoning you. You've had a crush on her for what, twenty years?" I put as much disgust and disbelief in my voice as I could. "I gotta tell you, I don't know if you're tenacious or just a masochist."

"I'm not going to let you ruin her life."

"You're the one who ruined her life, Danny. You crippled her that night when you convinced her she'd been driving the car. So maybe you were right when you said you put her where she is today. There's a reason she's never broken through to the top level: She's riddled with guilt. She feels like she doesn't deserve success, Danny. And that's on you. That's all your fault."

"No. No it's not. I helped her get started in comedy. I'm the one who is always there for her. Me!"

I felt flecks of spittle hit my face and took a step back. I had to get him to confess to killing Darlana. I had decided to work my way around to it, first getting him to own up to the blackmail, then admitting he had been driving the car the night of the accident. That was step two. I was hoping once he started talking, he wouldn't stop. But Darlana's murder was the big one. Steps one and two were just groundwork.

"Why'd you do it, Danny? Juliet wasn't driving the car that night, was she? You were and you'd been drinking. She hadn't. All you had to do was place the thought in her head that she had been the one driving."

"That's ridiculous. Juliet was driving that night." His eyes darted off to the side and I knew he was lying. "Besides, she was cleared of any wrong-doing."

"How much time did you have before the emergency vehicles got there? You must be a pretty good hypnotist to have planted the idea so quickly and so deeply."

"That would be unethical."

"So is drinking and driving. Illegal, even." This time I moved closer to him. "I wondered what changed a year ago to trigger the blackmail. So, I asked Juliet. New therapist. A therapist that uses hypnosis. That must have been terrifying for you. How long before the truth would surface? The blackmail really kept her on the ropes. And she'd go running to her bestie Danny for help. Each time, you'd reinforce the suggestion. How much time did you spend undoing any progress she made?"

"I didn't do—"

I didn't let him finish. I kept pushing. "Come on. You've already admitted to the blackmail. Juliet told me that you would hypnotize her to help her anxiety during exams. You probably worked with Darlana, too, implanting that thought so she'd back you up."

"I didn't have to put Darlana under. She was passed out in the back seat. She didn't know who was driving."

"But she figured it out."

"No! There was nothing to figure out. Juliet was driving. Darlana was just after the money."

"Why'd you do it, Danny?"

His hands were shaking and his face was so red I could almost feel the heat coming off him.

"I didn't do anything."

"You were driving that night. You planted the thought in Juliet's head that she had killed that man. For twenty years she has carried that guilt. Twenty years! You don't love her. You never did. All you've done is take her money and her peace of mind. There's something intrinsically wrong with you Danny; women sense it. I bet you don't get a lot of second dates. Underneath that nice guy exterior, you're just another creep. That's why Juliet never loved you and never will."

He lost it. Unfortunately, he lost it on me. His fist connected with my face before I knew it was coming. I stumbled backward and he was on me, his hands around my neck. I made a choking sound as I went down. He had me pinned to the floor. I was gasping for breath and trying to fight him off at the same time. All my senses seemed sharper. I could feel the battery pack digging into my back. The lights in the room hurt my eyes.

"You stupid bitch. You're ruining everything, just like Darlana. She wouldn't get out of the way. She was all about the money. When Juliet told me Darlana tried to blackmail her, I knew she had to go. I gave her a final ride on a dolphin." He laughed and the sound chilled me to the bone. Then my world went black.

I came to looking into Nick's very worried brown eyes. There was a lot of activity going on in the room. I could hear a struggle and people shouting. Juliet was telling Danny to just stop. *Good luck with that*. I tried to sit up but Nick put a hand on my shoulder.

"Not yet. You were out for more than a few seconds there."

I looked around at a sea of faces: Gabby, Roger, even Philipa.

"Did they get him?" My voice was barely a whisper.

Roger looked over his shoulder. "Just about. He's not going anywhere."

"Where's Luke?"

"First through the door," Roger said. "As soon as it started happening, Gabby called Stavon to get Security here. It was all pretty fast." He looked around again and scratched his head.

Nick looked at Philipa. "I'm sure Security has called for police, but see if you can get an ambulance here, too."

Philipa nodded her head and left.

"Who got hurt?" My voice was weak and raspy.

"You did, you idiot!" Gabby said.

"Oh. Right." I watched Philipa check with Security, nod in acknowledgment, and then she went out of the room.

I closed my eyes and took a deep breath. Three people said my name at once. Opened them again.

"Just messing with you." I wasn't. My head hurt. I wanted to cry. I really wanted to sit up and not have people staring at me. "I missed the fun."

"Yeah, Luke got off some pretty solid hits," Roger said.

"So did you, Roger," Gabby put in. Roger shrugged but he looked over at me. I winked.

"We actually had to pull Luke off Danny," Nick said. "He seemed to take Danny trying to kill you personally."

He watched me carefully. I just nodded.

"Can I sit up now, please? And water."

Gabby was on the floor on one side of me, Nick on the other. A bottle of water appeared fairly quickly and I took a long swig. It hurt going down. Nick had his flashlight out and started checking my eyes.

"No concussion," I said.

"Not this time. Some petechiae. Throat is a bit bruised. And it looks like you took a hell of a hit here." Nick's tone was clipped as he cataloged my injuries. He very gently touched the place where Danny had landed his punch. I winced.

"Some days are diamonds."

"Not funny. This whole thing was... I was an idiot to go along with it."

"Welcome to me." I took another sip of water. "Anybody have some aspirin or something?"

Gabby looked at Nick. "Acetaminophen okay?" and then started digging into her handbag. I realized she was sitting on the floor.

"Oh Jeez, Gabby! Your dress!"

"What? This old thing?"

I laughed and it turned into a choking fit.

"No one say anything funny for a few minutes, please."

"Uh, Kasey?" Roger made a circle with his right hand, indicating the room. "Comics?"

It took a short while for the police to arrive. Luke and Juliet had come over for a minute to check on me and then they were called back to deal with Security. I asked Nick to cancel the ambulance.

"Not my call. The hotel needs you to be officially checked out. And I'm not licensed in California." He seemed a little too pleased about it.

"I'm not going with them. They can check me out right here. It's a wasted trip." My throat was sore. I was hoping the acetaminophen would kick in sooner rather than later, but it was taking its time. I felt better sitting up and I had a chance to look around the room.

I could see Danny through a sea of legs, sitting on the floor, his hands zip-tied behind his back. He caught me looking and glared at me. I shivered. Then someone moved in between us.

Nick put his suit jacket over me and looked around. "We need a blanket."

Gabby and Roger jumped up to get one.

"No, I'm good. Just a momentary thing."

Nick looked at me. "You know, rejecting help when you need it is not a flex."

"I'm not flexing. I'll be fine in a minute or two. I grew up with four brothers."

"Did any of your brothers ever choke you to the point of unconsciousness?"

I sighed. "No." It was more of a mumble than a word.

"Then stop being a jerk. We will get you checked out and if the EMTs say you're good to go, we'll leave it at that. But Kasey, this could have turned out much worse. He could have snapped your neck in the same amount of time."

"But he didn't."

Nick glared at me.

I nodded. "Point taken."

He held my gaze. I saw him swallow hard and he closed his eyes for a second. He took a deep breath and let it out slowly. "Let's get you to a chair like a normal person. Which you are not."

I laughed and he gave me a wry smile.

Philipa came through the door followed by the EMTs. She must have been sent out to guide them back. I nodded my thanks and she retreated. Luke and Juliet were talking with the police and I heard one of the cops ask if there was a recording. Juliet and the cop left the room. The detectives from this morning showed back up. It looked like we had ruined their evening, or maybe not, since we had found their murderer. They met with the cop who had been first on the scene, then questioned the hotel security guard, and Luke. The EMTs got done poking and prodding me. My pulse rate was high (no kidding) but everything else seemed okay. Once they started packing up their equipment, the detectives came over.

That was another round of questioning. Danny was arrested and escorted out. Juliet was back and talking with the second detective. The detective took some close-up pictures of my face and throat.

"Where'd you get the black eye?" he asked.

"I came back to my room the other night and someone had broken in. Probably Danny. I interrupted him."

"You're just a walking crime scene."

"Thanks."

I was on my second bottle of water and was thinking I'd have to pee soon. I checked the time on my phone.

"Are we keeping you from something important?" the detective asked.

"No."

He proceeded to deliver a lecture about getting involved in police business. Then he asked me if I wanted to press charges against Danny.

"I have a flight home tomorrow. Most of us do. If you need me to press charges, I will, but I think you have more than enough to hold him."

The detective nodded. "We have a report of it. If you change your mind, this is a felony assault. You've got three years to file."

"So, if for some reason your case falls apart, you can call me."

"Appreciate that."

"Detective?"

He looked at me.

"Don't let this case fall apart."

"Don't want to come back to sunny California?"

"I've had better times at the dentist."

He didn't laugh. "Everyone's a comedian," he grumbled as he turned away.

And then, the room cleared out. Juliet went out with the detectives, patrolmen, and Security. Danny was on his way to lock up. My headache was starting to retreat just a bit.

We all looked at each other.

"I guess that's it, then" Roger said. He looked around for confirmation.

"Feels a bit of a let-down," Philipa said.

We all nodded.

Juliet came back into the room.

"Is the party still going?" I asked.

"Are you kidding? Everyone out there wants to know what happened."

"Are you ready to tell them everything?"

"I was actually very okay with admitting to the accident. Once I made that decision, I was scared, but I felt like something had lifted. Danny never admitted he was driving the car that night but it makes total sense. I had a flash to that night, but I don't know if it's true or

I just want it to be true. Either way, there's nothing to be scared of anymore."

"Let's do this then."

We walked down the back corridor and went in through the side door. The party was still lively, but there was more talking than partying going on. Every head turned our way. Juliet turned around and I flipped her mic battery pack on. She walked onto the stage.

"So, perhaps a few of you were wondering..."

People laughed but there was a general surge towards the stage. Juliet told the story. People went quiet. When she got to the part about why she had set up the private showcases, I saw people nodding their heads. She apologized profusely.

Someone shouted, "We love you, Juliet," and she started crying.

"Gabby, quick!"

Gabby reached into her bag and brought out a little package of tissues. I brought them up to her and turned to go. She grabbed my hand.

"You're not going anywhere." She wiped her face and took a deep breath. "The rest of you get up here."

The guys hung back just a bit, letting Gabby and Philipa go first. We were all assembled and looking at each other sheepishly.

"For almost the entire three days of this seminar, Kasey and her friends have been helping me figure out who was blackmailing me. Danny Schillingford has been arrested for blackmail," she paused for just a second, "and the murder of Darlana DeLuz." There was a moment of shocked silence and then people started talking all at once.

"Suffice it to say, that while we tried to run things to schedule, there was a lot going on behind the scenes."

People weren't ready to laugh yet but they quieted back down.

"Kasey figured out that Danny was behind the blackmail and she came up with a plan to get him to confess. And, congratulations, you were all witnesses so thank you."

She put her hands together in appreciation and people responded by clapping. She let the applause die down. "What you heard over the sound system was Kasey literally putting her life on the line to help me." She looked at me. "There are no words to thank you for all you've done. All of you."

She took half a step back and made a little shooing wave for me to speak. I didn't know what to say. I cleared my throat and heard the sound go over the loud speakers.

"Glad the mic didn't get crunched in the brawl." My voice was still hoarse and raspy. People looked at me expectantly. "First rule of comedy: Don't break the mic."

I got a nice laugh. It gave me a couple of seconds to think. Juliet was not the only one with a lot of people to thank.

"I came to this seminar to learn about the business of comedy. And I did. But I learned something else, something more important. Rob said it several times in his sessions. We also saw it played out in that the instructors who were here this weekend were Juliet's friends, some from way back."

"Some only pretending to be friends." Juliet said.

"Well, yeah. Maybe not *best* friends." We looked at each other and laughed.

"The point is that we're not in competition with each other. People don't only go to see one comic. They don't watch only one TV show. There's room enough for all of us. And it works so much better if we help each other out."

"We need to have each other's backs." I pointed at the others. "These guys... and ladies all had my back. Completely and without hesitation. And they literally saved my life tonight. So, big thank you to them."

Big round of applause on that, with lots of whoops. I waited.

"Comedy is hard. Business is hard. We don't need to be hard on each other. This weekend, we had comics helping us out by sharing their knowledge and their experience. I hope that we will all pay it forward and lift each other up." People clapped and I got a few whoops. I looked over at Nick. "I also learned that we need to allow ourselves to be vulnerable, to be real, onstage and off. That it's okay to ask for help when we need it."

He mouthed 'thank you' to me.

"I got a lot of help from these people." This was going on too long. My voice was giving out. I needed more water. And possibly something stronger. "Anyway, so much of the time in stand-up, you feel like you're out there on your own. Look around you. There's a hundred people in this room. At least a couple of you are going to hit it big." I paused. "My name is Kasey McCormick. K-A-S-E--" I got the laugh and a nice round of applause.

I stepped back and let Juliet take it from there. We trooped off the stage as soon as we could. Juliet thanked her assistants and the AV team, then brought up Rob and Mo and thanked them.

I looked around at my friends. "I don't know about you guys, but I could use a drink."

My mic was still on. Oops.

"Champagne please!" Juliet called from the stage. Within a few minutes, the catering supervisor brought several bottles of champagne to our table, along with glasses. I used the time to get the mic off me and Roger ran it over to the sound guys.

Juliet, Rob, and Mo joined us for a toast. Juliet raised her glass. "I cannot thank all of you enough. You have gotten me out from under not only the blackmailer, but all that guilt."

"Think of the money you'll save in therapy fees alone," Roger said.

"Maybe a few more sessions to figure out how I could have missed how toxic Danny was."

"Not a bad idea," Gabby said.

"Well, I feel like a total imposter," Philipa said. "I didn't do anything."

I looked at her. "You're the one who cracked the case!"

"How? I didn't even know anything was going on."

"You told me that Danny and Darla had a magic act. When you told me about the hypnosis, that's when I put it together."

Philipa tilted her head. "I did."

"Yeah, you did!"

"Oh, in that case, more champagne please."

The champagne flowed and somehow we never got around to dinner. I crawled into bed that night and slept through for the first time since I had arrived in California. I finally adjusted to the time zone and I was leaving.

Chapter 29: Friend Code

"But hypnosis can't make you do something you wouldn't normally do. Or can it?" Philipa asked.

It was Monday morning and the six of us were sitting in the back booth of the dining room, taking full advantage of the breakfast buffet.

"Danny couldn't have hypnotized Juliet to kill the guy, but he could take a bit of the truth and plant a different story about how it happened in Juliet's head. Darlana's, too." I had done some Googling on hypnosis before the mixer.

"But why was he blackmailing her?" Roger asked.

"Another level of control," Nick said. "It reinforced the story he had placed and it scared Juliet to depend on him more. He set himself up to be her hero. If she needed him and he helped her, he figured she would finally see him as the guy she wanted to be with."

"Incel," Philipa muttered.

"He figured she would fall in love with him out of gratitude," I said.

"But it's not really love; it's need," Gabby said. "Two different things."

Roger picked it up. "Want is more of a conscious choice."

I was watching Roger and Gabby. He leaned in and whispered something in her ear. She was smiling as she looked down into her lap.

"Want is better than need, but people often want all the trimmings that come with a person, not the actual person." Nick might have had a trace of bitterness in his voice.

"Their perception of the person," I said. "And then they discover this person is not who they thought they were and feel betrayed." I was thinking of Stavon.

"When it was really stuff they had made up about the person in their own minds," Philipa said. "Been there."

Luke had been quiet, but now he spoke up. "Sometimes people expect you to be a certain way because of your looks. For better or worse."

"Or because of your resume," Nick put in.

"And we can play into it or opposite to it, if we're thinking along the lines of honing your persona."

"That's why the persona has to be an actual part of yourself, otherwise it won't work," Philipa added.

"And it can backfire," Luke said.

I shook my head at him. "Ya think?"

"Sometimes people do misrepresent themselves, though," Gabby observed.

We all said "Chad" at the same time. Then started laughing.

"I'm starting to feel sorry for him."

"He doesn't get it."

"Which means he doesn't get it, if you know what I mean," Philipa wiggled her eyebrows.

"Ewww."

"All this love stuff makes my head hurt. It's much too complicated for me." I speared a piece of French toast, swirled it in a pool of syrup and popped it in my mouth. My diet only varies so much.

"And some people just avoid and deflect," Luke's statement was barely audible.

"Well, yeah. Speaking of, where's Amber this morning? It looked like you two were hitting it off." I beamed at him.

"Amber may have had some issues..." Luke trailed off.

"Some?" Philipa actually snorted. "Kasey, remember that guy who was supposed to go up before you?"

"Yeah. Topher. Something."

"While we were drinking last night, Amber confided in me that she had gotten Topher drunk before the showcase. Actually, she was rather proud of herself." Philipa drank some coffee.

I looked at her. "That's kind of weird."

"Oh no, honey. It gets weirder." Philipa looked at Luke.

"Amber thought if you had to go up sooner than you expected, you wouldn't be as good—that it would throw you off." Luke shook his head.

"Why would she care?" I wrinkled my nose.

"Really, Kasey?" Philipa gave me the side-eye.

"Well, it wasn't a competition." I was still confused.

"Not what she was competing for," Nick observed.

"Ding! Ding! Ding! We have a winner." Philipa was downright gleeful. "I waited until she hit the ladies' room and told Luke. I know it's against the Girl Code..." she held up her right hand, "but I figured Luke has had his share of psycho females for a while."

"And the warning was much appreciated," Luke said.

"I don't know Luke," I said. "She's an improvement over the last one. At least Amber wasn't trying to kill you."

Luke pretended to write on his hand. "Try to date women who don't want to kill you. Thanks for that pro tip."

We all laughed.

"I think I'll just focus on my career right now." He shook his head.

Philipa looked at her phone. "Crap. I'm scheduled for the next shuttle. So great meeting all of you and let's keep in touch. For real."

There was a lot of hugging and good-byes. Gradually the group split up. Roger and Gabby had decided to stay a couple of extra days. Luke had an appointment set with the agent from the showcase. I suspected Gabby did, too. They all wandered off together, leaving Nick and me at the table.

"I need at least one more cup of coffee."

"I'll sit with you. My shuttle isn't for another hour and a half."

We looked at each other. I felt some regret. I looked at his hand.

"Keeping the ring on, I see."

He looked down at it. "It's a good reminder. Keeps me from stepping out before the divorce is finalized."

"You don't need a ring to remind you."

He shook his head. "No, I don't. Up until this point, I hadn't even been tempted."

"Sorry about that. Wearing it does have the added benefit of keeping women away."

He nodded. "Not as much as you'd think. But it's a way of filtering out women who don't respect marriage vows, for sure. Once burned..."

"Been there. Not married, but it was a long-term relationship. It's not fun. Mostly you feel like an idiot. Fortunately, one of my girlfriends clued me in fairly early on. And that, was that."

"Girl Code?"

I nodded. "Maybe we just need to change it to Friend Code."

"The man was an idiot."

"Absolutely. As is your wife."

"Thank you."

We were silent for a moment. I stood up to go.

"For comics, our timing sucks," he said, standing up. We started moving towards the exit.

"I was just thinking the same thing."

"I tell you what. Once I am free and clear—"

"And over your rebound dating," I interrupted.

He laughed. "Definitely. I would like to take you out on a proper date. Would that be alright?"

"That would be better than alright. Though there is a bit of a distance problem."

"I'll fly you up."

"For dinner?"

"Well, we could probably make a weekend of it."

"Moving kind of fast there, Slick."

He put his hands in the air, as if surrendering. "All aboveboard. I'll get you your own hotel room. We'll do the city. Have fun."

I gave him the side-eye.

"No strings. On my honor." He crossed his heart.

"Deal. Get yourself single first."

"You've given me some incentive to move a bit faster."

"I'm not sure how I feel about that."

"Look. The marriage was done. The paperwork was already being drawn up by my lawyer. It's going to be a shitty next few months and you've given me something to look forward to. So, thank you."

"I'm not *that* great a date."

"I think we'll be fine."

We were standing near the elevator banks and we were standing too close to each other. All I wanted to do in that moment was kiss him. I could feel the heat of his body and I could feel my body reacting, wanting him to make a move and at the same time, the voice in my head was begging him not to. *Keep being the good guy.*

"You feel it?" His voice was a bit hoarse.

I nodded.

"Hang onto the feeling. We'll put it to good use."

"Sometimes I hate being an adult."

"Me, too." He cleared his throat. "I need to take a walk and clear my head."

I nodded. *And I need to take a cold shower.*

Keep In Touch

Want to know when the next Kasey McCormick Mystery is coming out? Or just like free, fun, bookish stuff?

Visit my website: https://bonniecavaliere.com/ and sign on for access to my monthly newsletter and the Freebie Library.

See you soon!

Bonnie

While you're here...

Other books in the Kasey McCormick Series:

Fez Up (Get it for free on my website!)

The Girl in the Pork Pie Hat